Judy Astley was frequently told off for day-dreaming at her drearily traditional school but has found it to be the ideal training for becoming a writer. There were several false-starts to her career: secretary at an all-male Oxford college (sacked for undisclosable reasons), at an airline (decided, after a crash and a hijacking, that she was safer elsewhere) and as a dress designer (quit before anyone noticed she was adapting *Vogue* patterns). She spent some years as a parent and as a painter before sensing that the day was approaching when she'd have to go out and get a Proper Job. With a nagging certainty that she was temperamentally unemployable, and desperate to avoid office coffee, having to wear tights every day and missing out on sunny days on Cornish beaches with her daughters, she wrote her first novel, *Just for the Summer*. She has now had nine novels published by Black Swan.

www.booksattransworld.co.uk

Also by Judy Astley

JUST FOR THE SUMMER
PLEASANT VICES
SEVEN FOR A SECRET
MUDDY WATERS
EVERY GOOD GIRL
THE RIGHT THING
EXCESS BAGGAGE
NO PLACE FOR A MAN

and published by Black Swan

UNCHAINED MELANIE

Judy Astley

BLACK SWAN

UNCHAINED MELANIE
A BLACK SWAN BOOK : 0 552 99950 4

First publication in Great Britain

PRINTING HISTORY
Black Swan edition published 2002

5 7 9 10 8 6

Copyright © Judy Astley 2002

The right of Judy Astley to be identified as the author
of this work has been asserted in accordance with sections
77 and 78 of the Copyright Designs and Patents Act 1988.

Set in 11pt Melior by
County Typesetters, Margate, Kent.

Black Swan Books are published by Transworld Publishers,
61–63 Uxbridge Road, London W5 5SA,
a division of The Random House Group Ltd,
in Australia by Random House Australia (Pty) Ltd,
20 Alfred Street, Milsons Point, Sydney, NSW 2061, Australia,
in New Zealand by Random House New Zealand Ltd,
18 Poland Road, Glenfield, Auckland 10, New Zealand
and in South Africa by Random House (Pty) Ltd,
Endulini, 5a Jubilee Road, Parktown 2193, South Africa.

Printed and bound in Great Britain by
Cox & Wyman Ltd, Reading, Berkshire

In memory of my mother,
Nora Fender 1921–2001

Many thanks to Adrian Lovett-Turner of Treescapes for our gorgeous prize-winning garden and to Susan Rose for amazing information on unexpected uses for dead wildlife.

And especially to my editor Linda Evans for her patience, sympathy and friendship.

One

Please yourself.

There were two ways of saying it. There was the peevish, sniffy inflection which Melanie Patterson remembered, from her teen years, as a razor-edged speciality of her mother. It was kept for those occasions (and pretty frequent they'd been) when there'd been something to be disapproved of: a skirt too short, shoes too high, a boyfriend too clearly after One Thing. The specialized tone was still in use. More recently, over twenty years since Melanie had left home, there was the house too close to the river (rats), the cat allowed to moult on the beds (fleas), the divorce (carelessness).

But there was another version of those words: the seductively drawn-out tone, the sultry emphasis on the indulgent, the luxurious, the sensuous, the time-for-yourself, the purr.

'Pleeeease yourself.' Melanie intended to do just that, savouring the purred version aloud as she switched on the TV then opened a family-sized packet of Maltesers. She leaned back on the sofa, shoved her feet under the velvet cushions and crammed two sweets into her mouth at once. Bliss. The chocolate seeped over her teeth and the honeycomb compacted and melted between her tongue and the roof of her mouth. Delicious indulgence. Delicious *all alone* indulgence for there was no-one to comment snidely about calories, no-one to say 'Are you going to eat them *all at once*?' in that eyebrows-up, pursed-mouth way that had been Roger's speciality. (Come to think of it, why on earth had she married someone so like her mother?) He was off her hands now, delivered till Death Did Them Part into the pale skinny-fingered paws of Leonora, probably at the stage – she glanced at her watch – where the registrar was asking the assembled company about Lawful Impediment. There wouldn't be any: Leonora would have had his decree absolute thoroughly thumbed-over by some family legal eagle, in case Roger was sneakily clinging to the means of getting out of doing the decent thing.

Here though, on a sunny afternoon with the warm autumn breeze billowing the blue linen curtains by the open French windows, the racing was about to start: first from Kempton and then the highlights from Lingfield. Melanie had a couple of quid each way on runners in all the day's televised races. It should be a good and lucky afternoon, as scanning the lists of runners had proved so serendipitously fruitful. Better experts than her might study form and weigh up the advantages or otherwise of the going being good to firm, but for Mel the most important aspect (along with the colours the jockey was wearing) was always the aptness of the name of the horse. In the 2.30 her cash was on Bridle Sweet, in the next she'd got Promises Promises, Lingfield had yielded Bouquet and she could hardly wait for Second Honeymoon in the 5.15. It was all so fortuitously close to perfect she'd almost gone for a seven-race accumulator but had baulked at the thought she could lose the lot in the first (Bridle Sweet being rather a desperate pun), and lack a reason to keep her interest up for the rest of the afternoon.

'I'm eighty-one you know!' The words sang out from over the next-door fence just as the runners were being cajoled into the starting gates for the off. Melanie could swear her curtains flinched at the shrillness of the sound. This was old Mrs Jenkins's version of 'Cooee', the summons for a few minutes' company, a word about the noise from Melanie's daughter Rosa's music or a little domestic job her increasingly arthritic hands couldn't quite manage. Melanie sighed and got up from the sofa. Whatever it was this time she hoped it wouldn't take long, not today. Please, she thought, don't let it be a long rambling letter from the daughter in Canada that would have to be read out slowly and carefully with detailed interruptions from Mrs J. to explain all the friends and neighbours chronicled so very, very thoroughly by Brenda. These were people Mrs Jenkins had never met, never would meet, but whose family histories she could recount as if they were her own.

'Everything all right?' Melanie looked out from behind the door to the head that nodded gently and rhythmically over the dividing fence at her. The sun glinted on Mrs Jenkins's glasses.

'I'm eighty-one!' Melanie knew this more than well enough, though she wasn't sure if it was exactly true. Mrs Jenkins had been applying this statement as a greeting for at least the past three years. When she got overexcited she could mention it (and one day Mel had counted) as much as twenty times in ten minutes. Opening the back door was always a risk, especially if

9

you were hung-over or generally feeling unsociable. Mrs Jenkins, who usually seemed to be a bit deaf (well, at eighty one . . .), kept an all-weather radar beam trained on Melanie's door. So very often when she dared to open it, the old lady was up from her Parker-Knoll recliner with all the swiftness of a puppy sensing someone whispering 'walkies!'

'Two children I raised, we didn't always have enough to eat but they were immaculately turned out, *immaculately.*' The script was always the same. Melanie smiled at the head that wagged to her across the top of the fence and the remains of the roses. The head looked a bit like a pale mauvey-grey shaggy mop on a stick. Mrs Jenkins's children may have been *immaculately* turned out but their mother's pension could no longer extend to a weekly shampoo and set, and neither did Social Services run to the grooming of the elderly. Her hair's bizarre shade of muddy lilac was courtesy of a stack of sachets that the Meals on Wheels lady's cousin Doreen had liberated from Luscious Locks, when she'd been fired for leaving a client under the colour accelerator for an hour and a half while she'd gone off to lunch.

'It's the bin bag dear, it needs to be in the wheelie thing.' Melanie opened the connecting gate, went through to the adjoining garden and quickly hauled the bag down to the communal walled-off area just beyond the back gate, being careful where she trod in her last-Christmas Toast catalogue cashmere mules, for Mrs Jenkins's small orange-bottomed poodle had been startlingly incontinent lately. Sometimes it sneaked under the fence and deposited a sly pile on Mel's scraggy lawn. With any luck it wouldn't be able to do that for much longer – Mel was about to treat her garden to a complete makeover. In celebration of Roger's deliverance to Leonora, Green Piece, a gardening company of the kind whose prices made Mel's stomach clench, was going to transform her outdoor space into a 30-foot-by-60 semi-tropical paradise full of palms, succulents and elegant rocks. It was a non-wedding present to herself. She'd make a note about the fence – the expensive artistry of this project did not allow for the waste contents of a dog being deposited on the newly laid pristine stones.

'Where's that hubby of yours?' the lilac head asked as Mel returned to her side of the fence and firmly closed the gate. Melanie had gritted her teeth already, knowing that would be the next question. It always was. Usually she just informed her neighbour, gently and with tact, for no-one likes to be reminded that their marbles are rolling away, that he'd moved out several months ago and was unlikely to be seen around this area again. Today, though, there was a new and delightful answer. She smiled as if it didn't matter. Because it didn't.

'He's gone to a wedding. His own wedding,' Melanie said brightly, leaning forward to pluck the last non-blighted rose from the fence.

'Oh! And couldn't you go as well, dear?'

'Well, no, not really. I don't think his new wife would like it. Spectre at the feast, that kind of thing. Rosa's gone, though, so she can tell me all about who wears what and take lots of photos.'

'Fifty-six years me and Teddy was married. I'm eighty-one now you know. . .' The voice trailed away as each woman returned to her solitary home, in Melanie's case with haste and anticipation, for there was a bottle of champagne in the fridge that would be nicely chilled. Leonora and Roger would be at the 'You may kiss the bride' stage by now, which had to deserve a toast *in absentia.* The champagne was Bollinger, for this was a special occasion, *very* special. Unfortunately it was also one of those bottles that was stubborn about being opened, as if deliberately giving Melanie a few extra moments to reflect that lone drinking was a dangerous and slippery slope.

'Listen you, I don't bloody care,' she told the bottle as she wrapped a tea towel round the cork for extra strength, tugged and tugged and hoped this wasn't an omen. She intended to enjoy this day to the full, she didn't want minor difficulties getting in the way. At last the cork grudgingly relented to allow Melanie to pour a first delicious glassful, and she settled back on the sofa just in time to see Bridle Sweet romp home at a neatly profitable 7 to 1.

'This isn't the first time I've been a best man.' Rosa picked at her pale green nail varnish as her uncle consulted his notes for the next line. She didn't know why he bothered, unless he was nervous or pausing for dramatic effect – it was obvious what came next.

'In fact . . .' oh yes, here it is, she thought, cringing in anticipation '. . . in fact this isn't the first time I've been Roger's best man!' He grinned around the room and his audience exploded into exaggerated hilarity. Rosa gazed down at the tablecloth, wishing she could find it in her to feel as wholeheartedly thrilled about her father's new wife as everyone else clearly did. It was more than a bit insulting really, she thought as she pulled a couple of daisies from the table's centrepiece, as if all the years he'd been with her mother had been wiped out as a lousy joke; as if *this* was the real thing, the other had only been an easily abandoned trial run and Melanie was quite justly rejected for . . . well, for Chrissake *look* at her. Rosa stared hard at the bride, who was being giggly with her matron of honour, their blonde hair swinging together at some daft private joke. Leonora's own whippet-thin head held a coronet of fat marguerites, as if she'd just minutes ago been sitting out on a summer lawn making herself an adult-size daisy chain. She was wearing the kind of dress that Melanie (and Rosa had a rare moment of mother-appreciation) wouldn't be seen dead in, which would be something good to report back to her. It was strapless, for one thing – a huge mistake, in Rosa's opinion, if your collarbones look like someone's shoved a coat hanger sideways down your throat and your spine is a bit on the roundy side. Someone should have told Leonora to sit up straight when she was little – it would take years of Pilates classes to sort that out. The dress was also a glaring bright pink like cheap bubble gum and over-stiff around the bust area, so that when Leonora turned herself sideways the bodice took its time to follow. There was a kind of darker pink chiffon bolero thing over the top, presumably an attempt at blushing maidenliness, which was a joke, Rosa considered with teenage scorn, seeing as Leonora must be about four months pregnant by now. It didn't show, though – you'd think it would on someone as skinny as that. I mean, she wondered, where was it? Perhaps it wasn't there. Perhaps it had all been a ruse, a way of getting Roger to commit. He'd never been quick off the mark with decisions – especially when it came to the women in his life. How many bloody Christmas Eves and day-before-bloody birthdays had he cornered Rosa in the last-minute late afternoon and

13

said, 'Your mother, she's always difficult, what do you think . . .' It wasn't her mother who was sodding difficult.

Paul had finished his speech. Dutifully, for she had no intention of making any kind of scene, Rosa stood along with everyone else and raised her glass to the happy couple. Roger grinned at the assembled staring throng, put his arm round Leonora and kissed her. For far too long, oh God, and quite obviously with *tongues*. Rosa put her hand over her face. People were fidgeting, murmuring, trying not to look. Wait till she told her mum, she'd howl!

'Shit! How *embarrassing*.' Rosa stared down at the now-shredded daisies that she'd somehow crumpled and scattered across the remains of her crème brûlée. Her fourteen-year-old cousin Joel sniggered awkwardly beside her and she gave him a sharp dig in the ribs.

'Sorry,' he chortled. 'But wrinklies, snogging. Worse for you, being your dad, I suppose.'

'Yes it fucking is,' she hissed, feeling fat tears welling up unexpectedly. She didn't want this. Everyone would think she was mourning the loss of something – a stable family life perhaps (huh!), her parents' togetherness (huh! again). Everyone would feel sorry for her, nudge each other and look at her, poor little only child, the lonely victim of divorce, having to hand over her dear daddy to a woman who was young enough to be her not-that-much-older sister. It wasn't anything like that. What she was really missing, now that Alex had dumped her, was being kissed in that way, by someone who looked into her eyes and wanted his mouth on hers at that moment more than anything else on the whole planet. It would be a long time before all that happened again for her. She was about to leave for university, the very next day. Alex (the bastard) had already said his goodbyes and made it more than clear that although it had been 'nice' (and how shaming to have wasted all those months on someone whose vocabulary was so inadequate), he wouldn't be expecting her to rush up to Oxford to see him every weekend, nor should she be expecting him to use his own student railcard in the direction of Plymouth.

'I'll always be *your* grandma you know, this doesn't change anything for us.' Rosa felt a soft patting on her shoulder and tried to shake her tears away out of sight.

'Er, like I know?' Rosa immediately felt sorry for her aggressive tone. Her gran was only trying to be kind.

'Yes, of course you do.' Helen Patterson's tone sharpened. 'What I meant was . . .'

'Sorry Gran, yes I know what you meant, it's all right.' Rosa gave her the kind of smile that had always so pleased older people when she was small. It didn't feel quite right, a bit stiff, but her grandmother looked a touch happier.

'And of course Leonora's really rather sweet, when you get to know her,' Helen went on. 'She'll make a jolly good little mother, I'm sure. From what she's said, it seems to be all she's ever wanted.'

'Not like Mum, you mean.' Rosa hadn't intended to say it but the words slid out like a cat through a suddenly opened window.

'Well, your mother . . . she always had other interests of course, her work. Not a bad thing,' Helen added hastily. 'Not in this day and age.'

'I expect Leonora will go back to work after a few months,' Rosa teased.

'Oh I don't think so! She'll want to look after the baby . . .'

'Properly?' Rosa supplied for her, smiling to take the edge off the word.

'Oh, you were brought up properly enough. It's the best anyone can hope for, in the end,' Helen conceded with only half a smile. Then she brightened. 'Now, that dress you've got on. Very pretty. I like to see you young girls in frocks with a bit of a flounce to them. You should wear that sort of thing more often with your lovely slim figure. All those baggy trousers you hide yourself away in, you won't get the boys interested going round like that.' Helen wagged a finger at her, its nail varnish in Belisha beacon orange to match the flowers on her broad-brimmed egg-yellow hat.

'I borrowed it, Gran. Me and Charmian and Gracie have one posh dress each for sharing out at stuff like this.'

'Oh. Couldn't you have worn your own?'

'Well I was going to, but it's black. Mum didn't think it would have been very appropriate. She said I'd look like I was making some kind of protest.'

'Yes, for once I have to agree with her. It would have been most unsuitable.'

The restaurant was gradually emptying. The tables were a depressing bombsite of crumbs, wine stains and abandoned boulders of fruitcake. Even grown-ups only ate the icing on wedding cake, Rosa realized, though surely it was the fruity bit that was for good luck, for fertility. Perhaps in this case they thought there wasn't much point even pretending to eat it. Fertility (if a bump on the front of Leonora ever actually appeared) had been tested and proved. The floor was a mass of party-popper streamers, dropped napkins and dollops of food deposited by Leonora's brother's three unruly small children. They'd be getting a new cousin soon; Rosa would be getting a half-something. It was a strange term, half-sister, half-brother, as if it was the new little person who wasn't quite complete, not the relationship. She wondered what she'd think of it, this little half-creature, whether she'd love it to bits and regret that she'd been blighted to be an only child all this time, or whether it would be removed enough to be of little interest. Either way, there'd be babysitting money in it for her, that was for sure. Leonora was only twenty-four, there was no way, however mumsy-wumsy Gran reckoned she was, that she'd be staying in every night for evermore. Dad would get what was coming to him: one way or another, at his age he was going to be permanently knackered.

When you're a grown-up it is permissible to ignore a ringing doorbell if you feel like it. It could be sheer bad manners. It might be a huge mistake if it's the man from the Premium Bonds with your cheque for one million pounds and an offer of counselling, but it is an option. Melanie thought of this as she picked her way past Rosa's supermarket boxes of university-ready baggage in the hallway, opened the front door and wished she hadn't. Sarah (whose favourite phrase was 'I'm your best friend', words with which she excused an alarming number of frank personal remarks) stood there brandishing a bottle of champagne (God, another one), a couple of takeout bags from The Good Earth and a sickening sympathetic smile plastered on like too much drunkenly applied lipstick.

'Er, I was just going out.' Melanie really didn't want to see anyone. There was still some of the Bollinger, a whole tube of cheese and onion Pringles to be got through without guilt, and for later she'd been looking forward to a whopping great soft fluffy omelette stuffed with crisp little flecks of bacon and some squelchy butter-sizzled mushrooms. It was too late now. Sarah had pushed past her in a flurry of long lion-tinted hair and a waft of Opium and was already in the kitchen, while Mel stood with the door still open as if expecting a retinue of Sarah's elfin helpers to file in after her.

'You can't fool me, you know.' Sarah's head was slightly on one side and the grin now went rather strangely from north-east to south-west. 'I know you must be suffering inside. You're doing Brave Face.'

Melanie felt herself scowling like a cross child. 'No, I'm not doing Brave Face, I'm doing Very Happy Face. I've just won fifty-six quid on the gee-gees and I was going out to collect my winnings. If Second Honeymoon hadn't been such an idle nag I'd have netted over a hundred. Still, it was an outsider, it's what you get.'

'Second Honeymoon?' Sarah raised her perfectly sculpted eyebrows and pursed her lips. 'There you are. You *were* thinking about him. You're all alone and wallowing in misery while your Roger's swanning about out there getting married to his little back-office slapper. I knew it. Hug?'

Sarah's flabless arms (Melanie couldn't help thinking of a wingspan, Sarah was so like a long pale bird, an ibis or crane perhaps) stretched all the way from the dishwasher right past the microwave. It was hard to move out of reach, but Mel didn't fancy a hug. She wasn't in the slightest need of sympathy so she ducked out of the way and opened the fridge, murmuring, 'He's not *my* Roger. Hasn't been for ages. In fact I don't think

18

he's capable of being anyone's, not properly. Leonora will find out in time – he's one of those men who always has one foot out of the door.'

As there was no chance of Sarah leaving without sustenance, and the smell of the classy Chinese takeout was too tempting, she might as well be hospitable. 'Here, put your bottle in the ledge thing, I've already got one open.' She unstoppered the Bollinger, poured a glass for Sarah and topped up her own.

'And drinking alone? That's not a good sign.' Sarah reached up to the rack beside the sink and took down a couple of plates.

'It's a perfectly good sign. How insecure and pathetic do you have to be to need the permission of other people's company when you fancy a glass of something?' Melanie rummaged in the cutlery drawer. 'I hope you've got some of those sickly little lemon chicken things in that bag.'

'Of course I have. I've got the duck and pancakes and the prawn toasts and the pak choi thing with the gloopy sauce. I'm your best friend, I know all your favourites. So what were you doing? Drowning your sorrows?'

'Joining in. If I couldn't go to the wedding and have a gander at all the frocks and stomp about being the Bad Luck Fairy and upsetting people, I could at least have my share of the booze. I had sweeties instead of cake. Anyway I do wish them well. Now that he's finally gone and done it he won't be coming round here every five minutes asking me if he's doing the right thing, wondering where it all went wrong or if his blue cashmere sweater might still be in the back of the wardrobe.'

'Is that what he was doing? You know that could

have been a cry for help, he probably wanted to come back. If you'd played your cards right, Mel, you could have got him back.'

Mel snorted into her drink. 'Back? What would I want him back for?'

'Company now that Rosa's going? Your old age? Sex? To buy you nice little bits and pieces and to go on holiday with and . . .'

'Enough!' Melanie laughed. 'All irrelevant, has been for some time, probably since way before Luscious Leonora was on the scene. No, I'm on my own and happy. I'm going to be fine. I've done my bit as half a couple. Rosa's off to university tomorrow so I reckon I've also done my bit as the downtrodden parent. From now on I'm going to celebrate being the Whole, Sole, *Me*.'

'Absolutely.' Sarah stabbed her fork into a piece of duck. 'But you won't want to be the whole sole you for long, you'll get bored, frustrated and lonely. So now all we have to do is find you some nice new man. I'll start shopping around for one for you *right now*.'

Two

When Melanie woke up the next morning she stretched out starfish-style in her kingsize steel-framed bed and looked at the telephone on the table beside her. She didn't need to unplug it at night any more for fear of hearing 'Hello sweetie, small problem . . .' from Roger with something on his mind at six in the morning. Time after bloody time she'd told him it was a) too early and b) nothing to do with her any more, but neither message had penetrated his brain. He was so much a creature of habit it still amazed her that he'd broken out of his neat routines (and so frequently too) in order to go about the business of adultery.

It was now twenty-four hours since his last call. Then he'd been a worried divorcé, still thinking it was a good idea to rely on his ex-wife to get things right for him. Now it was just bliss to know he was safely on his honeymoon a whole continent away, and enormously unlikely to find an excuse to phone. Of course, it could be quite funny (for her, but not for the new Mrs Patterson) if he did: she could just imagine Leonora on the last day of the holiday, scanning the itemized phone calls listed under 'Extras' and realizing he'd called his ex-wife on a daily basis. Probably, though, given the age gap, Leonora's sweet blond little head wouldn't be allowed to be troubled by the sight of a bill, and she certainly wouldn't be asked an opinion on whether it would be a better deal to pay with Visa or Amex, as Mel had been over the honeymoon booking.

Roger's call on the morning of the wedding had been to ask Melanie if you were supposed to give a present to the young woman acting as Matron of Honour even when it was just a registry office wedding and supposed to be completely informal, and if you were, would a silver yo-yo from Tiffany be all right or should it be something less frivolous, seeing as a wedding was supposed to be quite a serious event. That had been only the last of a constant stream of doubts and questions he'd presented her with ever since he'd moved out all those months ago. She'd been hugely amused by the bit about a wedding being 'serious', given that he'd taken a determinedly flighty attitude towards marriage itself. Still, she'd been outstandingly patient with him and his phone calls, even the time he'd phoned late at night (and more than a bit drunk) to ask whether it was usual for pregnant women to feel sick in the evenings instead of the mornings. She'd pointed out at the time that as a way of informing her that his new girlfriend was pregnant it lacked a certain something in the subtlety-and-sensitivity department. His genuinely bemused response of 'Oh does it? Sorry,' scuppered any final doubts as to whether she might be better off with rather than without him.

Sarah really hadn't got it entirely wrong. Possibly if Melanie had made all the right moves Roger might be lying next to her at this moment under the goosedown duvet. He'd be doing that thing with his foot, the thing she hated, running his calloused sole up and down her calf as if checking how efficient her last leg-waxing had been. He was one of those men who took no notice at all if you mentioned that something annoyed you and would they please stop, which in itself was way up on the List of Annoying Things, possibly at number one. He refused to keep any telephone numbers stored in his head either, even frequently asking Mel, phone already in his hand, for his own mother's number, as if it was entirely her responsibility to keep track of that sort of thing. *Her* mother had been completely on his side when she'd grumbled about that one, coming out with her famed, 'Well, men have so much to think about . . .' as if it was a wife's job to scoop up all the sundry bits of domestic information that men couldn't be bothered to file in their memories and have them ready for instant reference, like an in-brain Psion. Men, of course, had to keep their intellects free for the kind of work that earned the household money.

Melanie had plenty going on in her own mind, work-wise, but as she didn't commute daily into central London in a suit, possess a briefcase, a pension fund or a set-in-stone retirement date to look forward to, there wasn't a hope in hell that her mother would ever call it A Job. Mel shared her working life with an invented woman: Tina Keen, the detective who starred in her novels and earned her a pretty good living. Tina specialized in solving gory murders of unlucky, down-trodden females, women who seemed to have been born victims, few being particularly grief-stricken at their loss, and whose grisly deaths required a stroppy champion like herself so that the men who'd carelessly wiped them out wouldn't walk free to smack someone else around just that bit too hard. Tina wasn't as sharp and scathing as Lynda La Plante's Jane Tennison, nor as forensically blood-soaked (or as bloody-minded) as Patricia Cornwell's Kay Scarpetta. Nor was her creator anything like as successful, although the work more than paid the bills. Tina was foul-mouthed, feistily bright in a non-academic sort of way and much given to sitting on bar stools and assuming (rightly) that men with recently committed crime on their minds would find it hard to resist dropping telling little hints about their misdeeds, over a couple of gins, to a woman whose legs were well worth looking at. Tina had starred in seven books so far and the eighth, *Dying For It*, was taking shape in Melanie's indigo i-Book upstairs in the study that looked out, through gaps between roofs and alleyways, towards the Thames. The room had once and too briefly been the nursery, ready to be decorated for Rosa's little brother, who had launched himself out into the cold world far too early to survive. A mobile of painted shells she and Roger had bought in Tobago to hang over the cot now chattered and clattered lightly in the draught by the window.

Cohabiting with Tina was a bit like being a child again and having an imaginary friend. Melanie had invented Tina's opinions (slightly dated Bolshie left-winger), her dress sense (skirts too tight for all the traditional police-style running about: she left that to the eager young detective constables) and her habit of smoking Panatellas over restaurant tables and being told off by smiling waiters on behalf of outraged but cowardly customers. Sometimes, out on a supermarket foray, Mel would drift off into Tina mode and start pulling from the shelves the kind of food her creation kept stocked in her fictional fridge. At the checkout she'd then wonder if she'd somehow appropriated the wrong trolley, as she unloaded onto the conveyor belt packets of chocolate finger biscuits (for dunking into strong black coffee and sucking at rudely among impressionable male colleagues), giant bags of oven chips ('virtually fat-free!') and luridly packaged yogurts as well as magazines full of soap-opera gossip and shimmer-tights in vibrant American tan. Once, contemplating the research involved if Tina had to investigate the macabre murder of a slimming-club leader, she'd been caught by her neighbour Perfect Patty from number 14 sitting in the car park munching her way through a box of miniature doughnuts.

'That your secret vice then?' Patty had called, as she'd strolled past pushing her virtuous trolley full of organic veg and free-range pasta.

'No, I'm thinking of joining Shape Sorters. Just fattening up first,' Mel had replied, realizing too late how little sense this made. Patty (sprayed-on jeans and skimpy lilac cardi) simply smirked, which Mel hadn't found too complimentary. Surely, by the woman-as-sister code, Patty should be protesting Mel's perfect slenderness and absolute lack of need to lose weight. OK, Mel had thought, wait till the next time she needs to borrow the drain rods . . .

Rosa had once dared to be a bit sniffy about Tina. 'Why've you made her such a gruesome old slag? You'll never get a telly series if you don't glam her up a bit,' had been her scathing words, catching Melanie at just the wrong moment.

'Because even old slags can have brains and intuition. This one's not only a shit-hot detective, she's paying all our bills and she'll put you through university, so a bit more respect please. And as for telly, she's biding her time, she'll get there.' Melanie had sounded surer than she was, defending her creation, for Tina really was a bit rough round the edges and her language was frankly only suitable for Channel Five, late night. It was a sore point: seven books down the line and not one had been optioned for so much as a pilot. 'It'll need some work . . .' her agent, Dennis, had said, without specifying exactly what sort of work he had in mind and whether it was down to Mel to do it, or someone else with TV-adaptation experience.

On this first morning of Roger-removed freedom, Mel shoved her huge white and black cat, Jeremy Paxman, off her legs and onto the floor so that she could climb out of bed. Now she was to be living entirely by herself without Rosa to wait up for at night, or needing to worry about whether she'd gone out and left her room full of burning candles, it occurred to her she could go on a course, learn the business of screen-writing and sort out Tina Keen's future for herself. Meanwhile, there was Rosa to prise from beneath her duvet. This was the day she was leaving for Plymouth – the mountain of bags and boxes in the hallway had to be loaded into the car. There would be arguments about what was to be left behind (for it surely wouldn't all fit into the Golf, even with the back seats down and parcel shelf out), some last-ditch bickering about money and then several hours of driving listening to music at a level that would shred her brain. Still, there was the wedding to discuss. If Rosa could be persuaded to part with information without Mel feeling like a Gestapo interrogator, that should keep them going almost as far as Exeter.

26

*　*　*

'What time is Rosa leaving?' Melanie's mother Gwen phoned as Mel was getting her chocolate croissant out of the oven.

Melanie looked quickly at the clock on the front of the microwave. It was already nearly ten and Rosa's thumpy footsteps had not yet been heard overhead, nor had water from the shower dripped through the ceiling lights onto the worktop – why did a plumber's promise to turn up on any given Thursday always come with the sinister rider 'All being well . . .'?

Mel replied, crossing her fingers that it would turn out to be true, 'In about two hours I should think. Did you want to say goodbye to her? Shall I call her down?'

There was a sharp intake of breath down the phone. 'Oh no! No! Just tell her I phoned, tell her good luck and to have a lovely time and work hard. I would send her a card, but you haven't given me her new address yet, so I can't.'

Melanie smiled to herself. 'You could have just sent it here.' She wished she hadn't said that; whatever her mother had decided was the right thing to do, there was no point in suggesting anything different.

'No dear, that wouldn't have done at all. It's so nice to have mail waiting for you when you move, it makes you feel at home. Just tell her what I said and that I'll be writing to her soon.' There followed a very firm click, as if the phone hadn't quite been slammed down at the other end but had come pretty close to it. Melanie took herself to the mirror in the understairs cloakroom, forced herself to breathe evenly and calmly and arranged her face into a smile, trying to relax the tense grimace out of it.

She asked herself: a) why she felt she'd been told off

and b) what on earth her mother thought she knew about moving house, she and Howard having occupied their leaded-light mock-Tudor house with its pretend cat stalking a bird on the porch roof since 1961. Conversations with her mother often affected her like this, leaving her feeling wound up and ludicrously frustrated, as if she was on the losing end of some word game for which the rules hadn't quite been explained.

'You need to let your anger go, take it to the mirror, watch yourself relaxing, setting it free, and replace it with inner, centred, calm,' Yvonne the masseuse at the gym had said the last time she'd attempted to knead a wodge of tension out of her shoulder blades. Re-interpreting it later, Mel had wondered if Yvonne had simply wanted her to shut up and listen to the whale music and leave her in peace to get on with her job, so she could drift away mentally to plan her holiday wardrobe.

Back in the kitchen, as centred and calmed as she was going to be for now, Melanie shoved half the cooling croissant into her mouth, choking slightly and sending a scattering of crumbs to the floor, which Jeremy Paxman pounced on and licked up greedily. Thoughts of her mother were still kicking about at the edges of her mind. Gwen Thomas tended to regard her older daughter as someone who had constantly failed to be the good example she should have been setting to her younger sister. She needn't have worried though, Vanessa had inherited all the conformist genes that were available in the pool and was, as Rosa had pointed out, so close to a clone of her mother that secret scientific pioneering could not be ruled out. Mel had a quick gleeful moment anticipating showing her parents and sister her garden when its makeover was finished, their horrified incredulity at the lack of flowers, lawn, bedding plants, proper British shrubs. They would chorus, 'Oh what a shame!' as if a gang of vicious vandals rather than the expert Max from Green Piece had ripped out and destroyed the shrivelled lavender and rooted out the matted clematis. They would predict gloom and failure for the graceful palms and chunky spiked agaves. Melanie, crossing her fingers briefly, hoped the climate wouldn't prove them right and that she wasn't relying too heavily on global warming not being a spiteful rumour.

'Who phoned? Was it for me?' Rosa, wearing one of her father's long-abandoned Led Zeppelin tee shirts, appeared in the doorway. Her long legs were bare and had the faded tan of late summer, and her arms were wrapped across her front against the morning chill. The scent of stale cigarette smoke and crowded pub wafted from her. Mel hoped she was intending to shower it all away: at least on day one it might be an idea to present herself to her unknown flatmates as someone reasonably clean and appealing.

'No, it was your Nana Gwen, wishing you luck.'

'Oh. Is she going to send me some money?' Rosa looked at Mel as if expecting the answer to be at least an instantly produced fifty-pound note.

'I don't know. Shouldn't think so, would you?'

Rosa switched on the kettle and spooned instant coffee into a mug. 'I don't see why not. Her first grand-child to go to university, it's a special occasion.' She grinned at her mother. 'I'll send her a card, a postcard of the Hoe or something, let her know the address. I bet when the saintly Twitchy and Witchy cousins go to uni she'll send them whopping great cheques.'

Melanie laughed. 'Poor Tess and William, do they have any idea you call them that?'

'Nah, though I wouldn't care if they did. So no-one else called?' Rosa was looking beady-eyed and eager over the top of her mug. Mel knew whom she meant: Alex might now be an ex-boyfriend but that 'ex-ness' hadn't been Rosa's choice. She kept hoping he'd change his mind, but he wasn't going to: he was a boy for whom life was a list of Next Things that had to be sought out and ticked off. For him now, the current Next Thing was Oxford and then on to a career in law. He'd turn up at Christmas, after the first term – both she and Rosa knew it, and one slightly pissed evening had giggled about it – with a neat-haired girl in baby-blue cashmere, a single slender gold bangle and sleek black trousers with a crease down the front. Rosa and her charity-shop treasures, her multi-pocketed low-slung baggy trousers and her trainers that were so very past their best would be laughed off as early experimentation, simply a way of finding out how to do sex just about well enough before moving on to someone who might need to be impressed into a Good Marriage. That, she and Rosa had damningly decreed, would last until, as a big-name lawyer in bored middle age, Alex was tempted into the thrill of some career-jeopardizing sexual naughtiness and was caught by the tabloids.

'Perhaps . . .' Mel started, then thought better of it. She'd been about to suggest Rosa might meet someone else, someone in Plymouth, but it was both too obvious and too trite.

'Perhaps what?'

'Perhaps we'd better get going. You don't want to be late.' *Melanie* didn't want to be late. She'd planned an overnight stop on the way back in a hotel near Exeter and she fancied a leisurely settling-in, a rustic walk in the late afternoon sun followed by a long hot bubbly bath with a couple of indulgent magazines, then a solitary delicious supper. She was going to practise hard this new art of being totally alone. Perfect Patty (who loved any chance to check out her neighbours' decor) was away for the weekend but her sister Vanessa had promised to call in and feed the cat. Melanie had quite easily impressed on her the folly of driving to Plymouth and back in a day. She hadn't mentioned the hotel with the 25-metre pool and Michelin-starred chef, for Vanessa didn't much approve of the pursuit of a good time. In case of emergencies she would leave the hotel's phone number, but wasn't going to feel any guilt for Vanessa assuming she was making a sensible but reluctant stopover at a Travel Lodge.

Rosa was taking her time brushing her long coppery hair. Clouds of ciggy-scented dust danced in the sunshine from the open door of the cloakroom. 'It's not like school, Mum. No-one's going to give me bloody detention if I'm a few hours after the deadline.' Rosa slammed the loo door shut behind her and flung the brush into her battered suede bag. 'Come on, help me load up. You can take the heavy stuff.'

Melanie shoved aside a box of books and picked up Rosa's guitar case. 'I don't think so. I'm old and decrepit, I need to protect my bones.'

Rosa grinned. 'God Ma, you're not going all menopausal on me, are you?'

Melanie hadn't even considered it. The very idea came as quite a shock. OK, so she wouldn't see forty again (or forty-three) but she still felt and functioned like a twenty-year-old. Her heart still quickened at the sight of a gorgeous young hunk, she'd never yet felt so out of place in Top Shop as to expect the Age Police to evict her at any moment and if she occasionally felt a bit hotter than usual she would put it down to excessive central heating, nothing more.

'No, I'm not going all menopausal as you so sweetly put it, I'm just old enough to choose what to lift and carry. And it is *your* stuff,' she told Rosa, picking up a small carrier bag full of what looked like old letters. She hoped they weren't relics of Alex. Wasn't university supposed to be about fresh starts?

Eventually the car was packed. There were no arguments about what would fit in and what wouldn't because Rosa simply doggedly arranged and rearranged the bags and boxes till they were wedged into place and the boot could just about be forced shut. Melanie noticed that the kitchen radio (the one she'd only that morning loaded with new batteries) was lying on top of a box of CDs and that back in the sitting room the video player had been unplugged as if in a half-hearted attempt at removing it. Rosa went back up to her room to check for forgotten essentials and came down the stairs looking thoughtful.

'Sure you've got everything?' Mel asked as she locked the front door behind her.

'Mmm. I think so. If there is anything you could send it down on an overnight, couldn't you?' Mel gave her a look. 'Please? And Mum, you won't get all upset when we get there, will you? I mean I'll be back in a few weeks. And I might phone you.'

'Might? Oh thank you so much. Yes, I'll probably cry absolute buckets,' Melanie teased. 'You'll be so embarrassed you'll be hustling me out of the door and disowning me.'

'Don't even joke about it.' Rosa scowled as she settled herself into the front seat and under the comfort of her headphones. Her fingers were pecking at her mobile phone, texting her loyal troupe of female friends (and especially best mate Gracie) who supplied each other with a constant running commentary on their lives. If Mel was as prolific with her Tina books as these teenage girls were with their text messages she'd be on her twentieth novel by now, no problem. Mel headed for the M3 and wondered what Rosa was saying, reluctant goodbyes or a sort of 'Yesss! I'm outa here!' Rosa had not since her mid-teens, been what a social worker would call a 'high divulger'. Whatever went on in her shaggy, foxy head was only rarely broadcast beyond the edges of the digital telephone networks.

The room in the hall of residence was smaller than Mel had expected, but cleverly put together like a half-size hotel one with a dolly-sized bathroom built into one corner. The block was so newly built you could still smell freshly dried paint. There was a sign at the end of the corridor just beyond Rosa's room, saying 'New Plaster – Do not kick the walls'. Someone had been a bit naive putting up a sign like that, she thought; competitive wall-kicking would almost certainly turn into a regular post-pub activity. In the room the pale wood-veneered wardrobe, desk, drawers and bed were all as a continuous fitted, immovable unit. The thought of mental patients or unstable prisoners flitted across her mind, folks who needed their furniture nailed down to prevent murder and maiming.

'Good grief, the luxury of it. Your own bathroom!' As Rosa hadn't yet made a comment, Mel filled the silence with over enthusiasm.

'Well, shower room, you couldn't swing a kitten.' Rosa looked out of the window. There was a glimpse of something silvery sparkling far away between the city buildings.

'And a sea view!'

Rosa scowled. Her mother was overexcited, fast heading towards being a liability. If anyone came out of any of the other rooms Rosa thought she just might have to lock Mel in the bathroom and pretend she was a mad intruder or a (very) mature student wandering around the wrong building. There was a smell of interesting smoke from along the corridor and she wondered why the alarm hadn't gone off – the rules in the booklet she'd been sent were very strict about smoking in the rooms. It seemed to be practically a chucking-out offence. She could hear music too: David Gray, which was a promising sign – she didn't want to be sharing with five swots whose idea of entertainment was something soothing on Radio 3.

'Shall I help you with the bed?' Melanie was delving into one of the boxes and pulling out pillows and the new packs of duvet covers and pillowcases. 'The plain blue or the stripey ones?' Rosa just felt exhausted. They'd hauled box after box up the two flights of stairs from the car. All she wanted to do was lie down on the unmade bed, among all the unpacked debris, and go to sleep for a couple of hours. Ideally, when she woke up it would all be done completely by magic. All her food and crockery would be stashed away in the cupboards in the big shared kitchen just across the hallway, all her clothes hung up, all her books lined up on the shelf over the desk and photos of her friends would be grinning down at her from the silly dinky pinboard that hung over the bed.

'Are you Blu-tacking stuff up?' A tall girl with streaky blonde hair appeared in the doorway, clutching a rolled-up poster. 'I'm Kate? Next room to you?' She had what Melanie called *Neighbours* intonation, every statement a question. Rosa looked shy suddenly, but smiled at the girl.

'I'm Rosa. I've only brought photos. Friends and that, I thought I'd see what the room was like first.'

'I think you're not supposed to . . .' Mel interrupted.

'Mum!' Rosa warned, picking up a carrier bag and clanking off with it to the kitchen opposite. Kate followed her and Melanie could hear the two of them laughing, could hear glasses being unpacked and put on a shelf and the fridge door opening. Rosa reappeared a few minutes later clutching a bottle of beer.

'I did the bed for you,' Mel said, 'but if it's OK with you . . .'

'It's OK Ma, you're allowed to go now. I'll be fine.'

Melanie didn't doubt it. Rosa allowed herself to be hugged but Mel could feel her eagerness to get to know her flatmates, to move in properly to her room and her new independent life.

'Shall I come down and wave you off?' Rosa offered.

'No, stay here and meet the others. Give me a call soon, I expect there'll be something you've forgotten.'

Melanie went back down the stairs to the small car park in front of the building, calculating that she'd just have time for that riverside walk if she put her foot down a bit on the A38. Her car was blocked in by a black Range Rover.

'Bugger!' she muttered, looking round for the owner. A tall man with a light blue sweater emerged from the building behind her, carrying an empty supermarket box.

'Sorry, I'll move it. Elly's stuff's taking forever to unload. She makes me carry all the boxes of books.'

'Sounds studious! I think mine's only brought a few novels.'

'Oh, I expect these are only for colouring in!' the man laughed. His eyes were the same smoky Gitanes-blue shade as his sweater. His hair was short and spiky and blond. Mel felt ludicrously fluttery. He was just the sort she'd fancy if she was . . . well, what? How much more available could anyone be than she was? No husband, no child at home – she even had what Rosa and her friends used to call a Free House. *He* wouldn't be available, though. There was sure to be a Mrs Spiky-blond-hair-and-blue-sweater. She was probably up there settling daughter Elly into her room, checking the cupboard space in the big airy shared kitchen and admiring (as Mel had) the new microwave, the cooker, the pair of fridge-freezers.

'So where've you come from?' Spiky asked, seemingly in no real hurry to move the car. The afternoon was still hot and sunny. Mel was anxious to get going.

'Richmond. And you?' she asked. Jeez, he was delicious-looking. What a smile, just enough of a tan, big elegant hands, bare brown feet in scuffed dock-siders.

'Oxford. Are you staying over or going back?' It was only conversation, not an invitation. But still . . .

'Er . . . I'm staying over. A place on Dartmoor.' So why not let him know, she thought, her fantasies leaping way ahead, the theme going: she told him where, he said oh yes, might see you later, she *did* see him later, an awful, thrilling lot of him and . . .

'Not the Inn on The Edge?' He grinned at her,

unlocking his car. She grinned back, nodded. Perhaps there was a God.

'We stayed there when Elly was down for her interview. Food's gone right off, the wife got food poisoning. We wouldn't go back.' He climbed into his car, then added, 'Though perhaps it was just a bad day. Hope you have more luck!'

Oh me too, thought Melanie, feeling more than slightly foolish. Me too.

Three

Gwen Thomas hadn't been inside a church since Vanessa's boy William's christening, but took it for granted that God was someone with whom she had an ongoing working relationship. Her personal mental portrait had him down as male (well of course), close to an Englishman's retirement age, thin and tall but slightly stooping beneath the burden of his responsibilities. Her God was dressed in a proper suit with a starched white shirt, just like the manager from the Barclays bank she'd wheeled Vanessa and Melanie to in their double pushchair, back in the days when you weren't separated from the counter staff by bulletproof glass and your signature didn't need to be backed up by a plastic card. God chronicled the world's fateful progress in massive ledgers using a black Parker pen and indelible darkest blue ink. He had a slow, solemn hand – what was written had been carefully considered, for life, death and the judgement of souls were not matters for haste or frivolity.

In the same way that she felt humbly apologetic for taking up his time if she ever needed the attention of her doctor, Gwen didn't trouble the Almighty with requests for unnecessary favours. She disapproved of those who were in the habit of wishing their lot was an easier, more prosperous one – you only got out what you put in. She had worked hard taking care of her home and family, reaped just enough in the way of material rewards, a healthy pair of daughters, three (so nearly four) grandchildren and a paid-off mortgage. Now that she and Howard were well into retirement she'd quite reasonably expected to be among the great band of elderly contented, smiling towards life's sunset with Howard at her side like the silver-haired couples in TV ads for life insurance. She should be able to look back and be pleased with having done her best, look forward and see herself and Howard enjoying an old age of shared interests, garden-centre visits and the loving attentiveness of their comfortably settled children. She didn't like to put it to God directly, because it was hardly the stuff of Third World debt, earthquake, famine or tidal wave, but, as she listened with slight disgust to some gynaecological frankness on *Woman's Hour*, she did wonder where things had gone amiss.

In the same way that she trusted God (though his ways were sometimes more than mysterious) to keep a guiding hand on the universe, Gwen assumed she'd continue to be the one who ran domestic life for herself and Howard until God decided which of them should be first to line up at St Peter's gate. The diary on the kitchen dresser was filled in by her, not by Howard. She would tell him when they were due at Vanessa's for Sunday lunch, when it was time to get the pelargoniums out of the greenhouse and repot them, when they should start going through the brochures and decide between Cornwall and the

Lakes. Howard deserved a rest from serious decision-making, after more than forty-five years at the Ministry of Health. When he went down to the corner shop to get the paper every morning, all he needed to do was choose between the *Mail* and the *Telegraph*. He could take the dog as well, make sure it went before it got back to the garden. Nothing trickier was required of him. He certainly wasn't supposed to come back with copies of *Maxim* and *Mayfair* and the smell of early beer on his breath.

If anyone was to blame it had to be Melanie. If she'd made more of an effort and hadn't let Roger go chasing after young things she'd still be keeping her family properly together. Rosa would still have a father on the premises to come home to in the university holidays, and Roger and Mel would be safely on the home straight. The fact that they weren't had unsettled everyone, especially, it seemed, Howard. Mel had had a secret gleeful look about her ever since Roger had wrapped his grandmother's Steinway piano in old blankets and called the specialist removers round to take it into storage.

'Oh the space! The glorious empty space!' Melanie had sung out, twirling round in the great gap by the sitting-room window on the day the instrument had been trolleyed out of her house. Gwen and Howard had been there at the time, invited for lunch, though Mel had completely forgotten in the midst of the upheaval. 'I should have got rid of it years ago!' It was obvious she'd meant more than just the piano. Gwen had said as much to Howard in the car on the way home, trusting him to be as appalled as she was.

'Good for her,' he'd declared instead, adding, 'and for him.'

41

Not at all the response she'd expected. 'But . . . what about . . .'

'What about what? What's there to "what about" about? Rosa's off to have her own life. She doesn't need parents breathing down her neck any more. Mel and Roger have grated on each other like sandpaper for years and now they've both got a chance to be happy. Good on them.'

He'd chuckled, Gwen recalled, as if somewhere deep down was their fulfilment of his own secret lost dreams. That was when he'd started to stay out for a couple of pints, the minute the pub opened in the mornings. Two pints just lasted through the sports pages of the *Telegraph*. 'Except on Saturdays,' he'd said unapologetically when she'd assembled the courage to ask what he thought he was playing at, 'that needs a whisky chaser – there's a few extra pages.' She didn't ask what it took to get through all the filthy magazines. Howard didn't know she'd found those. He could hardly expect her not to, though: he knew her domestic routine and she wasn't yet feeble enough to abandon the turning of the mattress once a fortnight. What her dignified God, the creator of all that was well-ordered, would make of it, Gwen couldn't bring herself to think.

It was getting on for 9.30 a.m. and Melanie's gardener was late. Max from Green Piece was due to bring round the finished plan he'd come up with after an initial discussion and a tour of the garden a couple of weeks before. Max, who, when they'd come to check out the job, had been the one of the Green Piece pair who'd done all the talking, had promised her 8.30 a.m. 'At the latest'. After they'd left, she realized she should have changed that to 'At the earliest', then she'd have known what time it would be safe to get into the bath without dreading the doorbell going. As a lone woman employing a team of potentially leery workmen, greeting them on day one wrapped in a towel and dripping Clarins bath gel all over the floor wasn't quite the coolly businesslike impression she intended to give.

Green Piece had been the fourth company she'd had round to quote for the restructuring of the back garden. The other three had been one-man businesses, and in turn each of these one-men had given her the sharp-intake-of-breath treatment, followed by a session of kicking at the crumbling garden path, a stamping on the threadbare lawn and a depressed shrug.

'Palms and stuff is a lot of hassle. If you want low maintenance, you want nice shrubs: bit of spotted laurel, escallonia,' the first decreed, adding – to bowl Melanie over with Latin – 'but if it's exotic you're after, you're sheltered enough for *fatsia japonica*.' The second had barely looked at the garden but grumbled that he'd never get his lorry round the back of the house, and the third said he might be able to let her have a few days eighteen months on, give or take. There would have been a fifth if the proprietor hadn't even refused to come out and take a look. 'We don't do Southernbrook Road,' a sniffy voice from Gone To Earth had told her on the phone. 'We are *landscapers*. Small back yards like Southernbrook are hardly *that*.'

Well fuck you, Mel had thought, plonking the phone down and going back to the Yellow Pages. Small back yard indeed. OK, her garden wasn't exactly stately parkland but surely town gardens had plenty of chic potential? They certainly did according to Roy Strong – Mel had done her research and reading. Wait till

43

Dying For It is peaktime viewing with an audience rating better than an *EastEnders* special and I'm the shit-hot new guest columnist featured in every magazine, she'd thought furiously. That prat from Gone to Earth would be knocking on the door begging to trim her hedge just so he could show off to his mates down at the swanky café-bar over his mozzarella and oil-drizzled tomato baguette with double espresso. She'd plunder the depths of Tina Keen's sharpest vocabulary to tell him what he could do with his dibber.

The doorbell eventually rang just as Melanie was delving in the drawer for a pair of tights. She was otherwise fully dressed after the fastest possible shower and the flinging on of clothes to a body still just slightly damp.

'Hi! Nice to see you!' she said as she opened the door, then stopped, declaring, 'Oh it's you!' on seeing Cherry, who, like Sarah, claimed to be her 'best' friend (they used to say 'oldest', it occurred to Mel, a term which seemed to have disappeared as soon as it became possible to construe it as not just meaning 'long-term').

'Yes it's me! Isn't it just as nice to see me as whoever you were expecting? Can't I come in?' Cherry was carrying a small pink and white cake box containing at least, Mel guessed, 1,000 calories, from Madame Blanc's patisserie. She flattened herself against the wall as Cherry pushed her way in and strode down the hallway towards the kitchen. 'I thought you might be feeling a bit down now that Rosa's gone so I thought we could go out and *do* something, you know, something girly just for *ourselves*. We can start with these.' She pulled plates from the rack over the sink and arranged a pair of delicate apricot pastries on them.

'Why do people keep feeling the need to feed me up?' Melanie asked, filling the kettle and reaching across to the dresser for mugs. 'Sarah brought me a Chinese to make up for Roger getting married and now you're consoling me for Rosa with cake.'

Cherry took a large bite of pastry, then, scattering crumbs, said, 'Well, I just thought you might need cheering up. You're not used to the lone life, not like me. Sorry if I've got it wrong. And I know I have because you were obviously expecting someone else.' She looked around the kitchen, her head going this way and that like a cat that's sure there's a loose mouse hidden in there somewhere.

Oh God, Mel thought, some people are just so over-sensitive. She handed a mug of coffee to Cherry and sat down beside her at the battered old elmwood table. Rosa's name was etched into the surface of the wood, down at the window end where she'd always sat for meals, first as a baby in her high chair then later in the cream wicker one, the arm of which she'd unravelled and snapped off in fronds by the time she was five. Melanie could see her vividly, twirling the broken-off strips round and round, curling them into rings round her fingers. It would be quiet without her, admittedly, but it was all right to have quiet, especially in the early morning, after all those years of 'Where's my home-work? Who's had all the milk? I need money! Quick!'

'I was only expecting the garden designer. He's late. He should have been here an hour ago and this isn't a very good sign.'

'Garden designer? Are you kidding? For a suburban oblong? What are you having done? Your garden always looks OK to me.' Cherry went to peer through the window, adding, once she'd noted the garden's obvious neglect, 'or it would if you put a bit of effort in.' Cherry turned back to face Melanie. 'You'd find it really quite good company, now you're on your own.'

Mel laughed. 'What? The garden? Don't tell me you actually talk to the plants, Chezza, that way lies royal madness.'

'No, I mean it's really absorbing, fascinating, watching the stuff grow, especially plants you've started from seeds. In spring, I race out every morning to see what's come up. It never fails to be a thrill. And in the winter you just leave the most tender ones in the greenhouse and ignore them while it's cold. All that's a lot more than can be said for men.'

'Ah now, men. I'm definitely not looking for one of those, not to keep anyway. Sarah thinks I should be leaping straight into the dating marketplace. I hope you don't.'

'Me? Hardly likely. You know me better than that.'

Mel smiled lazily. 'Though I did see one I rather liked the look of down in Plymouth. And, you know, for one gorgeous moment I thought he was going to be spending the night at the same hotel as me. I was just getting all geed up about possibilities when . . . well, nothing. It wasn't to be. Pity, I could do with just one little chance to see if I've still got any pulling power.'

Cherry put down the remains of her pastry and stared at Mel. 'But suppose he *had* been going to stay at the same hotel? Just suppose you'd met him in the bar, maybe had dinner with him . . .' Melanie watched, amused, as Cherry screwed up her face in concentration, forcing her imagination to take the scenario to its luscious and wicked conclusion.

'Go on, Cherry, don't stop now. We've had all this marvellous food, now what?' Mel prompted. 'Do I get offered another drink? Spot of brandy? Bit more champagne? Do we have it in the bar or take it up to the room? And are we heading for his room or mine?'

'Yes but you wouldn't have, not really,' Cherry decreed, sipping quickly at rapidly cooling coffee. 'Would you?'

'I might have. What's so wonderful is that there's absolutely no reason why I shouldn't.'

'Apart from nasty infections, guilty conscience, a sort of shabby, used feeling the next morning?'

Melanie laughed. 'No chance. For one thing, to deal with the first there's condoms.' She hesitated for a moment, for she didn't actually carry a supply of those around with her. There'd been no reason why she should, so far, but perhaps it wouldn't hurt to pick up a few in the supermarket, distribute them around her handbag collection. 'And as for the rest of the list, well – I'm a free woman. I can do whatever, or whoever, takes my fancy. I have this awful feeling I'm going to end up like a car that spends all its time in the garage. The least I can do is rev it up now and then and take it out for a quick run, make sure the engine still ticks over.'

'And to hell with the consequences.'

'There wouldn't be any consequences.'

'There's always bloody consequences.'

Cherry had been bitter and bereft for too long, Melanie considered, as she poured more coffee. What was it now, six years since Nathan, her partner of fifteen years, had gone to visit his brother in Australia – 'Just a couple of weeks, Chezzie, I'll be right back,' – had met an irresistible stewardess on the plane and married her in Hong Kong a month later. Cherry had wept and wailed tumultuously for over a year, giving herself up completely to sorrow, betrayal and anguish. Melanie and Sarah and many others had worried about her, concerned that she was turning her grief into her life's work. She couldn't have felt worse if Nathan had died, in fact she once told Mel after too much gin that she'd feel better if he had: 'At least that way I wouldn't feel so *rejected*.' After a hefty legacy from her grandmother, she'd given up her job as a legal adviser and devoted herself to the solitary life of a slightly tragic widow, all kitted out with a pair of Siamese cats, life membership of the National Trust and Friend status at the Royal Academy, the Tate Gallery and the Royal Horticultural Society. She filled the hours that might have potential for loneliness with painting meticulous, highly detailed studies of small wild animals, every claw and whisker in disconcertingly perfect place. They sold well as greetings cards and she was starting to get illustration commissions. Cherry obviously now thought of Mel as being in the same boat as herself – or at least alone on a raft that made up life's flotilla of solitary souls. It wasn't like that at all. Mel was delighted to be alone; she'd chosen it. She was happy that she and Roger no longer had to play along with the roles allotted them in their long-ago wedding ceremony. Leonora could do all that stuff now. See if *she* liked being expected to function as a walking Filofax.

The doorbell rang again, breaking an edgy silence. 'Oooh, my horny-handed man of the soil at last!' Mel leapt up and raced to the door. She didn't want to glance back and see Cherry making that familiar pinched face. It was enough that she could see it in her head as she went down the hallway: the glum, disapproving look, the determination never ever to consider as an option, not even just slightly, anything to do with sex, love or involvement with a man ever again. Mel wasn't exactly looking for any of that either, but she wasn't going to barricade herself emotionally against every thrilling possibility of dalliance. How depressing would it be, she thought, to shut up one's personal sex shop permanently, to deny yourself the possibility of any kind of closeness to another human being ever again, just in case it all went so horribly wrong?

Roger didn't like this much heat. When he stepped out of his fan-cooled hotel room into the blistering sun he felt immediately drained and exhausted. He held his wrist as he walked, checking his pulse, feeling that it must be rising closer to danger levels with every step he took. He could almost hold the steamy air in his hand, and drops of moisture trickled between his shoulder blades, seeped round the waistband of his shorts and behind his knees. He wondered, as he walked slowly towards the dining terrace for breakfast, how it was that everyone else looked as if they could function perfectly normally. The hotel specialized in luxury spa treatments and fitness programmes – some body-perfect fanatics were even getting up at dawn for God-awful sessions of what was unappealingly (and not jokingly) listed as Boot Camp in the exercise programme. How anyone could do press-ups, aerobics and a five-mile run to the town and back before breakfast was completely beyond him.

Leonora seemed to be blissfully content. She'd stopped feeling sick but hadn't yet got to that cumbersome stage in pregnancy where women start to have miserable sessions of staring into the wardrobe, flicking the clothes up and down the rails, searching for something that fits. He'd named that the Expensive Stage – Melanie had hit the shops with the fervour of a desperate raider when she'd been expecting Rosa. And then after the birth she'd said she never wanted to see the clothes again – so it was a whole new set for the next pregnancy. He could understand that she hadn't wanted to see those ever again, not after what happened. He'd taken them all to the nearest Oxfam shop in a couple of bin bags, handed them over to the gentle custody of a grateful volunteer. Mel had cried, told him he should have taken them further afield, afraid she'd have to face the poignant sight of her redundant clothes hanging in the shop's window or drooping pathetically on the putty-skinned old-fashioned shop dummy with the stiffly posed fingers, reminding her that it had all been for nothing. The possibility of something as awful as the death of a baby happening again was something he and Leonora hadn't discussed. She didn't have a lot of curiosity and simply hadn't mentioned it. He put that down to her being still young enough to be almost totally self-absorbed. And things went right for the young, didn't they? They didn't go round looking for life's disasters – if they did they'd be born with zero ambition and terminal timidity.

In the comparative cool of the dining terrace Roger helped himself to mango, pawpaw and pineapple from the buffet. He was hungry now and quite fancied a proper cooked breakfast – he could smell crisp bacon, toast, hash browns. He would be sixty-five when his new child was fifteen: 'An old pensioner – if you live that long!' Leonora thought it amusing to remind him, whenever he fancied something dangerously cholesterol-filled. She seemed to think it was a huge joke. But it wasn't funny at all, not when you really,

really wanted a couple of fried eggs, sausages, tomatoes and a big helping of potatoes sautéed with onions.

'Are you there? I'm eighty-one!'

'Jesus H., what's that?' Max wheeled round at the sound of Mrs Jenkins from her side of the fence. The orange poodle yapped a more hostile greeting. Melanie wouldn't have fancied Max's chances if it chose that moment to wriggle under the fence and go for his leg. It amazed her that this tall, gangly, wild-haired (weren't bleached blond dreadlocks a tad unexpected on white blokes past forty?) man, with a quiet, rather intellectual demeanour more suited to a speciality book dealer, should be perfectly capable of serious ground-clearing, heavy duty earth-shovelling and the installation of concrete posts where necessary. Beneath his ancient soil-encrusted guernsey (and it was *darned*! Who darns, these days? Did he live with his aged mum?) he must have muscles like Geoff Capes.

'That's my neighbour, Mrs Jenkins,' Melanie explained, turning to seek what the lilac curls bobbing about just beyond the fence needed. 'Are you all right?' she called.

'There's a man in your garden, dear.' Mrs Jenkins was glaring through the tangled roses at Max.

'Yes, it's all right – he's here to look at the garden, see what needs to be done.'

'You should let me have a word then. You were never any good with plants. You can't go wrong with delphiniums.'

Melanie rather thought she could – she'd bought any number of them over the years and every single one had gone to fatten the slugs and snails in gardens for

51

miles around. She was convinced they made special journeys, tipped off by garden-centre slug-spies that she'd just parted with another sixty pointless quids' worth of fresh leaf-stock for them to munch. Perfect Patty, only four houses away, had an entire bedful of delphiniums, immaculate flower-spikes pointing obediently heavenwards.

'I tell you what, I'll pop in and see you later,' Mel told Mrs Jenkins. 'Tell you what Max and I have decided,' she said, disentangling herself from what could become a decidedly cross-purpose conversation.

Max consulted the drawing on his pad. 'If you think you could run to a couple of pretty decent-sized *Washingtonias* over there,' he pointed to the corner by the back gate, 'plus a clump of those classic Cornish palms, the *Cordyline australis*, fast-growing and not too pricey, and some of the biggest *phormiums*, that should soon screen the garden off from the alleyway and the backs of those garages in the next road.'

'What about the manky cherry tree by the back gate? It's been unhappy for years but don't you have to get permission to cut it down?'

'It's a fruit tree, so it's no problem. And those young sycamores can go, they're just weeds.'

'Right. So what's staying?'

Max looked at her over his reading glasses. The look was an amused one, as if all this time there'd been some major, important point that she'd been missing. 'Nothing.'

'Nothing? Not the roses, not the clematis or the horrible lavatera?' This was bold stuff. Her father would have heart failure.

'Absolutely nothing,' Max insisted. 'Your garden is having a completely fresh start.'

*   *   *

Melanie sent Tina Keen up a ladder in a dusty attic room above a coffee shop from where she peered out of the window between the slats of a chrome Venetian blind. Melanie stopped typing and thought about how much the scent of cappuccino would take the edge off her detective's concentration. She could have let her have a coffee and a sandwich sent up from downstairs – but then someone on the staff would have had to know she was there, and that someone might just be the killer. Perhaps she could have brought a flask in with her, before the evening shift in the café had started. But Tina wasn't the flask type, not unless it was of the hip variety and filled with five-star brandy against an evening stake-out chill.

Melanie sat back in her chair and gazed out of the window. It was dusk, but she could just make out the Thames shimmering between the houses beyond her back garden. The tide was high and parked cars down by the bridge would soon be sitting like small metal islands in the water, the tide creeping up their wheels, under the doors and then soaking the floors. Later, the river would slink away again, leaving the road fresh and wet, the cars' tyres glistening clean stark black. Their oblivious drivers would return, would drive away, wonder about the strange noise from the exhaust, gradually realize that the floor was wetly tacky and that there was a smell that hadn't been there before. That was what she had to get into this chapter, she thought, as she started typing again. When Tina and her DCI went down through the back of the coffee shop after a long and bad-tempered fruitless watching session, the terrible realization that the next murder victim was already lying dead and cruelly mutilated in

53

the cubbyhole beneath the stairs would have to seep into their senses like the stench of rotting river water.

It was close to midnight when Melanie finished working for the day. The heating had gone off hours ago and her fingers were starting to set into cold curves over the keyboard. She hadn't eaten since lunchtime and her stomach was telling her it was painfully empty. Down in the kitchen she opened the fridge and found a big slab of Cheddar, which she grated over a couple of thick slices of bread. She shoved the lot under the grill and poured herself a generous and well-earned glass of red wine. Outside some kind of animal life skittered about and a cat yowled a raucous warning to an invading creature in the garden. Mel sat rigid at the table, not looking at the uncurtained window and waiting for her heart to stop pounding. That was the problem with writing about the most terrifyingly gruesome things that could happen, you never stopped imagining the worst. What was important, she told herself as she switched the grill off and topped up her wine glass, was to switch her mind off along with the computer. Tina Keen and the macabre, murderous world she inhabited were only pretend. Really.

Four

Melanie had left the radio tuned to Radio Four and when she returned home and switched it on she could trust it not to be blaring out Chris Tarrant at full volume. She also knew that if there'd been bread in the cupboard before she went out to the gym in the morning, she'd be able to have toast when she got back. These small truisms occurred to her as she got into the car and chucked her bag onto the back seat. Superficially trivial facts like these represented significant milestones – with Rosa occupying the house no such things could ever be counted on. No item of food was safe, no last half-inch of milk, no final scrapings from the marmalade jar or sticky crystals from the bottom of the sugar bowl. Before, when Mel had gone out in the morning, she'd had to gamble with herself whether it was worth calling in to the corner store to do a quick restock in case she felt acute exercise-induced near-starvation after her workout and swim. There'd be that nagging thought in the back of her head that in the cupboard the loaf was down to barely more than a drying heel – just enough for a desperate snack – but only for one. Rosa, who, when Melanie left would have been fast asleep and dead to all but her dreams, would be up before her mother got back, scavenging the kitchen for something sweet and filling. Toast, with honey, jam or marmalade, was what she craved on waking. And back into the fridge would go an empty, scraped-out jar, back in the cupboard would go the bread wrapper containing only crumbs. Empty banana skins would be replaced to blacken and seep their sweetly rotting aroma on top of the fruit bowl.

'At least she puts things away,' Sarah had commented, watching Melanie one day as she discovered a pair of completely empty ketchup bottles in her store cupboard. 'Mine just leave everything scattered around like a burglary gone wrong.'

'I wouldn't call it "away",' Mel had replied. 'Throwing the empties in the bin would count as "putting away". I blame all that emphasis on recycling and conservation at school – she finds it just about impossible to consign anything to the trash.'

Today Melanie had left the kitchen as tidy as a show house. And when she got home it would, so long as robbers hadn't come ransacking, be just the same. She smiled broadly to herself and, as the car slowed to join the queue at the traffic lights, she realized an entire grumpy bus queue was staring at her and judging her to be mad. One member of the queue was Ben, the school-bound son of her neighbour, Perfect Patty. As the car drew level, the boy glowered at her, slouching his shoulders into habitual teen sullen mode, but then suddenly he smiled back at her in recognition. Astonished at this transformation from hunched hostility, Mel waved, lowered the window and called to him, 'Ben! I'm going past your school, would you like a lift?'

The boy flung his scuffed bag into the car and folded his long self in after it. He brought with him the scents of a recently smoked cigarette, hair gel, and a lemony tang of deodorant. He was only a couple of years younger than Rosa, approaching A levels next year, Mel guessed, but, as his school still demanded the wearing of a uniform right through to the bitter end, he looked a lot less grown-up than Rosa had at that age. No wonder he usually seems so surly, Melanie thought with sympathy, it must be tough being seventeen and having to face the mean suburban streets each day in a red and black striped blazer.

'You going to the gym? That one behind St Dominic's?' he asked, glancing at her Nike bag on the back seat.

'I am. But I don't go as often as I should.' She laughed and prodded her thighs, encased like over-stuffed sausages in workout leggings. 'In my job there's too much opportunity for sitting around and letting the legs spread.'

Oh God, why had she said that? She could feel herself going ludicrously pink. Perhaps (vain wish) he'd passed that age when just about anything was remotely *double entendre*-ish? Unlikely, especially a boy at a single-sex school without the scornful but essentially more mature presence of girls. Or perhaps the comment had passed him by. A woman of her age, well, probably he wasn't even listening. Teenage boys were a bit of a mystery to her. The only one she ever had any dealings with was her nephew William, but he was only fourteen and not communicative unless a conversation contained the word 'PlayStation'.

'So wassit like down the gym? D'you do weights and stuff?' Kind boy, she thought – he couldn't possibly care less what she inflicted on her flabby body in the gym. Patty and David had obviously passed on to him their good-manners genes.

'Well, I usually start off with the bike for twenty minutes, then do a circuit of various machines, some stretches on the mat and then if the pool's not too crowded I have a swim.'

'Is there a sauna?'

'There's two, one in each changing room.'

'In each?' Ben looked puzzled.

'Men and women. Separate.'

'Oh. Right. Yeah well I suppose they would be.' She'd reached the roundabout where commuters were doing their daily resentful battle with school-run parents, and couldn't take her eyes off the teeming road to glance at his face, couldn't guess whether he was laughing (at her?) or (his turn) blushing.

'Well, this isn't Sweden,' she teased.

'Nah, shame.' He *was* laughing.

The traffic thinned as they left the main London-bound road. Assorted boys in the same red and black as Ben sloped along reluctantly towards their school day. Some hung about in groups in shop doorways, swigging from drinks cans like the winos on the Green. Younger ones play-punched each other and chucked their bags around. Next to her, Ben watched them. 'Pathetic,' he murmured at the scene in general.

'Where do you want me to drop you? Somewhere safely past the school gates?' How uncool it was, or not, to be seen in the company of a middle-aged woman (who looked decidedly early-morning and *sans* make-up) she had no idea.

'No, the gates are fine. I don't have a problem being

seen with you . . . unless you do of course . . .' He was openly mocking her now.

'I'll get over it,' she told him, stopping the car.

As he got out he hesitated. 'Thanks for the lift and . . . er, I know it's a bit of a cheek but do you often go to the gym? I mean, winter's coming. It gets wet and cold at the bus stop . . .'

'OK, OK, if I'm going I'll look out for you. But I don't always go at the same time,' she warned.

'Cool, good enough.' He treated her to a final smile as he turned and sauntered through the gates, and Mel was left with a Cheshire cat-like display of the most perfect teeth modern orthodontic treatment could provide.

Sarah's car was parked as close as she could get to the gym's doors. Mel parked the Golf between a pair of the massive tank-like vehicles favoured by the women of the area – yuppie trucks, Rosa called them. It must have been raining when Sarah arrived, either that or she had slid out of the car all geared up and ready for the cross-trainer in her little pink Nike shorts and cropped-off vest and didn't want the outside world to catch sight of her exposed tummy. Sarah's gym outfits, particularly the lime snake-print leggings, it occurred to Mel, would sit neatly on her Tina Keen detective. Sarah and Tina had similar clothes taste and both were skinny, wiry women, though Tina was a few inches shorter and a good bit faster-moving. If the two had to escape from a burning building, Tina would be swifter off the mark, out of the nearest window, pausing only to pocket her cigarettes and shimmying down a drain-pipe as if SAS-trained. Sarah would be sizing up all possible exits for the one that would do the least damage to her nails.

Mel took her time in the changing room, shoving her reluctant feet into her state-of-the-art trainers that were far too high-tech for the paltry amount of exercise she took in them. She almost felt sorry for them, for the lack of decent challenge she offered, their soles barely scuffed from sauntering round on the gym's carpets as she took her time ambling between the weights machines, stopping for chats here and there. The most she asked of these shoes was that they didn't slip on the pedals of the stationary bike as she watched Lorraine Kelly organizing viewer makeovers on GMTV.

'Oh, you're here! Have you been in yet?' Sarah, her face flushed as seaside-rock pink as her outfit, bounded in and flopped down on the bench next to Melanie.

'No. I just got here. I gave Perfect Patty's boy a lift to school.'

'Huh!' Sarah snorted. 'His school's only next door, it's hardly out of your way.' She poked a sharp finger into Mel's leg. 'You're slacking. We need you toned and honed for the meat market. And book a sunbed, manicure and facial too. If I'm going to relaunch you as a desirable product I want to have something good to sell.'

'You don't give up do you, Sarah?' Mel stood up and went to the mirror, tying her hair back into a scrunchie. 'I'm really truly not looking for another man. I'm living completely on my own now for the first time since I was – well, ever, really and it's great. Let me just enjoy it, OK?'

'OK.' Sarah sighed and looked sulky. 'But – if you won't go out with boys will you come out with the girls? Our dear old school's having a final reunion. They're closing it for good, knocking the place down

60

and building something – social housing I think – so will you come to that? Thursday week?'

'Now that you've got time on your hands . . .'

It was something Melanie wasn't supposed to have. It was too much along the lines of Pleasing Herself. Perhaps it had been a mistake to drop in on her mother on the way back from the gym. It gave a bad impression of careless leisure to be frittered away at sinful will. Mel and Gwen sat at the small round table by the window in Gwen's kitchen. In front of them was a two-cup cafetière, a small floral plate (intertwined morning glory), with chocolate chip biscuits arranged in a circle, overlapping as exactly as if a practised card sharp had dealt them out, and a glass bowl containing the kind of sugar that reminded Melanie of miniature grave-chippings.

Gwen Thomas sipped at her coffee and gave Mel a beady glance over the fluted edge of the cup.

'I wasn't exactly rushed off my feet looking after Rosa, you know, Mum,' Melanie told her. 'I mean she is nearly nineteen, and has been telling me she has a life of her own for the past three years at least. Most days we just crossed paths once or twice on the way to the fridge.'

Gwen laughed. 'You'll be surprised. You think there's no difference but when the washing machine's half-load button is permanently on, and when it's taking three days to fill the dishwasher – then you'll know you're really on your own.'

Melanie took a deep breath, forcing herself not to protest. There was no point. 'OK, so what is it you want me to do with all this time?'

Gwen took a deep breath. 'It's your father.' She

looked down at the table and her fingers picked at bits of sugar that weren't really there.

Mel felt cold suddenly, sensing disaster, illness, death.

'Dad? Is there something wrong? Where is he, by the way, has he gone to the garden centre again?'

'Garden centre! I wish it was the garden centre.' She looked at Mel, glittery-eyed but defiant. 'He's at the pub. Takes the dog every day and goes to the pub. He's there hours. Comes home reeling.'

Melanie tried to imagine her father blind drunk. It wasn't easy, even for a woman who made a very good living from exercising her imagination.

Carefully, she put together a picture of the man she knew so well. It was like painting by numbers, with the finished view so familiar you barely had to refer to the chart. There was the cricket-club blazer, faded navy corduroy trousers (baggy and faded at the knee), soft brown and cream check Viyella shirt, Marks and Spencer V-neck brick-coloured wool-mix jumper (only three-ply, he hated anything heavyweight), thoroughly polished slip-on shoes. Having carefully assembled this portrait, she set her father down on the road out near the parade of shops by the crossroads and tried to send him tottering along the pavement, one hand in his pocket, the other outstretched to ward off obstructions he might not see in time.

'Aren't you going to say something?' Gwen prompted, while Melanie was still sorting out her mental pictures.

'Er . . . are you sure?' she said eventually. 'I mean lots of people like a bit of an appetizer before lunch and, well, he's retired, there's no reason why he shouldn't. He can even sleep it off in the afternoon if he feels like it.'

'*I'm* retired!' Mel's mother got up abruptly and started bustling the coffee things together, practically hurling them onto the draining board. '*I* don't go getting plastered in the middle of the morning. There are things to do!'

There weren't things to do though, really, Melanie thought. Her parents always seemed to be filling in their days, as she assumed all the other non-employed elderly did. They devised time-consuming routines to occupy the hours. Gwen hand-washed her dusters every week, even though there were rooms in the house where the air was barely stirred enough to gather dust. She ironed underwear that could (possibly should) be simply fluffed and folded straight from the dryer and put away. Her father swept fallen leaves from the garden every single morning, from the first autumnal flurry right through to the first buds of spring. Once, Melanie had commented to Vanessa that it was as if the virtuous pursuit of good order would keep them alive longer. Vanessa had been sniffy about that, saying they'd never been the sort to take to the idle life and weren't likely to start now. If one of them declared they fancied simply lying on the sofa for an afternoon reading a novel, the other would probably decide their spouse was sliding into terminal decadence. Active body, active mind was the thinking of the generation that might have vanquished Hitler, but now feared senility invading by stealth.

Melanie's mother whisked away their coffee cups, donned her rubber gloves and briskly swished the crockery around in the suds-filled bowl in the sink. Gwen had never got the hang of modern detergents. Melanie had marvelled over many years at the great alp-like crests of soap suds that resulted from the prolonged squirting of the Fairy bottle. 'It's hard water,' Gwen had argued, when Mel had tried to tell her that you needed the merest gentle splash of liquid these days to get the same results as twenty years before. Change of any sort alarmed and unsettled her. Just now Melanie could feel her confusion about her husband's behaviour. Howard was doing something different, something that was just for himself. He hadn't consulted his wife, hadn't invited her to join him for these morning drink sessions. It was almost as if he had been her tame pet, but had started reverting to the wild and behaving in a way that didn't respond to the old well-tried training techniques.

'Have you talked to Vanessa about Dad?' Mel asked. She could imagine her sister's reaction and had to stop herself smiling: Vanessa was of the 'Stop it at once!' school of behavioural therapy, applied with no expectation of argument to her pair of seemingly angelic (but to Mel's mind rather suspiciously quiet) children. She'd quite easily use the same strategy on her father, as if he was a naughty child who would keep climbing over the gate and making for the dangers of the main road.

'Vanessa's got her own family to deal with. I'm only mentioning it to you because you *haven't*. Well, not any more.' Gwen sighed, as if the goings-on of the world were suddenly an exhausting mystery to her. She peeled off the pink Marigolds, folded them neatly and placed them next to the yellow plastic scourer in the china sink-tidy, taking refuge in small, familiar kitchen rituals.

Mel bit her lip and tried to feel that she hadn't been mildly insulted. Something was her fault. Losing Roger was her fault. But it was only her mother (oh, and of

64

course Vanessa) who made her feel he'd been 'lost'. It was too dramatic a word for their reasonably contented separation. 'Losing' was for something that left you with real, heart-clutching emptiness. Like her son, that tiny, barely formed baby with skin the colour of fury, so thin that between the tubes and dressings she was sure she could see right through him. Time to go, she decided, getting quickly out of her seat, time to get back to Tina Keen and the mutilated teenage hooker stuffed under the café stairs.

'I'll have a think about Dad,' Mel said as she briefly kissed her mother's powdery cheek. 'I'll ask him if I can come to the pub with him one day and see what he's up to. Perhaps he'd just like a bit of time to himself.'

'To himself? Whatever for?' Gwen said as she opened the front door to see her daughter off the premises. 'You get plenty of time to yourself when you're widowed. It's not something you go looking for, Melanie, you'll find that out for yourself one day.'

It was cold in the aircraft's Club Class section, which cancelled out any extra comfort that the legroom and not-bad food gave. Roger could swear there was a freezing draught whistling in from the window beside him. Leonora slept peacefully, stretched out beneath her airline blanket as if she was in the best kind of bed. In fact, he thought, as he checked his watch for the hundredth time, for the price of this upgrade he could have bought a bloody excellent top-of-the-range mattress.

The cold Atlantic blast was aiming at his left calf and making him shiver. Roger wasn't a happy flier at the best of times, always expecting the big tin tube to give in to gravity and plummet to earth. He could see drops of something (not rain, could it be rain?) trickling down the wall beside him. This couldn't be right, surely the plane should be completely sealed? He wondered about calling the stewardess, but was terrified that these small wet drops really were a cause for concern. He could imagine the stewardess's panic-stricken shriek, all the passengers waking, the shouting, the confusion, the praying – the end. Definitely if he made a fuss they'd crash. If he ignored this, the plane would fly on. Whether he said something or not, though, there shouldn't be little gaps where the outside could let itself in. Suppose something gave way under the pressure. Wouldn't they all be sucked out? He tightened his seat belt, then felt under Leonora's blanket to make sure hers was secure. The stewardess, catching sight of his hidden hand snaking across her body, gave him an uncertain little smile. Let her think what she liked: he was too old to explain himself away.

Leonora smiled in her sleep, content, confident, sure of her happy future. Roger, meanwhile, twitched his feet up and down, rotated his ankles, went on to worry about deep vein thrombosis and about whether he really should have eaten the chicken risotto that now lay so heavily in his stomach. Most of all, though, he worried about whether the plane's oxygen supply was enough for the fragile growing baby, because, as he (and Mel) knew too well, there were things that could go catastrophically wrong and, as Leonora's pregnancy advanced, it seemed more and more to Roger as if with this extra chance of producing a little life, fate was being teased and tempted. With wicked disloyalty, he wished Melanie was next to him right now. Not as a replacement for Leonora, but just to talk to about all the worry-things. She'd know whether it was all right about the leaky plane, that was for sure. If she took one quick look and said, 'Condensation,' that's exactly what it would be. If she said, 'Hmm, not sure,' he'd worry on. You knew where you were with Mel. He hoped, he really hoped, as he looked at Leonora's smooth young trusting face, that he'd manage to know where he was without her.

The trouble with working late was that sleep wasn't as easy to come by as when you packed up earlier and gave yourself several hours to loosen the brain. On nights like this, when Mel's head was still buzzing at 2 a.m. with the work she'd just finished, she could quite see the point of proper office hours. She realized, as she lay in bed staring at the shadows on the ceiling, that she shouldn't have gone to bed straight after the cheese and pickle sandwich. If it was true, as her mother had always said, that cheese last thing at night gave you nightmares, she wouldn't mind at least getting to sleep so that she could put the theory to the test.

It should have been the quietest part of the night, too. Instead she could hear the distant whoopings of a group of revellers who must have managed to persuade some unlucky pub landlord to host a lock-in. There was the special night-time traffic as well: she could hear the rhythmic whine and clunk of the bin wagon collecting rubbish from the back of the shops and restaurants on the main road a couple of streets away. And along with them was the metallic clanging of heavy-load trolleys delivering to the fast-food res-taurant at the end of that same block.

The whooping gang were getting nearer. Melanie tensed as she heard glass breaking, somewhere at the far end of the road near the lane that led to the river. There'd be graffiti by morning too, she guessed: some indecipherable teenage tag scrawled on a house-side, applied with far more speed than artistry.

Mel turned the pillow over to cool her head, lay on her side and tried to settle. Thoughts about Tina Keen still raced around her brain. There could, she thought, be a way of using these early-hours rubbish collections to find her way to the killer. Mel herself wasn't yet sure who'd done it. She preferred to use the Ruth Rendell method of plot formation: if she knew from the start who the culprit was, a reader could work it out too. It made the job more interesting, but definitely tiring. Sometimes she envied writers who had every chapter mapped out, complete with character sketches and plot summaries. It would be like having a good map to follow in a country you'd never visited. The way she worked, she just had to rely on instinct and a reasonable sense of direction.

The whooping gang were quite close now. She put her hands over her ears and tried to shut them out. She could smell the lavender water she'd sprinkled on her pillow, and wondered if its soporific qualities had possibly been exaggerated. But then she'd defy any herbal tincture to lull away the new sound of a car screaming at full throttle down the lane. It sounded mildly familiar, even being over-revved. A Golf, she identified, at last feeling mildly dreamy.

A Golf? Her Golf had been parked in front of the house, in its usual place just under the chestnut tree. Wearily, knowing exactly what she'd find, Mel climbed out of bed and went to the window. 'Oh, great,' she murmured as she dialled 999. 'Bloody frigging great.'

'We don't usually come out for cars.' The large gingery sergeant, who looked as if retirement wasn't that far off, accepted a third biscuit and stretched his legs out under the kitchen table. Melanie assumed she was to feel privileged.

'So why did you?' she asked.

'Well obviously it's because you're on your own, love. We have to check you're not unduly distressed, or that there's not something else you haven't felt able to mention.' Ginger sounded like a patient teacher, going over something for the fiftieth time with a bunch of trying pupils.

'Like what? There isn't anything else, it's just the car that was stolen.' Melanie, having waited well over an hour for the honour of this police presence, was more than ready for sleep now but felt she should make the most of the visit's research possibilities. She knew plenty (definitely a lot more than the average citizen would want to know) about police procedures and protocol, but the real-life character traits had to be grasped as and when.

Sergeant Ginger gave her a bless-your-sweet-innocence smile and explained, 'Well, your car might have been taken by an abusing partner. You could be covered in bruises and not finding it easy to divulge the real problem.'

'Yes, but, well I appreciate all that but truly, as you can see, I'm fine. The car was just taken. I was just trying to get to sleep at the time.'

'Even so.' Ginger Plod sipped at his well-cooled tea. 'Crime is always a shock. Do you have anyone you could get to come and stay with you? What about a neighbour? Boyfriend? Best pal?' He looked as if he rather hoped she'd fall sobbing to the floor. He had a kind, round, placid face. She hoped he wasn't disappointed by his job – he looked as if when he'd joined the force he'd given 'Helping People' as his main reason for doing so on the application form. His shoes were wonderfully polished, as if compensating for the laxity of discipline in the modern cop.

She smiled at him, hoping to express thanks for his concern along with reassurance that she didn't need it. The cat came rattling through the catflap and although it was tempting to say she was going to cuddle up in bed soon with Jeremy Paxman, she no longer had the energy for explaining the joke.

'I'll be fine, really. And please, I don't need Victim Support or counselling – I know it's always offered, but it would be wasted on me. It's not as if I've suffered . . .'

The policeman gave her a disbelieving look. 'Everyone's suffered, one way or another,' he declared as he stood up. 'The trick is to admit it.' He put on his cap and headed for the door. 'There's such a thing as being too independent, you know,' were his parting words. Mel thought how very like her mother he sounded, promised she'd bear it in mind, then went rather crossly back to bed, falling into a deep sleep just as she was wondering where the hell her insurance details were.

Five

Being eighty-one (or thereabouts) didn't stop Mrs
Jenkins being an early riser. She liked to be up and
ready to greet the postman, always opening the door to
take in her mail as if her letter box had been sealed up
or she was protecting the poor man's fingers from her
poodle's savage teeth. Often she was disappointed –
too frequently he cycled on past without even junk
mail to deliver, not so much as a pizza menu or an invitation to take out a bank loan. She liked to be waiting
on the step, though, just in case there was something
from Brenda in Canada. And when there was, as today,
when an autumn breeze wafted in through her open
door and chilled her vein-knobbled legs beneath her
old plaid dressing gown, she needed to know immediately what the news was from her daughter, so she
stepped over the low wall and knocked hard on
Melanie's door.

'It's seven o'clock!' Melanie yawned, wrapping her
robe tightly round her against the cool, damp air. This
counted as more of an interrupted night than an early
morning and was to be grudged, even to a needy neighbour. After the previous week, when the car had been

stolen, she'd gone into a kind of jet lag without the fun of travel. It was becoming a routine, working late and then staying up for a good relaxing while, well into the early hours, flicking through cable-TV films to find the ones she'd missed first time round. She'd also started to make her way through the red wine that Roger had told her was definitely not for drinking *yet* (so when? Suppose they died first?) and ate bizarre sandwiches from whatever was left in the fridge. The night before had been salami, artichoke hearts from a jar whose sell-by date she now wished she'd checked, topped off with tomato and a couple of slices of mozzarella. Cheese, she'd found, did not give her bad dreams. Only the thought that Roger might resume his habit of loading her with his life's minor hiccups caused her to half-wake in the night. She could have solved this by switching off the phone, but there was Rosa in Plymouth to consider and the rest of the family too – the moment she was out of contact there would be sure to be some dreadful emergency. She could just imagine Vanessa, tight-lipped outside a hospital ward, hissing accusingly, 'We did try to phone you . . .' as if instead of innocently sleeping she'd been out on the town, having careless rampant sex with a coked-up young stockbroker newly trawled from Stabbers nightclub out in EC-something. This morbid worst-case dreamscape was completed by her mother, pale and sorrowing in the background, clutching a poignant black bin bag containing her freshly dead husband's clothes, his watch, four back teeth (on a plate that had click-clacked and never really fitted), signet ring and the loose change that always weighed down his left trouser pocket.

'I've had a letter, dear.' Mrs Jenkins tottered past

Melanie and made her way straight to the kitchen, where she sat down at the table and ripped open the envelope. She held out the pages to Melanie and looked across at the kettle.

'Cup of tea?' Mel asked, obediently.

'Thank you dear, and if you've got any bread I wouldn't mind a slice of toast to go with it. Whatever it is in tea, it needs something to mop it up or it's funny on the insides.'

'OK, toast it is then.' Melanie cut a couple of slices of her favourite rough-hewn wholemeal and hoped it wasn't too challenging for Mrs Jenkins's tender 'insides'.

Mrs Jenkins's daughter Brenda had strangely old-fashioned handwriting. It was spiky and slanted keenly to the left, like wind-battered trees struggling to survive in coastal areas. Mel could imagine Brenda at school in the 1960s, being told off in Handwriting Practice for the exaggerated backward slope, the almost apologetically undersized script, for not rounding her o's and e's properly. Possibly the girl had been left-handed – whatever she was, she was fluent enough in her middle years. Page after page of turquoise hieroglyphics challenged Mrs Jenkins's failing sight. It seemed bizarre to Melanie that Brenda kept so fervently in touch with her mother, chronicling her Toronto life so thoroughly but being ignorant of the fact that her mother could now read only from the Large Print section of the local library. Perhaps it was just as well this was the case, otherwise Mrs Jenkins would be perusing the cheap-flights sections at the back of the Sunday papers and wondering why she was never invited to cross the Atlantic on an out-of-season special offer. Brenda's letters were always crammed with news of recently acquired material goods – particularly hearty outdoor equipment which made Mel feel she was reading through the L. L. Bean catalogue. This time there was husband Hal's new hunting rifle, a couple of Arctic-quality sleeping bags, the winter cover for the pool, son Barty's drop-head car – second-hand, but with scarlet leather seats. How much could a few hundred dollars for her mother's air fare hurt?

'They're so far away,' Mrs Jenkins sighed now, gazing out of the window past Melanie as if Toronto might just come into view on a passing cloud. Melanie stopped reading and poured her aged neighbour another cup of tea. It was all she could do, really. Mrs Jenkins didn't want to hear her making suggestions about visits, raising hopes and possibilities that just weren't going to happen.

'You must miss Brenda a lot,' Mel said, cursing herself for the inadequate platitude.

'Well yes I do, but you want them to get on in life,' Mrs Jenkins said. 'You don't want to stand in their way.'

I would, Mel thought fiercely, I'd stand in Brenda's bloody way with a return ticket and the grandchildren all lined up before it's too late and they're all rushing over here for the funeral. Depressed, she returned to the letter and continued, '"*And the big news, I saved it for last! Hal's got a business trip to Europe so I'm coming with him for a visit. School will be out by then so Barty and Lee-Ann will come too . . .*" They're coming over!' Mel couldn't keep her astonishment out of her voice. 'They're coming to see you!'

'They'd better hurry up then, I'm eighty-one, you know.'

*　　*　　*

Max from Green Piece was not what anyone could call a speedy worker. On his initial inspection visit, he had been accompanied by a business partner who hadn't appeared since, and Max seemed to have taken on all the work himself and occasionally went missing. Beyond Melanie's back gate was a skip that was only very, very slowly being filled with the rejected contents of her flower beds. If he didn't get a move on, the whole lot would have rotted down and be ready for digging back in as compost. Max had given her a quote for the entire job so he wasn't, thank goodness, being paid by the hour, but she couldn't help suspecting that he was spreading his services out, working on at least two other jobs at the same time – for clients who were clearly more important, or more profitable, than she was.

'It's always the same,' Sarah told her over coffee at Costa's in Richmond. 'It's what they do with lone women clients – plumbers always tell you they need a vital part and don't come back for a fortnight, leaving you with a defunct boiler and a dripping tap. Remember Cherry's kitchen?'

Melanie did. When Cherry was renovating her flat, post-inheritance, she'd existed for two months with a kitchen that was no more than a sink and a plank. Bare lethal wires poked from the walls and ceiling, the flooring was rough broken concrete and there was a lurking smell of drains. She had become a world-class expert on takeout pizzas: 'I could go on *Record Breakers*, if it was still going,' she'd complained. 'I could tell you what it was and where it came from and its fancy menu-name blindfold.'

'She got quite plump at the time,' Sarah reminisced,

not without a note of sly pleasure.

'Mmm,' Mel agreed, giving her own left thigh a testing squeeze. It felt too soft. One week without the car meant no trips to the gym. She could have cycled, her conscience told her, or taken a bus (lined up at the bus stop with Ben and his schoolmates – would he speak to her if she did? Or just skulk and glower, praying fervently that she wouldn't single him out?) But that would have taken half the morning, time when she could be writing . . . or having coffee with Sarah.

'So you're coming tomorrow night? To this reunion?' Sarah reminded her.

'Yeah, OK. What do we wear?' Mel giggled 'Old school hat? Do you remember those straw boaters? They made good frisbees.'

'They did. I remember boys at the bus stop nicking them off our heads and whizzing them into the road under cars.'

'And all the goody-goody girls kept theirs on with elastic under their chins.'

'Do you think they'll all be there? All the smug ones, the ones who never rolled their waistbands over so their skirts were up to their knickers?'

'Sure to be. They're just the sort who'd be bound to turn up. It'll be a sea of Jaeger and Country Casuals and clever ways with scarves.'

Sarah downed the last of her coffee. 'It's really the old members of staff I want to see.'

'Most of them are probably dead. Or at least as old as dinosaurs.'

'Not all of them. I wonder if that cow who taught us maths is still alive, the one who said one day that I was so hopeless I'd never get a job in a bank.' Sarah giggled. 'I got detention for asking her if that was a promise.

And what about . . .' she hesitated. Mel watched a frown of concentration collecting across her face. She knew what Sarah was thinking. She'd already thought it herself: what about Mr Nicholson (geography), passion fodder for just about every girl who'd read past page forty-six (and studied the accompanying photos carefully) in the school's biology textbook.

Sarah snapped her fingers, making Mel jump. 'Mr Nicholson – geography. Mr Knickers-off. He looked a bit like a cross between Jim Morrison and that bloke off *Magpie*, all long curls and leather. We all fancied him. I think some girls even got lucky, so rumour had it.'

Mel sipped her coffee and avoided Sarah's eyes. 'I don't suppose he'll be there, but if he is at least he won't be a dinosaur. He wasn't much older than us, not really. If you think, we were what, sixteen, when he arrived? It must have been our O-level year. He can't have been more than twenty-three.'

'You're right, that's barely any difference. Poor bastard, newly qualified, far too good-looking and thrown in to face being adored by seven hundred adolescent girls. He liked you, Mel, I remember that. Did you and he ever . . .'

'He gave me a lift home sometimes – it was only because he was going that way, no special reason.'

She'd lied a bit, because if she'd told the truth Sarah would ooh and aah and demand to know a) full details and b) why she'd kept it a secret from her very best friend for so long. She wasn't sure herself – at the time it was because it was so delicious (and Neil had said essential) to keep it a secret, and since then . . . well, it had simply never come up. Till now.

Sarah sighed. 'I remember he had a nice car, a red MG – we could hope for no greater sophistication back then. Such a tragic waste – him, not the car. He could have given us all far more of an education than just teaching us about contour maps and the exports of Argentina. Do you think perhaps he was gay?'

'Couldn't tell you.' (Almost true, *wouldn't* was closer.) 'He won't be there though, I bet. He could be anywhere by now. He could be working at Roedean and still being adored.'

Sarah laughed. 'No, he'll be bald, paunchy and depressed about the State of Education Today. And he'll have a saggy wife who's not a bit like all that luscious teen crumpet that we were.'

'What a terrible fate. Poor sod,' Melanie sighed.

'Yeah. Poor sod.'

The nice ginger sergeant was on the answerphone when Mel got home. 'Your vehicle has been located in an undamaged condition,' he said in that mechanical, stilted way, like police being interviewed on TV. Mel felt rather disappointed: she'd seen a cute little Audi in the car showroom round the corner and had been planning to call in and chat to the sales staff. She'd never bought an absolutely brand new car, one that smelled only of fresh, clean, unsullied upholstery. Every car she'd ever driven had carried beneath the over-lavish air freshener a history of the fast food and cigarettes and sweat and particles of life from the previous owner. Roger had been one of those people who (like her mother – again) considered the depreciation during a car's first year was so enormous that it made far better sense to go for something which was – in his words – 'slightly used'. An unfortunate, sordid little term, she thought now, reminding her of the time they'd spent the night in a bed and breakfast in Lyme

Regis, and she'd been more than suspicious that the sheets hadn't been changed since the previous occupant. He was probably right though, boringly, sensibly right, she conceded, as she looked up the number of the police station in her Psion: a new car was surely a piece of wanton extravagance. Nice, though. It would have been fun to look through a brochure, to be offered options like leather seats (in pink? purple?), a sunroof, alloy wheels (whatever difference they made) and an unfathomable choice of in-car entertainment systems.

The Golf had been found tidily parked in a cul-de-sac near Basingstoke. Nothing had been taken from it, according to Sergeant Ginger, who was keen to assure her that even her packet of Everton mints was still untouched in the door pocket.

'And are the cassettes still there?' It was hard to believe that anyone willing to nick a car wouldn't think to pilfer the contents.

'In the glove compartment? There's about a dozen of them listed here. Were there any more than that, in a bag or something?'

There weren't. Her taste for the Beach Boys' greatest hits, vintage Hancock comedy shows and the complete works of Duran Duran had been scorned. Rosa would have been in full agreement with the car thieves, she thought, wondering as she often did about the Youth of Today. A more fitting, dramatic finale for the faithful Golf would have been for it to end up a gloriously burned-out shell, abandoned at a skewed and dangerous angle (possibly upside down) in a lay-by somewhere way up near Carlisle. It should have had a thrilling adventure as the unwilling but speedy and reliable accomplice to a stunning bank raid. Investigating officers could perhaps have found a few suspicious bloodstains, traces of cordite . . . It was all the fault of the books she wrote, she thought, as she went up the stairs to have a good look in her wardrobe and see if it suddenly and magically contained an outfit that would make her the envy of all those ex-contemporaries from her schooldays. Deciding what to wear was going to be almost as tricky as working out how Tina Keen was going to pinpoint the murderer.

'I didn't think there'd be this many,' Sarah whispered to Melanie as they went in through their old school's main door and followed the sound of high-pitched, exclusively female conversation to the hall. Melanie hesitated by the door, reluctant to launch herself into this chattering and colourful throng. Dress-code-wise, the majority seemed to have gone for the smart, bright, on-the-knee suit. There were no scarves that Mel could see, cleverly knotted or otherwise, but there were a daunting number of scrubbed teeth on show: every woman she looked at seemed to be beaming far too eagerly. A hundred different perfumes almost knocked her out, too, successfully quashing any stale lingering scent of school lunches.

'Can you see anyone?' Sarah murmured.

'Bloody hundreds. Can't you?'

Sarah punched her arm, just sharply enough for Mel to be sure there'd be a bruise on its way the next day.

'No, idiot, people we know!'

Mel couldn't. And, apart from a gaggle of ladies so ancient and wizened they could have passed for founder pupils, it looked as if most of those present were younger than her and Sarah. Instantly, she felt like a sad (in the Rosa-used sense) middle-aged divorcée with nothing better to do in the evening, and her morale sank even lower on considering that this was the truth.

'We shouldn't have come.' She turned in panic to Sarah. 'It's a nightmare in there. I feel as if I'm going to be signed up for a netball match any minute.'

'You'll feel better after a drink.' Sarah grabbed her wrist and pulled her towards the back of the hall, where the thickness of the crush suggested the welcome presence of a bar.

'Why are we here?' Mel hissed, as they sipped at unchilled Chilean white that Sarah had obtained by shimmying her slender self through a mass of softly padded bodies.

'You're here for a giggle and for a bit of research. I'm here to show that maths bitch that you didn't need to understand bloody quadratic equations in order to have a gorgeous life. We're here together to prove how successful and wonderful we are, swans among ugly ducks.'

'So that'll come under "showing off" then, will it? "Swanking", as my mother would put it?' Mel felt depressed, surrounded by all these brightly chirping females. She wished she was home, lying on the sofa with Jeremy Paxman and watching *Changing Rooms*. She could just sneak out – Sarah was being picked up by her husband Nick later, so Mel was going home alone anyway. Sarah was right, though, occasions like this were good for a writer's research. She'd do some listening in on other people's conversations, see if there were any gems to pick up and store for later. Around her she caught the odd phrases: talk of families, careers – years and years of catching up bundled into sentences that had to be few enough to hold their

81

listeners' attention, but full enough to convey an impression of a top-grade A level in Life. The really insecure simply wouldn't have turned up. The ones who were still looking for themselves, for love, for fulfilment, wouldn't have dragged all that tatty baggage along to be picked over like reject jumble tonight.

It was a perfect event for Sarah, with her massive house by the park, pair of children brilliant in both the sporty and academic areas, and a husband with an account at Tiffany's, who brought home loving little trinkets so often that if he was married to Mel she'd be convinced he was having an affair. Melanie thought about her home, that, comfortable though it was, could be less shabby round the edges, her devastated garden, the just-successful-enough career that could be more dynamic, her husband who was now someone else's and her daughter who pecked out her life in text messages. Sarah had disappeared into the throng, presumably in pursuit of Mrs Golightly (maths) with a view to showing her how well her bank statements added up.

'Good grief! Surely it's not Melanie? Melanie Thomas?'

Why was it 'surely not', Mel wanted to know. She put on a cheerful smile and looked at the man standing in front of her. He was one of very few males in the room, someone's husband, she assumed, hoping it wasn't someone she'd been out with long, long ago and impolitely forgotten.

'Sorry – er . . .' Good grief, she suddenly thought, surely not Neil Nicholson (geography)? His face was less youthfully sharp, his brown hair (no longer curly) had a hint of streakiness that could be the beginnings of grey, but the grin was familiar, a slightly mocking, urbane know-all look that had had several hundred silly schoolgirls wishing he'd share some very private non-geographical tuition time with them.

'Mr Nicholson! Well, I didn't expect to see you here!'

He leaned forward and she caught a familiar memory-tweaking scent of Gauloise.

'You always called me Neil out of school,' he said, teasing her.

'But we're in school now, aren't we?' She cursed herself for sounding so pert – not something particularly becoming in anyone over fifteen. So he still favoured leather, she noted, though now it was a puppy-soft black jacket, DKNY she'd guess, rather than the battered old flying jacket he'd worn in all weathers and which, he'd told her during one of the lifts home, had annoyed the head of the school no end.

'I think we're each now supposed to be amazed at how little the other has changed,' Neil said. 'You first.'

Mel laughed. 'After twenty-five years? Would you still want to look like Jim Morrison? And are you going to tell me the puppy fat will disappear in time?'

Bugger. She wished she hadn't said that. Now he'd think it had been an astoundingly major event in her life, that scorching summer day close to the end of term when he hadn't driven her straight home but had put the car roof down and taken her for tea and ginger cake and a bit of a lie-down among the ferns near the Windmill on Wimbledon Common. She hadn't had sex before. Well – she didn't (quite) get it then either (which was disappointing) but it had been close enough to rate a seven out of ten in her diary that night. He'd been the one to hold back. It might have been fear for his career or it could have been the off-putting virginal presence of her school uniform, the blue and white button-through check dress with its little-girl Peter Pan collar. She'd lain back on the grass, still and passive and barely daring to breathe while he'd unfastened all the buttons down the front, peeling the fabric apart, then staring at her pale sun-starved body as if she was a box of chocolates and he was wondering where to start. That was when she'd started gabbling about being fat, putting her hands over her tummy and pushing it flat. 'Typical woman,' he'd said, gently pulling aside her broderie anglaise bra and kissing her left breast. 'You always imagine you're less than perfect.'

She'd never told anyone, but whenever lurid news of an offending teacher reached the press, she was reminded that these days that lazy and usefully instructive hour on the common could have got Neil fined, finished for ever in his profession and quite possibly enrolled on the sex offenders' register, even though she'd been close to seventeen.

The chatter volume was rising as more women arrived in the hall.

'Have you had a look round the place? Has it changed much?' Neil asked.

'I've only been here about ten minutes. In fact I was just wondering why I bothered. I came with Sarah, remember Sarah Michaels?'

Neil shrugged and shook his head. 'Most of them are a blur, to tell the truth. Not you, though.' Mel felt absurdly pleased, conscious that she was rapidly regressing to daft-schoolgirl level.

'Come up to the staffroom – there's better wine up there, and we can do some catching up. Unless you're desperate to hear the speeches?'

Melanie wasn't. She had a feeling that her feet

(crammed into kitten-heeled slivers of scarlet velvet from L.K. Bennett) quite literally wouldn't stand for the reminiscences of the three surviving retired head teachers. Neil took her hand and whizzed her through the crush, up the stairs by the music room and left into what had been the Staff Corridor.

'We were only allowed to come up here in dire emergencies,' she told him.

'That was so we staff could have a fag in peace,' he said, opening a door and leading her into a big untidy room.

The faded beige walls had brighter, grey-edged patches where posters had been, like skin that's been too long under a plaster. There were pin-scarred naked noticeboards and scruffy old armchairs were dotted around randomly, with faded seats dented and battered as if weary teachers had gradually moulded their personal shape into each one over too many years. On a big central table (which Mel noticed was as heavily biro-ingrained as classroom desks) a stack of used glasses and several empty bottles showed that the staff returning for the occasion had got themselves well fortified before facing the throng of eager Old Girls in the hall.

'There's plenty left under here,' Neil said, delving beneath the table and hauling a bottle of red wine from a cardboard box. 'This OK for you?'

It crossed Melanie's mind that last time they'd met she wasn't old enough to drink. She hadn't, then, yet found any alcohol she liked and when he'd once taken her to a pub (at a safe distance from the school's catchment area) she'd chosen cider and sipped her reluctant way through half a pint, hoping that the taste would grow on her.

Neil and Mel selected the least unappealing of the chairs and sat down. From the hall below them high female voices could be heard enthusiastically belting out 'Jerusalem', the hymn with which each school term had opened and closed.

'So . . .' they both said at the same time. Mel laughed. 'No, you first. You don't have to say much, just your life in half a dozen sentences. Then I'll do mine and we can see if there's anything left over. Just one thing, though, how many others of us pupils did you take out and seduce?'

'Now I didn't seduce you,' Neil insisted. 'I wanted to but . . .'

'Actually, why didn't you?' Mel was curious.

'Scruples.' Neil grinned. Mel spluttered into her wine. 'Scruples? I don't think so!'

'No, truly. About being caught, being found out, being fired.'

'Oh, *those* kind of scruples, those of a true gentle-man! You haven't answered the question, Neil, how many dozens of other girls . . .'

Neil groaned. 'Don't even ask – but it was only those first couple of years. I did manage to grow up eventually.'

'Married?'

'Yes – then divorced. And you?'

'Same.' Mel sipped her wine, marvelling at how few words twenty-odd years had been condensed into. From beyond the door, a collection of footsteps was making its way along the corridor. There was the sound of voices heading towards them.

Unable to face what could only be the post-speech dignatories, Mel looked around for an escape route. Neil grabbed the wine bottle, took her hand and quickly led her to the far side of the room, where a door led to what Mel remembered as the school's sanatorium – an over-grand term for the small airless cell with no windows.

'The old sanny! We used to hate being sent in here,' Mel whispered as the chatty volume increased in the room they'd just fled from. 'It was just like prison. We'd put up with any amount of pain rather than be sent here.'

A door on the far side of the little room would have led to the corridor, if it hadn't been locked.

'Bugger! What now?' Mel sat down on the narrow rickety bed that was probably the same one on which she'd squirmed with pain during her first period. It was covered with an ancient blanket and several heaps of what looked like old report books, the ones that had held each girl's entire school progress record. Neil shoved some of the books aside and sat next to her. 'We could go back through the staffroom, brazen it out. Or we could wait.'

'If we strolled out of here they'd think . . .'

'Mm, they probably would.' The two of them were in danger of giving away their presence by a fit of giggling. Mel picked up one of the report books and opened it, in an attempt to stop feeling hysterical. Inside the booklet's cover a black and white photo of an unknown teenage girl stared out, looking defiant. 'Janet Silverman, Four B,' she read. 'Remember her?'

'No, she was before my time.'

Mel flicked through Janet's records. 'She was good at geography, an A every time.'

'Mm. Shame I can't take the credit.' He was close to her, reading over her shoulder. That sharp tang of Gauloise was taking Mel right back.

'You know, you really should have . . .'

'Pity we never . . .' They'd spoken together again. Neither sentence was finished as Neil leaned closer and gently kissed the edge of Mel's mouth.

So this is what it's like, this no-commitment instant sex, Mel thought an indecently hasty few minutes later, as, on the small tatty bed, with her former headmistress only feet away on the far side of the door, she lay beneath Mr Nicholson (geography), with her knickers on the floor gathering old school dust.

Six

'I had sex with my old geography teacher last night.' Mel, her voice light and jolly, tried out this forthright revelation on Jeremy Paxman as she sliced open a sachet of Whiskas for him. The cat was only interested in food, and continued going through the twice-daily routine of granting his owner some small display of affection, plaiting himself round her legs and purring. 'I hadn't seen him for twenty-five years. Probably won't ever see him again, either,' Mel continued as she put the bowl down on the floor. She wondered what all this would sound like to another human, how she would react if, say, it was Cherry telling her this.

'Are you appalled, Jeremy? Do you think I'm a desperate old slapper?'

The cat shoved his greedy face into the malodorous mess, the purring continuing in fits and starts as he guzzled. She could hardly expect him to be the slightest bit interested. Cats, she thought as she switched on the kettle, didn't have to agonize about whether a spot of instant, no-commitment sex was or wasn't a good idea. They didn't talk about it, analyse it, wonder if they'd done the right/wrong thing and what would happen next, if anything. Unlike humans they were allowed to put nature first and knew exactly what they were there for: when the opportunity to procreate arose they simply took it and then scarpered without a backward glance. Morals, squeamish considerations about pregnancy, disease and guilt and a follow-up date out of politeness just didn't get in the way. Lucky buggers – though, in Jeremy's case, not so lucky: the cat had been neutered at six months. She tickled the top of his wide black head. No wonder there was no response: he didn't have a clue what she was talking about.

Ben was at the bus stop again as Mel made her traffic-snarled way to the gym. She tooted the horn and watched him taking his time to recognize her. He looked even more hunched and skulking than ever, as if he was trying very very hard to pretend he was somewhere else, anywhere but at a chilly bus stop on his way to school.

'You look a bit down,' she commented as he dropped his long body onto the passenger seat. He shrugged and folded his arms defensively, as if scared she expected full-scale confiding as payment for the ride.

'Bloody school. Bloody exams, bloody parents.' It all tumbled out like a long verbal sigh. Mel wished she hadn't said anything. His proper response should have been a smile, a shrug and a 'Y'know how it is' to which she could have grinned back and said something equally meaningless like, 'Yeah, isn't it though?'

'Exams this year?' she asked, pulling up to yet another traffic-light queue.

'Every year. All the time. AS, A2, whatever, till next year when they change the system. Again. Too late for our lot. And when I'm home . . .' He was really warming up now, hadn't even said hallo, how are you. Oh the glorious self-centredness of the young, only themselves to think about. Not that different from me, in fact, Mel admitted guiltily to herself.

'What's wrong with home?' she asked slyly. Please God, let it be possible that Perfect Patty was not entirely faultless as a mum? Could a woman who'd single-handedly cooked twenty-five Victoria sponges for the local retirement home jubilee party have failings? Mel hoped so: for Patty was also a woman who could barely bite back a request for guests to remove their shoes at the door for fear of a grain of mud sullying the textured cream Berber, and really did need her devil side exposed.

'They're always *on* at me. Well Mum is, Dad just grins at me like it's sympathy, but he's just being lazy and scared of her. She goes, "Haven't you got any homework, Ben?" and, "It's so important to *read round* a subject, Ben."' Mel laughed at Ben's too-accurate mimicry of Patty's deceptively soft-spoken tone of benign but determined dictatorship.

'Come on now, she's only got your best interests at heart.'

'That's something else she always says. And she says it in that way like she's just a bit *disappointed*.' Ben looked despondent, suspecting he was travelling with a closer ally of his mother than he'd assumed. It didn't stop him continuing, though, he was in full grumble mode.

'And she's always on my case about the computer. She's made me put it downstairs in the kitchen so she can make sure I'm not getting into porny chat rooms and then *she* chats all through my work. Yak yak sodding yak. Can't wait to leave.'

'What, school or home?'

91

'Bloody both. Soon as.' Ben sighed so deeply Mel feared for the total collapse of his lungs.

'Rosa's computer is still in her room – she's using the university ones. You could come and use it if you want.' What the hell had made her say that? What was she thinking of, volunteering to have another rangy, permanently starving teenager hanging about and making the house reek of unsavoury trainers? What happened to delighting in all that blissful personal space and time?

Ben's face whipped round to study hers, to see if she meant it. She smiled at him, and marvelled at the way a teenage mood could lift so instantly. 'Could I? Really? What, like any time?'

Mel hesitated, wondering what she'd let herself in for. Perhaps he *would* want to spend hours searching out Internet totty, tapping out his life in chat rooms and e-mails like Rosa did. Perhaps he'd want to know what she had in *her* computer, maybe think it was OK to wander in and out of her study asking her how far she'd got with Tina Keen's new case or, worse, read stuff over her shoulder. On the other hand he seemed so miserable, and she had offered. She'd just have to make a few ground rules.

'Yes, but phone first – and it's only for work, no hours on the Internet.'

'Cool. I'll be round tomorrow – I've got this French lit. essay to finish. All I get at home is Mum twittering on about when *she* was doing André Gide at school.'

Melanie dropped Ben off at the school gates, where a couple of his mates were leaning against the wall waiting for him. As she pulled out to drive back into the main road she could hear their over-loud male laughter. She glanced in her mirror at them; the two who weren't Ben were gazing back at her, grinning and doing that kind of poorly co-ordinated shuffle that joshing boys did when they were being dirty-minded and jocular. Ben was striding away from them. She couldn't see his face, couldn't see whether he was distancing himself from their comments. He probably was, she thought, though whether out of horror at the very idea of his middle-aged neighbour as schoolboy fantasy fodder, she'd never know.

Sarah's Freelander was in the gym car park – close to the door, so she must have arrived early again. Melanie hadn't spoken to her after the Neil-in-the-staffroom incident. When she had ventured back to the main hall – rather shaky on her feet, and mentally, and quite possibly physically, rather dishevelled, Sarah had been ensconced in the centre of a group that Mel identified from the safe distance of the doorway as most of the star hockey team from their fourth-form days. As just about anyone could have predicted, they'd grown into a sturdy bunch of broad-shouldered women with no-fuss haircuts. One or two, who were standing with their feet planted solidly far apart, looked as if they still pounded up and down a pitch most weekends. She would hazard a guess that they in their turn had become games teachers and married the kind of men who enjoyed having their lives run for them like a fixture list. Mel had baulked at the idea of joining the group, especially as she'd hardly got her breath back from the brief but intense exertions. Instead, she'd caught Sarah's eye across the group, mimed what she hoped was a convincing oncoming migraine and waved a quick goodbye. A fast escape was better than facing Sarah saying archly – and far too loudly – 'And where did *you* get to all this time?'

In fact, as she drove slowly into the car park, she wasn't sure she could even face it now. Sarah would be flexing away on the cross-trainer, watching her skinny but muscular frame in the mirror. She'd see Mel and shriek, 'Bone to pick with you, sweetie!' and every head in the room would turn and stare as Sarah leapt off the machine and hustled her out to the locker room. And she'd have to tell her – Sarah would pull that 'I'm your best friend' number and out it would all come. She wouldn't be able to lie, either – people who've known you since before your first period tend to notice when you're telling whoppers. It wouldn't be like telling the cat – Sarah wouldn't just ignore her and go in search of a coffee and a bun. She'd want to know all sorts of gruesomely intimate details. She'd ask questions. Her eyes would be shimmering with eagerness to be Told All. For a woman who would far rather, as she'd once put it, have a facial than a fuck, Sarah's interest in other people's sex lives seemed almost fetishistic.

Melanie turned the Golf round and headed back to the road. She didn't want to go straight home again, either. That would seem so pointless, and besides, it would only depress her if she got there and Max hadn't turned up yet with the new York stone slabs for the garden (without which, according to him, no further progress was possible). She'd forgotten to bring her mobile phone, but Cherry wouldn't mind an unheralded visit. She always said that her kind of meticulous painting was the one art form where you really could do two things at once – listen to the radio, make mental shopping lists – be lied to by your 'oldest' friend.

* * *

94

Roger stopped the car at the end of the road and parked in the residents-only section at the end of the small row of shops. He noticed the laundrette had closed down, and felt a small tingle of surprise that it could have happened without him being around to know. Not that it *should* have been a surprise – this was hardly bedsit-land; most houses in the area had what Mel called a futility room, fully equipped. The shop doorway was boarded up, paint-flaked and shabby, and its windows were covered with posters warning the world not to stick up other posters. Between the smart deli with its £30-a-litre olive oil and authentic French rustic bread, and the chic greengrocer who sold organic herbs by the fresh-picked bunch, it looked like a grumpy vagrant who had strayed into the Royal Enclosure at Ascot.

Roger bought a parking ticket from the machine outside the delicatessen. It still seemed a strange thing to do – for so many years he'd had a residents' permit. It had actually been the last bit of his connection with the area to go and he'd almost been inclined to renew it secretly the last time it expired. He didn't need one at the shiny new Esher house – with the integral garage and gravelled driveway there was room for an entire dinner party's worth of cars down at their end of Balmoral Close.

Leonora's parents had bought the house outright for their treasured daughter. It was in her name only – Leonora's father had punched Roger on the arm in a slightly harder than jovial manner and said, 'Well, better to be safe, eh?' as if Roger was a serial divorcer, likely to run off with half the takings the minute the ink on the marriage certificate was dry. The house didn't yet feel at all like anything Roger could call home – Leonora and her mother Maureen had chosen it together from a brochure of newly built executive homes and had marched about in their stabby high heels on the new pale floorboards, clutching swatches, making unchallengeable decisions about fabric and paint and carpets.

Leonora had let him choose the crockery that went on the wedding-present list and had given way (after some pouting and sulking) when he'd put his foot down about the lime-green leather sofa. Citrus yellow wasn't what he'd call a compromise, though. In fact all the house's furniture seemed bizarrely hotel-like and came from stores that were unfamiliar to him. Melanie had veered between forays to IKEA or Habitat interspersed with junk-shop treasures. Leonora had peculiarly grown-up tastes, exactly like her mother's, and liked things in 'sets'. She'd chosen a chilly slate-topped dining table with eight matching wrought-iron chairs, the fat, frilled cushions of which didn't make up for the feeling that the whole ensemble was intended for a far sunnier climate than Surrey's. He and Melanie had never had matching chairs: the big old scratched elmwood table in the kitchen was attended by their collection of Lloyd Loom antiquities. The cat slept on all the cushions in turn and shed fur. Roger wondered what would happen to Leonora's frilled fancies when the new baby started smearing goo on every surface. She would be a demon with the Dettox. Back at the old house there was probably still the odd crust of Farex filling in the chair weave, like mortar in a badly pointed wall.

Roger knocked on Mel's door. He could have phoned, he knew that, but the urge to show off his honeymoon tan was just too great. And it wasn't as if they weren't still friends. Everyone was amazed at how amicably they'd parted. There was no reply. He could see Mrs Jenkins's lace curtain flicking urgently back and forth, and he waved to show he'd caught her snooping. He knocked again, harder. Sometimes Mel didn't answer the door if she was working, saying that if it was important enough they'd knock more than once or come back later. Eventually he was rewarded by the sound of feet and the door was flung open.

'She's not in,' said a tall wild-haired man in a mud-splattered sweatshirt. 'She's gone down the gym, I expect.'

'Don't you know?' Roger asked, taking in the fact that the man was wearing thick tweedy socks but no shoes. Presumably a lover then, he thought, feeling ludicrously betrayed.

'No. I don't. I'm the gardener,' the man said with a shrug. 'Who shall I say called?'

'Oh, er. I'm Roger.'

'So *you're* Roger!' The gardener's face was lit by a massive smile, one that Roger didn't much like, for it contained too much of something that looked like flagrant amusement.

'What are you doing to the garden?' Roger asked. Mel hadn't said anything. And the bit between the gate and the front door looked just as it always did – unkempt and overgrown, almost to the point where it could qualify as a stylish meadow effect.

'Come through and have a look.' Max opened the door wider and led Roger through the kitchen.

'Here we are. A long way to go yet, but we're getting there.' Max shoved his tweedy feet into a pair of muddy green wellingtons and opened the back door.

'Jesus. What the buggery's going on?' Roger felt

sickened, outraged. It was like suddenly meeting a much-loved old friend who'd become wasted and raddled with disease. Where was the clematis he and Mel had chosen together? The roses with wittily appropriate names they'd given each other on anniversaries, the long lavender hedge that had been back-breaking to clip into shape each autumn and the lawn with the struggling beige patch where it had never recovered from being under Rosa's sandpit? He felt sad, full of impotent anger towards Mel. She was destroying such a huge part of their life together.

'She said she doesn't want to do mowing, or weeding or pruning any more,' Max explained. 'She said it's chuck-out and makeover time, and to be honest I think she was right.'

'Right? What would you know about it?' Roger turned on him, wanting to smack his fist into the placid, good-looking face and do it the same kind of serious damage that Max had done to his garden.

'Palms, bananas, some bamboo, pebbles, that kind of thing.' The man seemed oblivious to Roger's fury. 'That's what we're going for.'

We? Roger had had enough.

'I'm leaving. Just tell her I was here.'

He stalked off back into the house, shaking with rage.

'Oh, and by the way, congratulations!' Max shouted after him.

'On?'

'The baby of course and the new wife. Mel told me! Nice one!'

Melanie did not intend to tell Cherry about Neil. Cherry would be 'disappointed' in her. She'd feel sorry

98

for her, thinking, wrongly, that she'd grasped at a chance for quick sex in the hope that it would lead to something, a relationship, snatched-at company for a few hopeful dates, even. She didn't want her thinking that because it wasn't even close to being true. She'd had sex with Neil because, as with climbers and Everest, he was there and she wanted to know what it was like, this casual no-responsibility sex business.

Mel wasn't surprised to hear Cherry shouting 'Who is it?' from inside the door. It wasn't that Cherry was terrified of being ambushed by a mugger the moment she let the chain off, it was simply more than likely that she'd got wet hair wound up in a towel or no mascara on.

'It's me. Melanie. Please let me in and give me coffee!'

'Oh. Mel. Well, OK.' That sounded a bit grudging, Mel thought, wondering if she should just make an immediate excuse, change her mind and go home.

'You should have rung!' Cherry opened the door and smiled. 'Come into the sitting room, I'll bring you coffee and cake.' Cherry pushed the sitting-room door open and almost hurled Mel onto the long blue velvet sofa.

'What's wrong with the kitchen? I've hardly ever been in here.'

'Oh, nothing! Bit of a state, that's all, I was just working on something and it's all over the place.' Cherry's hands were indeed freshly paint-splashed. If they hadn't been, Mel would have suspected she'd got hidden in the kitchen the kind of lover that might be a touch embarrassing to introduce to friends: a hired stud perhaps, or a beefy female biker. Whatever paint she was using smelled peculiar too, there was a sharp acetic whiff in the air that reminded Mel of dead things in the school biology lab. Cherry shut the door firmly on her guest, leaving Mel's curiosity to rise like boiling milk. She'd give her a few minutes to feel secure and then pounce.

'So what kind of cake have you got?' Having given Cherry a mere thirty seconds, Mel wandered into the kitchen on the pretext of seeking food.

'Wow, look what's come in!' Mel stopped still in the doorway and pointed. On the table, right in the middle of Cherry's scattered paint tubes and brushes, sat a small grey squirrel clutching a walnut.

'What? You weren't supposed . . .' Cherry, who was dealing with the kettle and had her back to the creature, turned, looking flustered.

'Ssh! You'll scare it out!' Mel whispered. The squirrel hadn't moved, literally frightened rigid, she assumed.

'Er . . . you weren't supposed to come in here.' Cherry banged the kettle down on the worktop (the precious pale green granite one that had taken six weeks to deliver).

The squirrel still hadn't moved. Mel crept nearer. On the drawing pad in front of the creature its portrait was half-completed, every minute variation in fur colour and texture faithfully copied, the tiny curved claws immaculately duplicated on the page. 'Hell's teeth, Cherry, it's a stuffed one!' she shrieked, having put out a tentative finger and touched its cold stiff paw.

'Mmm. Not exactly.' Cherry was looking furtive. 'It's not quite stuffed, not unless you count the coat hanger. I didn't want you to know about this – no-one's supposed to see.'

'See what? That you've got a dead squirrel in to

paint? What's wrong with that?' Mel assumed she'd found it in a junk shop. There was something else she'd seen, though. 'Er, what's the thing with the coat hanger?'

'Well, it wouldn't sit up, even though it's crammed with formaldehyde – there's hardly an inch I haven't injected. So it's got a wire hanger up its bum.' Cherry clattered around with the coffee equipment, refusing to meet Melanie's eyes.

Mel laughed, sounding slightly manic. This all sounded like the sort of ghastly torture that she'd invent for one of Tina Keen's more gruesome dead victims.

'Injected?' she queried. '*You* injected it?'

'I bought a big bottle of the stuff a couple of years back, and I get diabetic syringes. I get through a lot of needles, coming up against bones.'

'Yeah, well you would . . . But where did you get the squirrel?' Mel asked, imagining a bizarre Bloomsbury shop that supplied artists' models of any species on demand.

'It was by the A3, quite close to the Asda at Roehampton,' Cherry admitted shamefacedly. 'And don't you dare tell anyone, especially Sarah. I'd never hear the last.'

'Roadkill. Hmm.' Mel accepted the mug of coffee Cherry handed her, but wondered about its chemical content. Wasn't formaldehyde hugely poisonous? Cherry's hands were still all painty. And she might have handled the squirrel, bending it and shoving it into position. She decided she could do without the cake.

'How else do you think I draw these creatures so accurately?' Cherry was defensive now. 'Did you think I copied them from a book?'

'I suppose that was exactly what I did think, if I thought at all,' Mel admitted. 'What else have you got?'

Cherry looked a bit shifty. 'Actually, I've got a lovely badger, in perfect nick, not a mark on it. I put it in a bag in the freezer but a fuse went while I was out and I'm going to have to chuck him out. Unless . . .'

'In the freezer? Next to your prawns and peas and pizzas?'

'Look, when you live by yourself you can do exactly what you like! I haven't got anyone here who gives a flying toss whether I've got a freezer full of caviare or carrion, so what does it matter? Anyway he's in a bag.'

'Oh.' Mel looked at Cherry, who was smiling at her in a horribly hopeful sort of way. 'Cherry, what did you mean by "unless"?'

'Well, I just wondered, seeing as no-one's going to be poking about in your freezer either, if you might just take him home and find a bit of room for him in yours. Please? Just till I've defrosted and got mine going again?'

Mel pulled a face. 'Ugh, Chezza, but it's a dead animal!'

'So's a leg of lamb.'

'A leg of lamb doesn't come with fur and eyes and teeth.'

'You don't have to look at him, oh please, Mel, I'll never get another one as good as this.'

Mel wavered. Cherry looked almost mad with eagerness. She could swear even the rather cloudy eyes of the squirrel on the table were staring at her, willing her to say yes.

'And no-one need ever know,' Cherry went on.

'OK, but only for a couple of days, right?' Mel

reluctantly agreed. The thing would have to come home in the car with her. She hoped it had been thoroughly disinfected. Suppose it had fleas?

Recklessly she went on, because somehow she couldn't stop herself, 'And you don't tell people that last night in the old school sickroom I had sex with my old geography teacher on top of a lot of abandoned school reports, OK?'

'Oh Mel, you didn't!' It was Cherry's turn to look satisfyingly horrified.

'I did. Because that's another of those things that we single folks can get away with. I really wanted to try free-range sex as opposed to the battery variety that coupley-types have.'

'You don't mean that, Mel, you're not really that hard.'

'I do and I am – well, I thought I was. Actually it was a bit of an experiment, to tell the truth, and I don't think it's something I'll be going in for. But at least now I know that, rather than wondering. Don't mention it to Sarah if you happen to run into her, OK? Or my mother. Now I'm divorced I think she considers I've been granted my virginity back again.'

'But why? I mean why did you do it?'

Melanie shrugged. 'Well, we just sort of started off and kind of carried on because it was all going pretty fine and before we knew it, we . . . er . . . He had a funny look on his face.'

'God, Mel, do I need to know this?'

'Probably not. It was as if he couldn't quite believe what was happening and half-expected me to call a halt any second. I must have looked exactly the same. There were people just the other side of the door – that gave it an edge.'

103

Cherry was, as predicted, looking disappointed. 'So you'll be seeing him again?'

'Possibly. I don't know. Only as a friend if I do. He's got my number but I'm not going into a state of teenage heartbreak waiting for a call. I'm not looking for a relationship.'

Cherry shuddered. 'No. Absolutely not. We're far better off without all that. You and I must go out together somewhere soon, just the two of us. I've had a couple of private view invitations that look interesting.'

'OK, that'll be great. Call me, let me know when.' Mel sensed that Cherry was hauling her back into line, pointing her towards a far more suitable occupation for the untethered woman than a crazed session of spontaneous sex. Obviously there was a set of behaviour rules for Cherry's type of man-free singledom that she hadn't yet read. She was pretty sure she didn't want to.

Melanie drove home with Cherry's badger in the car boot, all wrapped up for decency's sake in a large Harrods bag. She prayed as she drove that it wouldn't turn out to be the day there'd been a massive bank robbery in the area and the police had set up road blocks to search every car for ill-gotten loot. On the other hand, it could be quite fun . . .

Seven

Gwen Thomas packed just enough for three or four days. That should be long enough to give Howard the fright of his life and make him realize she meant business. She wasn't going to share her husband with a bunch of lewd and naked women, even if they did only exist between the glossy pages of a magazine. It was them or her – and frankly it shouldn't be much of a contest. Howard would come to his senses fast enough: these paper women weren't going to pop round and cook him a proper shepherd's pie.

He hadn't even had the grace to look embarrassed. Not so much as a hint of an apology or a stumbling explanation or excuse. He'd just brazened it out and had a go at her for snooping under the mattress. How exactly, she'd like to know, could going about your usual household duties be snooping?

'Can't a man have a bit of privacy?' he'd demanded, grabbing the magazine from her hands and storming out to the garden shed. He probably had a huge collection of the filthy things out there. They could be stacked high, the pages going clammy in the damp air, hidden under last year's growbags. She'd have to tell

Melanie the entire shaming truth now, because Melanie would never believe Gwen would walk out over Howard drinking a couple of pints on a daily basis. She didn't want Vanessa to know though, definitely not. Melanie had a lot more experience of the real world and she did write very peculiar books, so her imagined world experience was much broader than most people's, too.

Vanessa lived a dolls' house existence, every day the same, all her family neat, good and perfectly behaved. She had a proper, tidy husband (though hadn't Howard been like that for most of his life? Hadn't her own life been a dolls' house one?), with unquestioning regular habits, who took himself off out of the way, as men should, at eight each morning and didn't come home till after six. And the children gave no trouble at all. They had excellent school reports, shown to her dutifully at the end of each July. Though she had noticed you never got a peep out of Theresa and William, not unless you asked them something direct like how's school, and even then they'd just smile as if it almost hurt and say 'Fine, Gran,' nothing extra volunteered. Blood from stones. You didn't know what they liked or who their friends were; they didn't babble on about some unseen Gracie or Holly the way Rosa always had. It would be quiet at Melanie's without Rosa, but it would give her a chance to think.

She could hear a car on the gravel outside – her minicab had arrived. She checked her purse – she wasn't used to being a taxi passenger and didn't want to fumble around in search of the right amount. As she heard the driver's steps approaching the front door she took a final look around her kitchen. The pink rubber gloves were on the draining board, lying folded together like a pair of sad empty hands. She hoped Howard would notice and think them poignant. Somehow she doubted it.

Mel was making Tina Keen feel queasy in the mortuary. It was the smell that got to the hard-bitten detective every time – the formaldehyde, the disinfectant, all the chemical aromas that didn't quite cover the creeping process of slow decomposition. It didn't matter how perfectly chilled the staff kept the corpses, Tina's nose, that could expertly identify Calvin Klein's Escape in a party-full of scented women, always picked up the tiniest underlying hint of rot. Mel's visit to Cherry's kitchen had been a useful reminder of the way the acrid scent permeated the air and made your eyes watery. It caught in the back of your throat in a way that made you long for fresh clean air to choke out the stench. It couldn't be doing Cherry's lungs any good.

Melanie stopped typing and went to look out of the window. Writing this section of the book, she was even making herself feel a bit sick. The mutilated young prostitute who had been discovered beneath the café stairs had over twenty stab wounds. Blood would have spurted all over the killer, so she had to find some way of getting him (or her?) off the street and well away without being seen. The killer had planned this, it wasn't a random act, so he'd have been wearing something over his clothes, something that could be taken off quickly, rolled up and shoved into a bag to be burned or dropped into a bin later; a boiler suit, maybe, or some kind of overalls – possibly even the kind of apron a mortuary attendant might wear. Now that was a thought . . .

Down in the garden she could see Max looking bad-tempered. The York stone slabs were bigger and heavier than he'd expected – he'd ordered an old imperial size that no longer existed and the nursery had delivered the closest metric equivalent. He and his reluctant work-experience teenage assistant were arranging the slabs in a rectangular path, trying to keep an even distance from the boundary fence and doing it by guesswork. From the window, Mel could see that the front and back sections weren't parallel. She'd have to go down and say something, or every time she looked at the finished garden from her study window the asymmetry would irritate her. Why hadn't they set out stakes with string guidelines and why did she have to be the one who thought of that? Still, Max was a useful and friendly man to have around the place – he'd seen off Roger, for one thing. It had made her smile, Max's description of Roger's proprietorial rage at the devastation of the garden. 'I thought he was going to hit me,' Max had told her over a mug of tea. 'I couldn't tell which he thought was the worst thing: the idea that I'd ravished his garden or that I might also have ravished his ex-wife.'

'Either way, it was none of his business,' Mel had laughed.

'Quite right. I think he realized that was exactly my opinion when I congratulated him on his nice new marriage-and-baby package.'

The doorbell rang when Mel was halfway down the stairs. She waited for a few moments, hoping it wouldn't be Roger back again. What had he wanted the other day? Surely he hadn't brought round his honeymoon photos to show her? The blurry outline of the head through the door's frosted window was someone smaller than Roger. It was someone fidgety, she could see, someone female. She hoped whoever it was wouldn't want to stay long – Tina Keen needed to be rescued from her nausea and moved back into her office where she could start shouting at one of her inefficient underlings, the one who'd stupidly rinsed the murder weapon under the café's hot water tap.

'Mum! Nice to see you, come in. Were you shopping?' Melanie indicated the bag her mother was hauling along behind her.

'This isn't shopping. It's a suitcase,' Gwen declared glumly, marching in past her daughter, quite effortlessly tugging the case over the step as if she was leading in an obedient dog.

It still didn't occur to Mel that anything was wrong. She simply assumed the case was empty – her mother often brought capacious bags round to the house in search of jumble for the Townswomen's Guild's fundraising efforts at the Scout Hut.

Gwen didn't stop till she'd dragged her burden into the kitchen and deposited it securely beneath the table, as if, left anywhere closer to the front door, it would somehow escape back to home and Howard.

'I've left him!' she announced loudly, removing her coat, flinging it over the back of the woven chair with the chipped pink paint and sitting down firmly.

'What, Dad? Left him where?' Mel assumed he was somewhere in the area, possibly in the bank at the end of the road – or in the pub indulging in his new pastime.

'I've *left* him, Melanie,' her mother went on. 'I can't live with him any more.'

She burrowed into the case. 'I found this.' The magazine was wrapped in a Sainsbury's bag, but even this

Gwen held at arm's length, as if in fear of contamination. 'It was under the mattress on *his* side of the bed.'

Mel flicked through the copy of *Mayfair* while her mother averted her gaze and caught sight of the pillaged garden.

'What have you gone and done out there? It looks like a bombsite. Your dad will be . . . Oh, what do I care what he'll be?' Gwen sniffed and turned away from the window, waiting for a reaction from her daughter.

'I really don't know what to say,' Mel admitted. 'Are you sure it's . . .'

'Who else's would it be?' Gwen scoffed. 'There's only him and me slept in that bed for the past forty-eight years. I was quite looking forward to our golden wedding. I'd been planning. It was between a function-room buffet at the Watermill or lunch at the Grange Hotel. They've a lovely conservatory. Oh well.'

She was slumped in her chair now, looking more defeated than Mel had ever seen her.

'I expect he was just feeling . . .' What could he be feeling? The word 'himself' came to mind, but would not be appreciated. Mel searched her mental thesaurus for something more appropriate. 'His age,' she came up with, lamely.

'We're all feeling our age,' Gwen snapped. 'We don't all want to hark back and make fools of ourselves in the process.'

Mel shoved the magazine into the bin and sat down next to her mother. 'You could have just ignored it,' she suggested. 'I mean, what he reads doesn't really matter that much, does it?'

'I don't think *reading* comes into it. It's just so

disgusting, so *degrading*,' Gwen insisted. 'I'm not having it in the house.'

In spite of trying to be soothing and sensible, Mel was actually close to feeling as shocked as her mother. Her own *father*? Getting off on soft porn? There was so much about people that you simply couldn't know. She hoped her father would never know that Gwen had come running to her with all this. He might be able to brazen out his new (if it was new) hobby with his wife, but having your daughter knowing your sexual secrets was something else.

'You'll have to go and talk to him, Mel. Tell him . . .'

'No!' Mel's hands went up in instinctive defence. 'No really, Mum, this is definitely just between the two of you. Perhaps you should go home, not yet but later this afternoon, and try and talk to him. Calmly, with a little sympathy if you possibly can. He's probably just trying to recapture a bit of what he felt like when he was younger. I'm sure there's no real harm in it. There must be millions of men . . . well there are, aren't there, or there'd be no market for the magazines. I bet you finding this one has really shaken him.'

Gwen sat tight, her pale lips thin and rigid. 'I'm not going anywhere. If he wants me home again, he can come looking for me. I'm not crawling back, not till I've sorted out what I think. He won't even have noticed I've gone yet, not till his lunch isn't on the table.' She glanced at her watch. 'Just gone half past ten. He'll be on his way down to the pub by now, getting him and the dog sozzled, as per.' She stood up, heaving herself out of the chair as if the effort had become almost too much. 'I'll go up and unpack. I don't suppose your spare bed's made up, so just tell me which sheets and I'll do it myself. You get on with

111

whatever you were doing, I won't be in your way. You won't notice I'm here.'

So that would be all right then.

Rosa wasn't sure if Desi was the best one from the flat to have taken with her to Sainsbury's, but all the others were out. Two of them had even gone to lectures. On the plus side, Desi was the only one in the flat with a car that could be relied on to get them both there and back, but on the downside, it seemed that a visit to Sainsbury's was as thrillingly novel to him as a seven-year-old's first-time trip to Disneyworld. He would be worse than useless and would be no good for anything but steering the trolley into old ladies' legs.

'It's down there, on the right, next to the round-about.' Rosa pointed out the store to Desi. You couldn't miss it, the building was a local landmark, a design statement of its time, its roof designed with great triangular white shapes that were supposed to represent sails. To her, in the mood she was in, it looked as if someone had sat on Sainsbury's roof, made a small Sydney Opera House out of bits of old Christmas card – and let them collapse.

'It looks like a row of big prawn crackers,' Desi commented, snorting at his own hilarity in that way that made you avoid looking at him in case stuff was cascading out of his nose. She clenched her fingers together and reminded herself it wasn't his fault his upbringing had almost entirely been at the hands of a starchy ex-royal nanny and a remote minor public school. It wasn't his fault that he was the one person in the whole world who thought Harry Enfield's Tim Nice-But-Dim was a terrific role model. Before he'd arrived in Plymouth, Desi hadn't ever even *seen* a prawn cracker. Now, unless someone did some food-shopping, he and his flatmates were in danger of living on nothing else.

Rosa consulted her list. It hadn't been her idea, this communal kitchen business. She'd been happy enough with the original arrangement – half a fridge plus a cupboard each for their food, all individually bought, cooked and consumed as and when each of them felt like it. She'd reckoned without Kate, though, or Rota-Girl as she now thought of her, who'd appealed to simple financial student greed and worked out how much they'd save by pooling resources and even, at night, actually cooking, eating together and then washing the dishes – there and then – according to who was designated on that day's list. The three boys had been easy to convince (Rota-Girl had mentioned the magic words 'extra beer money'), Jemima spent all her time with her boyfriend and didn't care, but Rosa wasn't happy. She'd come away from home to enjoy being independent at last, to eat when and what she fancied with no-one going on about vitamins or fruit, and to sleep late with no-one nagging her. She wanted to exist on Rice Crispies if she chose, or Scotch eggs from the Shell garage up the road, followed by a Dime bar or six.

She'd pointed out the hitches such as: what if you were out a lot? What about Will being vegetarian? What about Desi, who thought a spatula was a shoulder bone and that roasting, steaming and boiling were Caribbean weather descriptions? But Kate had a weird, non-verbal approach to conflict. She just sat silently, like someone in the middle of yoga, and studied your face while you protested. You ended up feeling that if you didn't agree with her there must be something wrong with you, with you *personally*, not with her point of view. And she had the kind of leggy, flicky-hair blonde good looks that made most women snarl. So naturally the boys in the flat thought she was the next best thing to having Claudia Schiffer sleeping down the hall. It would be almost worth buying a mouse to release into her room, having first laid bets that she'd be the type who'd jump on the bed squealing the minute she saw it. Rosa also knew, though, that if a wild mouse turned up when no-one else was around, Kate would calmly and capably pick it up with bare hands and chuck it out of the window. One day, Rosa predicted, if the direst forms of Thatcherism ever made a comeback, Rota-Girl Kate would be in sole charge of the nation.

'We can't park here,' Rosa said as Desi nosed the Clio into a parent-and-child space.

'But it's got a picture of a shopping bag on wheels,' he protested.

'No Desi, that's a drawing of a baby buggy, you know, a pram thing? Like for babies?'

'Right. I see.' But from where Rosa was sitting, Desi looked as if he didn't, quite.

As Desi parked the Clio in a more distant space, Rosa thought of her father, who would soon be perfectly entitled to park in the buggy-pictured slots. She could imagine him worrying that people might think he was the grandfather. He'd be sure to have the full state-of-the-art kit for this baby: a truly fancy pram with lots of add-on bits, like a detachable car seat and a smart rain cover. It would have cashmere blankets. Later, he'd buy Leonora one of those cool three-wheel strollers because she'd start talking about getting her figure back and would keep mentioning the idea of power-walking through the park. She wouldn't actually do anything so energetic, though, or if she did it would be without the baby, and in the comfort of the nice warm luxury hotel spa that she'd been talking about at the wedding. Rosa felt small stirrings of pity for her dad. He'd be on a hard-work treadmill for ever now, shoring up the mounting expense of keeping Leonora and this new child. She hoped it wouldn't be an only one, like she'd been, though; she could do with a sympathetic brother or sister right now, someone she could just phone and moan at, grumble about trivial things (Rota-Girl, Desi's inability to tell a lettuce from a cabbage, the permanent smell of sock from Paul's room next to hers). As she pointed Desi in the direction of the cheapest yogurts she had one of her occasional what-if moments, about what it would have been like if her little brother had survived. He'd be fifteen now, shambling around and crashing into things as he grew too fast. He'd have spots and huge hands and probably barely speak beyond a hostile grunt. Except to his sister: he'd love his big sister. And she'd love him.

'Is this the right rice?' Desi cut into Rosa's thoughts. He was holding up a packet and looking worried.

'No, Desi, that's for rice puddings. We need this one, the basmati.'

'Oh, but . . .' Desi slowly put the packet back on the shelf and reached for another.

'But?'

Desi grinned shyly. 'Thing is, I actually quite fancied a rice pudding. One like . . .'

Rosa took pity on him. She would never subscribe to her grandmother's men-need-looking-after creed, but sometimes Desi resembled a confused Martian on a reluctant exchange visit to Earth. 'One like home,' she finished his sentence for him. 'I know, Desi, it's all right, put it in the trolley.'

You're a soft sod, Rosa, she told herself: now you'll have to phone home and find out how to make rice pud.

When she'd said, 'I won't be in the way,' Gwen really meant, 'Look at me, Melanie, look how carefully I'm tiptoeing round the house!' From her study, close to lunchtime the next day, Mel could hear Gwen very slowly filling the kettle, as if by running the tap at no more than a trickle it would make less noise. Cupboards were being opened and closed with all the stealthy concentration of a burglar who suspected a guard dog might be dozing within savaging distance.

She heard the back door creak as it was opened, and from her desk Mel watched Max's face light with a broad and cheerful smile. Another cup of tea. That must be about the seventh Gwen had given him and Luke that morning. It accounted for the downstairs loo flushing every twenty minutes.

Tina Keen had returned to HQ from the mortuary. Mel got her stripped off in the locker-room shower and allowed all trace of the air of death to trickle away down the grubby drain. Tina sploshed Clarins Eau Dynamisante shower gel all over her body, reminding Mel that Tina's creator was about to run out of the same product. Several times in her books she'd mentioned by brand name the odd luxury items – Pol Roger champagne, Bendicks Bittermints, La Perla underwear – for all of which she was enthusiastic herself, in the fond hope that some eager young executive might take it into his head (it would certainly be 'his', a woman would see straight through the ploy) to send her a complimentary boxful of goodies. This craven product placement hadn't yet worked, but at least Mel felt she was granting Tina the benefit of items she herself would prefer.

She allowed Tina to dress (it wouldn't do, somehow, to leave her shivering) in lavender satin underwear, a simple though decidedly clingy tee shirt and a suit that she hoped would pass for Armani, then closed down the computer and went downstairs. The noise in the kitchen was reaching a crescendo: her mother was in search of lunch.

'Haven't you got any soup?' Gwen asked, as Mel came into the room.

'I don't think so, unless there's some instant packet ones in the cupboard,' Mel told her. 'Look, there's a couple of things I need, so why don't we go into the town and have lunch at Fasta Pasta? My treat?'

'Oh, I don't know.' Gwen looked flustered. 'I'm not keen on all this spaghetti sort of thing. I'd rather just have a sandwich, I think. I've found plenty of tuna.' She had, too: at least seven cans of it had been extricated from the cupboard and piled high on the table.

'Well, it's one of those things you always pick up in the supermarket, isn't it?' Mel grinned at her. Her mother gave her a look. 'So's soup,' she said, and Mel started counting to ten.

'Are you there?' Mrs Jenkins's lilac head bobbed up and down by the fence. Mel opened the door. 'Yes, it's OK, I'm here. Are you all right?' she called back.

Mrs Jenkins unhooked the gate and came through, shooing her little dog back to its own side. 'I don't want him getting anything on his paws,' she explained, glaring at Max and Luke and their soggy mud-pie heap of concrete with which they were filling in the gaps

117

between the stone slabs. She followed Mel into the kitchen.

'They're making a big mess out there. My daughter Brenda will be looking down on that when she comes to visit,' Mrs Jenkins told Gwen.

'It *is* a mess, you're quite right,' Gwen agreed. 'I don't know when they'll ever get it finished. Or what it'll look like.'

Mrs Jenkins, happy to have found a like-minded ally, sat down at the table and picked up the top tin of tuna from the pile. 'You don't see so much salmon these days,' she mused, perusing the label and screwing up her eyes to read 'dolphin friendly'.

'Mrs Jenkins, this is my mother, Gwen Thomas.' Mrs Jenkins looked at Mel as if she was crazy. 'I know that. You've got her nose.' She turned her attention to Gwen. 'I'm eighty-one you know.'

'That's a good age,' Gwen commented obediently.

'No it's not. It's a bloody terrible age. But Brenda's coming over in two weeks *and* with the children.' She got up and peered into Mel's bread bin, hauling out a large linseed and soya loaf that Mel trusted to ward off any pre-menopausal forays of symptoms. 'Shall we have a sandwich, dear? Though this bread's got a lot of seeds. They'll get under my plate. Haven't you got any Mighty White?'

'No, sorry, I haven't.' Mel watched as Mrs Jenkins ran her fingers over the bread's surface and the little seeds fell off into the sink. Her mother watched, hungry and eager.

'This is better.' Mrs Jenkins showed Gwen the bald bread surface and the two of them nodded together, solemnly.

'OK, I'll make you a sandwich.' Mel took the bread

from Mrs Jenkins's gnarled fingers, wondering if she should go out and round up Max, Luke, possibly Perfect Patty from number 14 and anyone else who might like to work their way through seven cans of tuna.

'No, it's all right, dear, Mrs Jenkins and I will be fine on our own.' Gwen was slyly insistent. 'Why don't you go out? Take yourself off to that spaghetti place you were just talking about. You could do with a break.'

It was like being sent out of the room for talking in class. Mel, feeling unwelcome and outnumbered in her own home, abandoned Tina Keen for the day, left her mother and Mrs Jenkins discussing their respective families, drove into Richmond and parked in Waitrose's car park. With no particular plan in mind she wandered down the road towards the shops. At Pret a Manger she bought a small sushi selection and a bottle of orange juice, then went and sat on a bench beneath a chestnut tree on the green. There was a breeze gathering, and every few minutes there would be a soft thud as a conker hit the grass.

'You don't want to sit there, love,' a man carrying a bucket and a short ladder called out to her as he passed the bench. 'You're right in the line of fire.' She didn't mind, she quite enjoyed the mild feeling of risk: most of the conkers were still encased in their spiny green shells, reminding her of mines that threatened warships in old films. She was also directly under the Heathrow flight path. Every sixty seconds a massive plane roared across the green, ripping through the otherwise tranquil air. There's no bloody peace, Melanie thought, as she got up and stuffed the sushi box into a litter bin. Across the road a coachful of elderly ladies was being unloaded for an afternoon theatre trip. Every one of them had a silvery-grey perm and she thought of Rosa who'd have given them one glance and muttered 'cauliflower-heads'. She strolled along to look at the billboards, see what was on – Maureen Lipman was starring in *Peggy for You*, about the theatrical agent Peggy Ramsay. Seeing this suddenly seemed a far more attractive prospect than trailing round the shops trying on clothes that she didn't particularly need.

Inside the cool dark theatre there really *was* peace. Now that Mel was sitting in the scarlet and velvet dress circle (a spritzer pre-ordered at the bar for the interval) with no need to make conversation or do any thinking, working or placating, she almost felt as if she'd run away. No-one knew where she was. No-one expected her to be anywhere, or could reach her by phone, fax or e-mail. She would do this more often – it was a delight to be able to be this spontaneous – and you could only do it when you had no-one to answer to. Around her the matinée ladies chatted away about plans for Christmas, plans for holidays and plans for further outings, and she relished her own silent moments by thinking about nothing at all. Then there was the moment of never-failing thrill when the lights dimmed and the curtain went up. Maureen Lipman sat silently on a sofa being Peggy Ramsay, theatrical agent, reading a script. Among the first words was 'fuck', and the audience of leisured ladies drew in its excited collective breath.

Eight

'Now no excuses, Mel sweetie – as you're so determined to be completely unattached you'll be free to
come to supper on Wednesday, won't you?' This was
Sarah's slightly less than gracious invitation to
Melanie on the phone. Mel was in the garden, sitting
on the wall and waiting to help Max spread bags of
pebbles between the new stone slabs. It was a soft
golden late October day, the kind that makes you think
summer is trying very hard not to give in to the
approaching winter.

Mel laughed. 'Does being unattached mean I can't
have a social life unless mates like you feel sorry for
me? Do I have to stay in and crochet in front of *Friends*
every night, eating lonely Mars bars and wishing I had
a mad New York loft existence?'

'Yes, it means exactly that – though actually that version sounds bliss. So you can come, then? I've got a
surprise for you . . . no, don't even try to guess, you
never will . . . just come. Don't bring anything, it's just
kitchen food. Cherry's coming too.'

'So it's feed-the-singles night, then?' Mel teased.

'What? Heavens no, anything but! See you on

Wednesday. Eightish. Oh, and wear something gorgeous . . . er . . . well at least not your old jeans, OK? Bye, darling.' And she was gone.

It was always a treat to eat at Sarah's. Mel was a lazy and reluctant cook, but Sarah excelled at the hostess arts that were currently scorned as being well out of fashion, making her guests feel that she'd really pulled out all the culinary stops for them. Her idea of a 'kitchen supper' was what would definitely qualify these days as the best parts of a full-scale dinner party, with elaborate table settings that had you convinced Sarah must have been a model pupil at a finishing school, stunning food, lavish and delicious wines, yet all without the tense formality that everyone used to suffer at such weirdly stylized events. In their own homes, Mel or Cherry might knock together a bubbling lasagne with salad followed by various fruits and cheeses, served casually on the scrubbed bare table for their guests. Sarah, on the other hand, would consult her many shelves of cookery books and come up with a menu that might well combine the trickiest of Raymond Blanc, Gordon Ramsay and Marco Pierre White. Napkins would be all of a match with the table-cloth, which would probably be something new in crisp rough linen from Designers Guild and complemented by a row of candles and tightly packed posies at intervals along the table – lilies of the valley, sweet peas, tiny pink rosebuds or the narcissi that don't smell of cat pee.

There was one aspect of dinner at Sarah's that intrigued Melanie: the instruction about what to wear. Sarah was clearly up to something – she must have found a free-range available male whom she considered the perfect new man for Mel, and she expected her to dress for the role of Woman Seeking Life Partner. Presumably she'd discovered a glut of spare blokes somewhere (where? the only massed lone men in this area lurked under the bridge and smelled of excess cider), and was having a last-ditch attempt at fixing up Cherry as well. She'd have to go through her wardrobe and come up with something appropriate – something that would look as if she was at least trying to obey Sarah's instructions, but which was also an outfit decidedly not aimed at seducing a fellow guest. Not an easy call.

Max hauled the last of a dozen big bags of stones from the back of his truck. 'Bloody hell, Melanie, I should be charging you . . . oh, what's that thing where houses fall into complete disrepair . . . dilapidations. That's the one. This job is wrecking my poor old body. I'll never be the same again.'

Mel watched him as he clutched his back like a massively pregnant woman. He leaned against the wall beside her, took out his tobacco pouch and started constructing a skinny roll-up. 'It's going to look superb, this garden. Excellent.' He nodded slowly, approving the work that he'd put in. There wasn't yet a single plant in sight. The York stone paths were now all laid, the beds round the edges of the garden were dug over and ready for planting, and in the squares between the stone there was a lining of black semipermeable fabric, onto which the bags of pale pinkish pebbles were to be emptied.

'I love this feeling of space. It almost makes me reluctant to plant anything at all,' Mel said, dipping her hand into the first bag of smooth stones and running them through her fingers. They felt warm and silky.

'That might be taking minimalism a bit far. But it's good to be able to see the scope of the place. That's what happens when you throw out all the dead wood. You have to be so very careful what you put back in.'

'Oh, I'm being careful all right, don't worry about that.'

'I'm not worried.' He turned to her and grinned, hesitant. 'I admit I had one or two doubts at first. Not about getting rid of all that stuff that was there. There's no point being sentimental about rose bushes that have got mighty infestations of black spot and rust like yours had, but – well – nothing but palms, bamboos and succulents. The complete banishment of blooms – that's a bit harsh.'

'A bit like "no flowers by request" at a funeral?'

'That's the one. I always think that's a bit unnecessarily miserable.'

'I don't think that's what Roger thought when he came round. I think he minded that I was uprooting something more than plants. Our life together. He's probably right.'

Max chuckled and coughed on his cigarette. 'Like I said, dead wood.'

'Mmm. Good title for my next book. I'll go and write that down.'

'If God was so all-powerful, why did he need to have a rest on the seventh day? And how did he know it was the seventh day – that would mean he must have invented counting before he'd made people, and stuff.' Ben was leaning against the door frame on the threshold of Mel's study, clutching a mug of tea. Using Rosa's computer, he'd finished his essay, checked his e-mails and downloaded ('accidentally', he planned to say if challenged) some blurry scenes of Dutch teenagers engaged in oral sex that didn't look as thrilling (to them, and therefore not to him) as he felt it should.

Mel, at her desk working towards the final chapters of *Dying For It*, glanced up at him. He was a good-looking boy, but still at the stage where he wasn't yet sure of this. He had a very angular body: other people leaned comfortably against things but he seemed to be propped awkwardly against the door frame like a series of precariously balanced planks. The obligatory tumbledown jeans he wore, and the droopy skate-boarder's fleece, couldn't disguise the lack of softness beneath. He was so different from the usual baggy-faced doughboys that she usually saw – the ones Rosa had always brought home. When they were thirty they'd have run to greasy mounds of flab, but Ben would simply be trimly muscled by then. For now, though, he looked almost breakable. Even his hair, fluffed up (many minutes of mirror and care, this) to look as if he'd just climbed out of bed fresh from a session with some raunchy girl-band singer, looked as if it might snap off halfway down its rough fair tufts.

'And do you think he hated Mondays too?' he went on. 'Because if he did, he should've just un-invented those.'

Mel considered for a moment. 'But then that would mean people would hate Tuesdays instead – and all the way through, and then there'd be no days at all and no time and nothing would exist.'

Ben gave this a few seconds' grave thought. 'Perhaps nothing does,' he concluded with a shrug.

Her mother had given her the raised-eyebrow

treatment about Ben's visits. 'I told you you'd miss having Rosa around. She's only been gone a few weeks and you're already filling the house with replacement teenagers.' Gwen delighted in what she saw as her fulfilled prophecy. 'You'll be getting a new man in your life next. You can be too independent, you know.' Melanie had joined in, laughing as she duetted the last sentence with her mother.

'No, no new men. Absolutely not. I'm going to enjoy being one of those women who is difficult to place at dinner tables but I've got a cab account so no-one has to drive me home. It's the way I like it.'

It didn't seem to be the way Neil Nicholson liked it, though. It might have been the polite thing to do at the time, but it also might have been a mistake, Mel considered, to have given him her phone number before fleeing home from the school reunion. He kept leaving messages on her answerphone suggesting that they do more catching up. He said it as if the two words were in ironic quote marks – implying with no subtlety whatsoever that he didn't mean talking about friends and family.

'It was good, but not *that* brilliant,' Mel told Cherry when she ran into her in Waitrose. 'I mean he *surely* has had sex that's more worth chasing for a repeat than that very brief and dusty encounter.' Cherry turned a bit pink and looked round quickly, checking no-one was within hearing distance: this particular branch of the store was highly likely to be full of people she knew – smart, affluent women with sharp haircuts, time on their hands and acute ears for gossip.

'Honestly Mel, you sound quite shameless!' she whispered.

Mel felt puzzled. 'Well, I am – in the sense that I'm

neither ashamed or regretful. I should have put it about a bit more in my youth,' she sighed. 'No-one thought anything of a quick fling then. I was such a goody-goody. Someone should have told me that when you're old you're not supposed to have sex without a very well thought-out reason, or at least a note from your mum. Talking of which, I've left mine in the Dickins and Jones coffee shop. I'd better go and fetch her before she eats all their Danish pastries.'

'But what about Neil — you're not going to see him again, are you?' Cherry sounded almost anxious as they pushed their trolleys towards the checkout.

'Oh, I should think so, perhaps just once. A drink or something, for the real sort of catching up, that's all.'

'It's never *all*, though, is it. Next thing, you'll be half a couple again and back to square one. All that *involvement*.' Cherry shuddered, as if she'd mentioned a dread disease.

Mel laughed. 'No, really — there'll be no *involvement*, that I can promise. I like being on my own. Now if I can just get my mother to take herself back home, everything'll be hunky-dee. See you tomorrow at Sarah's.'

By day three of his wife's absence, Howard was phoning every couple of hours, at first trying to sound jolly and normal and as if he'd just remembered they'd run out of tea bags and wanted to remind Gwen to pick some up on the way home. Gwen pointedly left the room when the phone rang, and Melanie tried at first to claim that her mother was out and let her father imagine she hadn't a clue why Gwen had taken off like a cross flighty twenty-something who'd discovered her new live-in boyfriend was a loutish slob. By the fourth call, Howard had stopped pretending and sounded pitifully pleading. 'Can't you persuade her? Can't you get her to come home?' Gwen was still adamant, flapped her hands frantically at Melanie and made goldfish mouths at her in her efforts to convey refusal to talk. When he called at 8 a.m. the next morning when Gwen was searching the fridge for marmalade without rind in it, Mel decided it was time to call a halt to her unchosen job as referee, told her father, 'Yes, she's right here,' and pushed the phone into her mother's upraised hand.

'Just give him a break, say you'll meet him,' she hissed, striding out of the room before Gwen could thrust the phone back at her again.

Melanie kept well out of hearing range and crossed her fingers briefly in the hope of a resolution. Her mother was wearing to have in the house with her: she kept turning down the thermostats on the radiators, washing up by hand instead of confining the used plates to the dishwasher ('hardly worth wasting the electricity, just for the two of us') and asking about what Melanie had planned for supper when they'd barely finished breakfast. God knew, Mel thought, what would happen if circumstances forced the two of them to live together permanently. It would be like having two stroppy tigers pacing in the same cage.

In her sitting room she bashed the sofa cushions back into shape and folded the silky scarlet throw that lived over the back of the battered old pink velvet chair. The night before, Gwen had pointed out that the chair needed re-covering. This couldn't be denied – it resembled an ancient and much-adored teddy bear, squashed and misshapen with clumps of stuffing leaking out. Mel had promised it a revamp, for it was one of her true treasures, but only when she had time to seek out the perfect same thrilling shade of faded Schiaparelli pink fabric that currently suited it so well. Her mother's suggestion – Dralon, hard-wearing, the colour of dark sherry that 'blends with anything, doesn't show the dirt' – had made her shudder and feel quite dejected – as if now all she had to look forward to was growing old and stocking up on serviceable, dull items that would see her safely to the end of her days and absorb all kinds of foreseeable spillage and leakage. She wanted to carry on choosing only the furniture that delighted her, practical or not.

The scene reminded her of when, a few years ago, she'd been choosing fabric to re-cover the sofa. She was captivated by an open-weave white linen, covered in massive blue twined tulips. She was perfectly aware, of course she was, that it wasn't at all practical. The label recommended it for cushions and curtains only. The assistant in the John Lewis fabric department smirked and ruled, 'You can't have this for *upholstery*, madam,' as if Mel was a total fool. Roger had pointed out that the cat would claw it to shreds and that it wouldn't survive the Rosa treatment for more than a year. A year was enough, for now, she'd argued. Fabric was mendable, cleanable and in the end replaceable. She'd stood her ground, bought it and the sofa looked magnificently showy, like a gaudy party frock at a rainy summer barbecue. The cat did pull out threads, Rosa's trainers did make grubby indelible marks, but Mel still loved the pattern – and it was surviving in brave splendour four years on. It was Roger who was no longer there. All things considered, she was glad she'd so determinedly pleased herself.

*   *   *

The most comfortable of her four pairs of black trousers would be just the thing, Mel decided, gazing into her wardrobe. Sarah would approve – she knew they were from Joseph, being the one who'd persuaded Mel to splash out and buy them. On the other hand, Sarah had demanded something special. Top halves were the important bit at dinners – they were the only bit of you that could be seen above the table – your lower half ideally needed something with a loose elastic waist so that you could be as piggy as you liked with the food. To be awkward, and something in Mel had the urge to be, she pulled out a mad skirt she'd bought in a sale on impulse. It was calf-length black net, spattered with velvet dots, nothing but layers of the softest tulle with bands of ribbon sewn on each layer's hem. And shoes – these had to be her most gorgeous silly zebra-print mules. The combination would convince Sarah that she was making an effort, all the way up from ground level, at frivolous glamour, though the wackiness would probably be off-putting to men who might fear bizarre sexual tastes to match the odd dress sense. A top was trickier. Sarah had a generally warm and welcoming house, but it was old and high-ceilinged and had sneaky draughts. Outside, the evenings were cool and fast heading towards what Cherry called the shivering season. Eventually she pulled a silvery-coloured low-necked cashmere sweater out of its summer wrapping. Sarah would give it a look, the one that said 'so last season, sweetie', but it was snug and slinky, sumptuous and comforting, and the low neckline was edged with a purple band from which dangled tiny shiny black beads that were quite fun to twiddle with when she had to sit still for any length of time.

One thing Mel had done that would get Sarah's approval was to have her hair cut. She'd ventured somewhere new that afternoon, a salon with black walls and the kind of music she associated with class A drugs, where Ellie, clad in a ten-inch skirt, padded silver moon boots and a cut-off top with 'Eat Me' written across it in studs, chopped Mel's shoulder-length grown-out bob into something gloriously messy, ragged-ended, and dead flat. It couldn't be more rock-chick if she'd asked Ellie to 'think Anita Pallenberg' (which she couldn't have done – Ellie being no more than twenty and unlikely to be familiar with Sixties icons).

'I thought you were getting your hair done,' Gwen commented from in front of *EastEnders*, as Mel presented herself for inspection just before the cab was due.

'I have. Don't you like it? It's exactly what I wanted, I'm thrilled.' Mel fluffed her fingers through the chopped-out ends.

'It looks very flat and tatty. You should have put some Carmens in it,' Gwen said, looking doubtful. 'You never know who you'll be meeting.'

Mel thought about this last statement of her mother's as she walked up Sarah's path. The path was lit by a couple of dozen candles that glimmered in blue glass holders, guiding guests across the front garden to the porch. Mel pressed the bell and leaned on the door for a few moments, collecting her thoughts. Sarah must have been reading an article called something like 'Make An Entrance' in a colour supplement. Mel suspected her of practising for Christmas.

'Melanie darling!' Sarah's husband Nick opened the door, head already sideways like a parrot to kiss first her left then right cheek. He was a bit of a background presence in Sarah's life – adoring, but so very hard-working somewhere financially important in the City that he was rarely around for enough collected hours for real friendship to develop. He was so much an absentee he had been known to have to frown and think deeply when asked which schools his children attended. He led her into the sitting room, where Sarah could be seen beyond the stunning Christopher Farr rug, looking gleeful as she poured champagne. The reason for the glee wasn't hard to decipher: sprawled comfortably across the vast cream sofa, looking pleased with himself, was Neil Nicholson. Cherry was on the far side of the sofa, gazing round-eyed at first Mel then Neil, her mouth twitching with the effort not to laugh.

'Mel! Look! Big surprise! Look who you missed at the reunion! Remember Mr Nicholson (geography)? Such a shame you had to leave early.' Sarah, almost shrieking with delight at her 'surprise', whizzed across the room and kissed Mel swiftly and triumphantly, grabbing her hand and leading her to where Neil was hauling himself out of the sofa. 'I was sure you'd want to see him again after all these years,' she hissed too loudly into Mel's ear. Neil grinned at her from the other side of Sarah. Mel could almost swear he'd also winked, but hoped it was a trick of the soft lighting. The sly bastard, she thought: those phone messages – he could have mentioned he'd be here.

'All these former pupils,' he said as he approached and kissed her cheek. 'So wonderfully grown-up. It makes me feel ancient. Hello, Melanie – I'd never have recognized you.' Lying sod, Mel thought, wondering at the same time why something smelled as if it was smouldering gently. It couldn't be Sarah's cooking – she simply didn't get these things wrong.

'Well hello, *Mr Nicholson*,' she said, becoming aware of the smoky air. 'How er . . . terrific to see you again.'

'Sarah, I think something's burning.' Cherry, next to a short, cube-shaped blond man in strange lime-green jeans, sounded as if the fire alert might be a point of urgency.

'Jesus, Mel, you're on fire!' Nick grabbed her from behind and flung her to the floor like an over-eager wrestler.

Melanie was indeed burning. Her beautiful, fragile net skirt must have brushed against one of Sarah's candles on the porch. Now she lay scrunched beneath Neil (again), who'd fallen on her swiftly to quench the flames, while Cherry and Sarah and the lime-green-jeans man squealed uselessly and Nick took aim with a tiny fire extinguisher. Eventually the fire was decreed to be out and Mel stood up, reaching warily behind her to see what she was left with in terms of clothing. There wasn't any pain, so she hadn't been scorched all the way to her skin. But behind her she felt no fronds of fabric – most of the back of her skirt had disappeared. Horrified, she clutched at her bottom – her knickers were still in place, that was something, but it wasn't much, given that they weren't the sort anyone would put on with the intention of them being seen. Beneath the mad floaty skirt was a pair of pants built for comfort: flesh-coloured, waist-to-thigh cotton-soft snugness – the sort that mothers of teenage girls used to urge them to wear against 'chills'.

There was a stifled giggle from Sarah. 'You'd better come upstairs and pick out something of mine. I think your skirt's definitely a write-off. Pity, it was so pretty.'

'Oh I don't know, you look quite fetching like that,' Neil commented, grinning lewdly. Cherry's eyebrows went up almost into her hairline, and Mel glowered at him.

'Honestly sweetie, just because you're living on your own there's no need to let the standards slip.' Sarah told Mel off the moment she'd got her into her bedroom. 'Those *pants*! Did you borrow them from your ma?'

'I didn't know anyone was going to be gawping at them, did I?' Mel giggled. 'Just as well I did wear them anyway, they've been an effective firebreak!'

'You should have had a leopard-print thong under that skirt, or something bright pink with marabou. I get you a nice suitable man and look what you go and do!'

'I didn't ask you to provide me with a man! I *don't* want one!' Mel protested, peeling off the charred remains of the skirt. It was clearly not salvageable, which was a shame because it had made her feel as if she was almost in costume, as if she was playing a far more frivolous and irresponsible person than she actually was. She'd have done her best tonight, played up to Sarah's expectations and flirted with Neil and also with Nick. She had a feeling that Mr Lime-Green wouldn't be too responsive. Now she was destined to spend the evening in Sarah's black trousers, which had lost a lot of their original stretch and which, Sarah being skinny-hipped, were a bit tight for easy eating, and she would feel far too much like her real self.

'So. How come you two missed seeing each other at the reunion?' Sarah asked as they eventually made a start on the lentil and pheasant terrine (Raymond Blanc). Mel glanced at Cherry, whose lips were clamped together to contain either laughter or the truth. Mel prayed she'd manage to keep both in.

'So many people, so little time,' she said almost truthfully. 'You were there, you know how it was. It was like a covens' convention,' Mel said. 'Does your school ever have reunions, Cherry?' She couldn't look at Neil but could sense him bursting with their sinful secret. It was a conspiracy she really didn't want, but it was far too late to state boldly, 'Well actually we did meet and we had sex in the old sanny,' and it would have a definite ring of unsavoury showing-off about it.

'I went to about six schools. My parents were forever in pursuit of the perfect city to live in,' Cherry said. 'They tried Oxford and hated it because they weren't part of the university; Bath but couldn't cope with the tourists; Durham was too cold and they've ended up in Canterbury, where they now say there's not enough, theatre-wise.'

'Ooh, I went to the theatre the other day – saw Maureen Lipman. Brilliant,' Mel cut in.

'Who with?' Cherry looked surprised.

'What, besides Maureen Lipman? Can't remember, I've kept the programme though.'

'No, you. Who did you go with?'

'Oh, no-one. I went by myself, on a whim.'

'By yourself? That's a bit sad, why didn't you ring me? I'd have gone with you.'

'So would I,' Sarah added. 'You don't have to do things all on your lonesome, you know.' She leaned across the table towards Neil and summed up, as if Mel wasn't there, 'She's divorced, you know. Remember I told you – husband recently remarried, having a baby.'

'But there wasn't time to ask anyone else,' Mel chipped in before any more bits of her personal history

135

could come out. 'It wasn't planned – I was passing the theatre.'

Just as Mel was feeling uncomfortably defensive and starting to wonder if perhaps she was getting a bit odd, Mr Lime-Green – who was called Lenny – agreed with her. 'I love doing things on the spur of the moment like that. And you don't have the hassle of date-arranging or thinking about whether to eat or not afterwards.' He leaned forward and grinned conspiratorially at Mel, who felt most encouraged until he added, 'Sometimes there are advantages to being left on the shelf, aren't there?'

Gwen wandered around her daughter's house dusting the tops of the many picture frames. Melanie had a lot of paintings, mostly unfathomable abstracts where the whole point, as far as Gwen could make out, was that the colours clashed. Whoever was doing the cleaning – and Gwen hadn't caught Mel or anyone else with a vacuum cleaner to hand during these few days – didn't seem to believe in getting to the bits where no-one could see. Hidden dirt, that's what it was. Gwen didn't trust it. Such stuff harboured germs. Neglect and decay were only a blink away.

At last, happy enough for now (the skirtings were another story but they'd have to wait till daylight), she ventured into the kitchen. Melanie lived on all the wrong food. She didn't even have proper mealtimes, just ate as and when. She was forever cooking up peculiar messes with pasta or standing by the fridge spooning up a yogurt. A body needed meat and potatoes and vegetables, separately laid out on a plate – that was what Gwen had raised her family on and it had done them pretty well. Vanessa believed in plain home cooking, too: her children had good solid constitutions, whereas Rosa often looked as if she was in need of a square meal. She doubted that Mel had the makings of a decent casserole anywhere, but it was worth checking the freezer just in case. If she found anything worth defrosting she could leave it overnight and have it in a low oven before lunchtime the next day.

As she'd expected, the icebox contained more frost than food. She unearthed some chicken wings (no date on the pack), a battered box of ice lollies (presumably Rosa's, but you could never tell) and a single cling-filmed trout. The big Harrods bag looked more promising – something delicious and costly from the food hall, she hoped. It was heavy, possibly a large ham, she guessed, her mouth beginning to water. She put it on the kitchen table, tipped out the contents, staring at the frozen badger for a few bewildered moments before letting out the most horrified scream of her life.

Nine

It was a pity about the badger – Cherry would not be pleased. If Melanie had only gone into the kitchen for a glass of water, instead of crashing straight off to bed when she came home from Sarah's, she might have been able to salvage it. By the time she found it, late in the morning, it was smelling like something Tina Keen's detectives might be called to deal with, and dripping liquid nastiness onto the floor. Even the cat was keeping his distance, staring in nervously from the garden side of the catflap. The table and the floor would need a thorough scrubbing with Dettol. Lying soggy amongst the badger's leaking fluids was the note from her mother, which was an exercise in suppressed outrage and must have taken some thought to construct:

'Have phoned your father and he is collecting me right now. Thank you for having me to stay. Mum.'

No love, no kisses. What Gwen had been doing poking about in the freezer was unclear, but Mel guessed accurately enough that it was connected with the notion of proper food.

Just as she was plucking up the nerve to grab the

beast (never had she been so thankful for her mother equipping her with rubber gloves) and stuff it into a double-strength bin bag, the phone rang. It was tempting to pick it up and simply state, 'I'm wrestling with a melted badger, please call later,' but if it was her publisher, agent or anyone else expecting her to make sense, this would not be wise.

'Hi Mel, it's Neil. Funny old evening, wasn't it?'

'Hello, Neil. I suppose you could call it that.'

'Hey, don't sound so po-faced – it was a hoot!'

'Well, my favourite skirt was burned to cinders, I was sympathized with for being "on the shelf" as the lime-green man put it, and I had to spend the evening pretending not to have seen you . . .'

'Let alone slept with me . . .' Neil purred, less seductively than he imagined.

'. . . well, "slept" isn't what I'd call it . . . I was going to say, not to have seen you for twenty-five years, when one of my two best friends was perfectly well aware of the truth and almost bursting blood vessels with the effort not to tell. Fun, then, if you like.'

'So Cherry knew the *whole* truth?' he chortled.

'Actually she did,' Mel admitted.

'I'm sorry about not letting you know I'd be there,' Neil went on. 'It's just that when you left the reunion I ran into Sarah and she was so insistent that I come for supper and not tell you. I could hardly tell her that we'd just missed all the speeches because we were . . . catching up elsewhere, so to speak, could I? That wouldn't be the act of a gentleman. Let me take you out for a meal – start again. Please? Or I could come to you, bring ingredients. I'm a brilliant cook, honest.'

Mel considered for a moment. If Neil was outside the house this minute she'd gratefully haul him in and get him to bury the furry corpse, but the idea of going out, making man-woman conversation and then finding an excuse not to have sex exhausted her. She'd tried the casual fling: it had been a one-off experiment that wouldn't improve in the repeating. She'd rather spend all her evenings, for evermore, working late, living on her mad sandwiches and watching post-midnight rubbish TV. But then she'd end up deranged. Alone, friendless, crazed and gibbering or even, she thought, staring at the rotting badger, doing weird secret things to dead animals.

'OK, next week, say Tuesday. Thanks, Neil, that will be . . .'

'Fun?'

'Yes. Yes, it will be.'

She'd changed. Leonora, Roger could honestly say, was no longer the woman he'd married. Mel hadn't done that – she'd been entirely, dependably herself from day one to day – well, zero was probably the right number in the circumstances. Her reliability was probably why he'd been so stupid as to take her for granted and cheat so flagrantly and so often. Leonora was no longer even a grown-up woman – not by his standards, anyway. She'd reverted to child-pet, to pretty-princess, to mummy and daddy's special baby girl. The house seemed constantly to be full of her parents; Leonora's mother dropped in most mornings, and left evidence of her visit in the form of cerise-lipsticked coffee cups lined up beside the sink – the opening mechanism for the dishwasher seemed to be a secret known only to Roger and the cleaning lady. Colin, her father, sometimes stopped by on the way back from the golf course. As he arrived home from work, Roger's heart would sink at the sight of Colin's Jaguar skewed at a proprietorial angle across the drive. He'd try, and fail, to squeeze his Passat between the car and the front door. Later there'd be a kind of back and forth dance-like skirmish of the cars, as Roger backed down the drive while Colin manoeuvred his vehicle round the central circular flower bed and inevitably (being by then more full of early evening gin than he'd admit to) ran over the surrounding stonework and crushed the struggling lavender.

Leonora hadn't been encumbered by these people when he'd met and dated her. She'd savoured their relationship being a secret one – a married man, so many years older, wasn't what her doting parents had had in mind for her. Leonora, now he looked back on that time, had treated the whole thing as a naughty game. She'd lied about him to her family, elaborately, for the sheer childish fun of it. He remembered how, when they'd gone away to Scotland for a weekend's skiing, she'd phoned her mother from their hotel bed and told her, in great detail, about the health spa she wasn't really at with a girlfriend who probably didn't exist. What, he'd asked at the time, had that been about? Why hadn't she just said she was going skiing with her boyfriend? She'd laughed, hadn't answered, distracting him by winding her slender legs around him and hauling him back beneath the duvet. Now that everything was official, he felt rather as if he'd been the prey and was successfully shot and bagged. He'd fallen for something – a woman who was a con, almost a joke.

And there was going to be this baby. He'd have to work hard at claiming it as his, for although there was no question about its actual paternity, he felt there would be keen challenge for what could only be termed 'ownership' from Colin and Maureen. He hoped for a boy, for the child's sake. Another girl would be too much competition for the role of household princess. The house, already awash with rather Eighties frills, would turn into a Temple of Pink. A boy might even the balance and give him an ally.

Leonora and Maureen were busy organizing the nursery. Occasionally Leonora would ask him to arbitrate: this shade of blue or that one, blinds or curtains. He didn't know how much difference, if any, his responses made, and suspected he was simply being asked out of politeness or to back up a decision already made. He flicked through a book of wallpaper samples that Leonora had left on the conservatory table. The book fell open at a page where the corner was turned down. The design looked vaguely familiar – white background with a watery pattern of occasional clouds, drifts of wave-tops and small children in sailing dinghies. Roger was surprised it was still in production. He and Mel had liked that one, all those years ago. It had reminded them of *Swallows and Amazons*. They'd ordered seven rolls of it and never collected them; they were probably still piled up in a stockroom somewhere, waiting to be pasted up in the room of the boy who would now have been fifteen and who would have covered this whimsical pattern with black paint and posters of pert girls. Roger wondered about the turned-down corner: Leonora must have got it on her list of possibles. Quickly checking that she wasn't within hearing distance, he ripped the page out, scrunched it up and shoved it in his jacket pocket. This was one decorating decision he was going to make by himself.

* * *

Cherry had forgiven Melanie for the loss of badger. And so she should, Mel thought, seeing as she had just bought her a substantial lunch at the River Café to make up for it. They were on their way to an exhibition, a private view held at the unusual time of 2 p.m. to catch, according to Cherry, the school-run-mother trade. 'They're the ones who make the decisions about what goes on the walls. And they'll all turn up because they're grateful to be asked to a grown-up event in the daytime,' Cherry told her as they walked up the Fulham Palace Road, looking backwards for an available taxi.

'I can understand that. When Rosa was little, the only discussions I seemed to have were with other mums who had some small person twined round their legs. You'd be forever saying something like, "Did you see that play on BBC2 last night no darling don't eat the ice cream from the wrong end." Completely mad conversations that were only half there and never went anywhere.'

'Well, I wouldn't know about that, but I know how to get a woman to buy a painting,' Cherry said, flinging out her arm to hail a fast-approaching taxi. 'And you'll like the artist – she paints domestic interior scenes, a bit like those old Dutch paintings but about this century instead. Great wobbling oversized women, every bit of cellulite on show, staggering beneath mounds of laundry, that sort of thing.'

The gallery was in the middle of a row of chic shops at the Notting Hill end of Kensington and was indeed, as Cherry had predicted, crammed with women clutching drinks and chatting to each other – few seemed to be taking much notice of the paintings. Mel overheard words familiar from the gym locker-room vocabulary range such as 'scholarship', 'au pair', 'exorbitant' and 'Sardinia'. Collectively, the women all looked remarkably similar – mid-thirties, predominantly pinky-beige in colouring, with chin-length highlighted English-mouse hair and ditsy little tight cardigans in sugared-almond colours worn over black trousers. Mel wondered how many of them had independent careers other than being full-time wives and mothers. She tried not to do them an injustice: any or every one of them might be a skiving novelist just like her, or an off-duty lawyer, a nurse or a night-shift police surgeon.

Whatever these women filled their daily lives with, the contrast between their sleek, well-kept appearance and the subjects of the paintings could hardly have been greater. The artist, as Cherry had told her, had painted big angry canvases crammed with ironic social realism (so Melanie read on the catalogue, and which she didn't feel qualified to dispute). She particularly liked a six-foot-square scene depicting a kitchen table piled high with family detritus. There were schoolbooks, a computer, newspapers, junk mail, a sleeping cat, half a Lego castle – anything but food – the table looked as if it had never been used for meals. In the corner, cowering against a big fridge, lurked a fat woman spooning baked beans into her mouth, guiltily, covertly, cold from the tin. It was a scene of true domestic desolation. Another painting showed a defeated-looking woman waiting in a long bus queue, clutching a toddler, a buggy and several bags of shopping. Close by, great hulking lads sped fast and free along the pavement on too-small Chopper bikes. The paint looked as if it had been applied with fury – great splodges and streaks of muted, rather ugly shades livened with the occasional startling bolt of primary colour.

'A dismal thing, real life, isn't it?' Cherry appeared at her side with two glasses of white wine.

'Not exactly a symphony of domestic bliss,' she could only agree, 'but I like these, they've got a lot to say.'

'Mel, this is Helena – she's the artist.' Melanie was surprised to find herself looking at a small slim woman with pale ginger hair scrunched back in a neat high ponytail. She was wearing no make-up, and her nose was dotted with the kind of freckles that little girls are usually reassured will disappear with age. The paintings with their fierce energy looked like the work of someone much bigger, and much older, too. Helena couldn't have been more than twenty-five, and surely hadn't yet had time or experience to become as domestically jaded as her paintings.

'Congratulations,' Mel said to her. 'These are terrific and I see you've sold a lot already. You must be pleased.'

'Mmm, I am! I didn't expect to sell this many – I just handed out invites to all the mothers at the gates of my son's school.' She leaned forward and lowered her voice to confiding level. 'I targeted the ones with the biggest cars, the off-roader types. I didn't dream they'd all turn up!' Helena was as excited as a child, high on her success. To Mel, she didn't look old enough to have a child, let alone a school-age one. 'How old is your son?' she couldn't resist asking.

'Eight. I know what you're thinking – I still get asked for ID in pubs. I did actually have him when I was seventeen. His dad's not around – it's just the two of us.' A girl approached carrying wine, topping up glasses. 'Goodness, I mustn't drink any more – I've got to pick him up later. Luckily the school's just round the corner.'

Melanie laughed. 'I remember that feeling. When you've had a lunch with a friend and you've shared a bottle, that's always the day Miss wants to haul you in to talk about the reading scheme.'

'Or the PTA rep starts a long spiel about the summer fête.'

'And you're standing there breathing so slowly through your nose you think you'll faint, but the alternative is to have it all round the staffroom that Rosa's Mother Drinks.' As if to confirm the truth of this, a woman behind Melanie could be heard saying, 'No, not for me, I'm driving,' followed by a swift recant, 'Just half a glass, then.'

Helena drifted away to be congratulated elsewhere, and Melanie felt peculiarly out of place. She was at a different stage from most of the women in the gallery. Their homes were full of the hustle of family life, their voices full of false complaint at how busy they were, how rushed life was. She was by contrast a slowed being, able to choose the hours she kept, the routines she set herself. She could live as mad as a skunk, pile old newspapers into string-tied heaps, keep garbage in carrier bags on the stairs, make smelly towers out of empty cat-food cans. She could, with only a small deviation of decisions, become a witch-creature, alone with her cat and frightening to children. She had an unsettling vision of herself as a much older woman – double-locking doors, fearful of strangers, wary of unexpected telephone calls, taking her handbag up to bed at night. She gave herself a small mental shaking.

This wouldn't happen. Definitely not.

'Will they know me? I'm eighty-one now, you know.' Melanie guided Mrs Jenkins into the Ford Galaxy she'd borrowed from Perfect Patty, and hoped there'd be room for all the luggage as well as Hal, Brenda and their pair of well-grown children. It would be pushing it a bit, especially if they'd brought with them bulky Canadian presents. Somehow she kept picturing them coming through the swing doors of the Terminal 3 Arrivals Hall with a mounted moose-head (shot by Hal) resplendent on top of the baggage trolley. A couple of bottles of duty-free and a bottle of unsuitable perfume hastily bought on the plane was far more likely.

'They'll know you. You don't forget your own mother,' Mel reassured her. 'And they've got photos of you, haven't they?'

'From Christmas. At our Brian's.' Mrs Jenkins went tight-lipped and folded her hands firmly round her handbag. At Christmas, at her son's house the year before, there'd been what Mrs Jenkins had called a 'misunderstanding'. It had involved money, of course, family disputes involving aged widows usually did. Mrs Jenkins had been protectively unspecific about the argument but had hinted that Brian was angry that she hadn't made provision for ensuring her home would not have to be sold if she had to go into residential care. He'd suggested remortgaging for an annuity, 'free-ing up capital' – Mrs Jenkins, vague as she sometimes was, had remembered the exact words clearly enough.

'I'll die in my own bed in my own good time,' she'd declared soon after New Year. 'And he can get his share of the spoils then.' Mel trusted that Brenda, so eagerly awaited from Canada, wouldn't prove to be just as graspingly cash-minded.

It was quite a trek from the car park to the Arrivals Hall, but Mrs Jenkins showed no sign of flagging as they walked. She was wearing her best winter coat – smart navy blue, teamed with a pink and mauve flowered silk scarf she had shown proudly to Mel when Brenda had sent it for her birthday. The colours went perfectly with her lilac-tinted curls, which she'd had specially shampooed and set at Luscious Locks for this great occasion.

'I hope the plane's not going to be late,' Mrs Jenkins commented as they took their places at the barrier rail alongside minicab drivers clutching name-boards.

'No, it isn't. Look up there, it says it landed about five minutes ago. Perfectly timed.' Melanie showed her the screen above them with the flights listed. Mrs Jenkins gave it a glance, then concentrated on the doors, catching her breath each time they opened to reveal another outpouring of weary-looking travellers. She was shifting from foot to foot, either with nerves or because her narrow navy shoes were hurting her bunions. Mrs Jenkins was usually only seen in either her tartan slippers or a pair of flat capacious moccasins.

'They might be quite a while yet, perhaps we should find you somewhere to sit,' Mel suggested, looking around for seats not occupied by sleeping, sprawled people who must surely be in the wrong part of the terminal.

'I'm not sitting down. I might miss them,' Mrs Jenkins declared, clutching hold of the steel barrier rail as if Mel was about to haul her bodily across the terminal.

At last, passengers started emerging, carrying duty-free bags emblazoned with maple leaves. Any minute now, Mel thought, feeling almost as nervous as her neighbour.

'That's them.' Mrs Jenkins said it quietly, not moving. A portly foursome wielding a pair of heavily laden trolleys was walking slowly down the aisle towards them. They gazed through the waiting crowd, scanning for the familiar face. Brenda, Mel could see, looked pale and anxious, puffy-eyed and lank-haired, as if the journey had taken eighty hours, not eight. Then her face lit up: 'Mom!' she yelled. Abandoning her luggage, Brenda defied her middle-aged bulk and leapt the barrier, clutching her mother to a stoutly filled orange tee shirt. Mrs Jenkins herself looked bewildered, crushed beneath Brenda's bulk. The rest of the family, equally sturdily built, stood around looking awkward. Melanie could only watch, as one by one the son-in-law Hal and grandchildren Barty and Lee-Ann kissed their aged relative. Apart from Brenda, who was now weeping copiously, they looked as if they'd just met a stranger. Which, of course, they had. It all seemed suddenly terribly sad: this family of remote and unconnected beings. Much as she relished being on her own, Mel hoped and prayed that Rosa would not choose to live so far away. Or, if she did, that she had a job with an airline and paid at least fortnightly visits to her old neglected mum.

Rosa took Desi for a walk along the Hoe. It was cold; the wind was blowing in sharply from the south-east and she wished she'd worn a coat. Desi was a good person to walk with: he didn't make daft comments about everything and everyone, nor did he, unlike just about every other student in the city, take a skate-board everywhere with him and try to impress her by doing silly tricks on it. Only the local kids were really good at it: the wannabe boardies were useless and kept falling off. There was this thing they did when they bailed, toeing the board up into the air and catching it, as if that was what they'd meant to do all the time. She knew it was just a scuzzy way of saving face when they were about to fall flat on their butts. At least two of their Hall's residents were going round with either a wrist or foot in plaster from trying to compete with the experts. The only students who were remotely com-petent were the ones who hung out at the Boardriders club, real surfers, body-boarders, windsurfers – people with years of balance practice. She and Desi didn't really fit among them – neither of them was what any-one would describe as sporty. Desi couldn't walk across a road without tripping over his feet, and Rosa's idea of exercise was tapping out texts to Gracie, who was now backpacking in Mexico.

Perhaps she should have taken a year out. Most of the others had been away since school and done some-thing mad in foreign parts. The parents of Rota-Girl Kate at the flat had shelled out £3,000 so she could impress with 'taught at a school up a mountain in Patagonia' on her CV. Two of the boys had done Australia, Sydney-to-Cairns, along with a thousand other kids from the British private education system. A gap year would have given Rosa time to forget about Alex. Even now she had to stop herself phoning his mobile just to hear his voice. She had stuff to tell him. Stuff he was going to need to know. One thing *she* knew, she wanted to go home. For good, not just for a weekend. This just wasn't going to work. If it wasn't for the feeling that she'd be abandoning Desi to a harsh and cynical world, she'd be on the next train to Paddington.

Gwen simply didn't mention the defrosted badger, so neither did Mel. In her parents' house all was its pre-pornography tranquillity. If something had been resolved, this had happened privately and would never be mentioned again. In the sitting room with its walnut sideboard hosting a never-changing parade of Mel and Vanessa's old school photos, Mel accepted a cup of tea, helped herself from a plate of bourbon creams and listened as Gwen told her about the holiday Howard had booked for them both, 'As a surprise!' Gwen was quite skittish about this, delighted that he could still astound her in good ways as well as bad. They were to go to Spain after Christmas, for a whole month – special pensioners' rates.

'It's an apartment – and there's two bedrooms, so we thought you'd like to come too, seeing as you're on your own.'

'Well – er, I don't . . .'

Gwen wasn't in any mood to accept the word no. 'Rosa will be back at university and you can bring that computer of yours if you've really got to do your work. A change will do you good. And it's not as if you've anything else to do.' She leaned forward, as if the world was waiting to hear, and said, 'You might meet someone. There'll be a lot of the more mature sort of men there.'

Mel doubted this: it was far more likely there'd be a surfeit of elderly ladies.

'I think perhaps I should leave them for someone else. I'm not looking for one!' How many times did this

152

have to be said? Mel was smiling, but her jaw was tense.

'It won't be all bingo and ballroom dancing, you know,' Gwen said. 'At least . . . I don't think it will.' She was finding room for doubts to creep in.

'Even if it is, we don't have to join in with all that. There'll be lots to do,' Howard reassured her. They looked more comfortable together than Mel had seen them in ages. Howard had carried the tea tray into the sitting room. He'd put it carefully on the table and then straightened the cushions on the chair before Gwen sat down. She was, Mel could see, conscious of being treated like someone bordering on regal, sporting a gracious smile like a minor royal on a walkabout, deputizing for someone grander. Even if she'd been desperate to spend a month in Spain, it would have been like tagging along on someone else's honeymoon.

'I tell you what, I'll look after the dog for you, then you won't have to worry about him,' she volunteered.

'Vanessa's having him. You have a think anyway, you don't have to decide today. There's Christmas to get out of the way first,' Gwen said, getting up and bustling back towards the kitchen for some forgotten item.

'Dad, I really would rather not come,' Melanie said as soon as Gwen was safely out of hearing distance. 'You don't mind, do you? I mean, I could come over for a weekend, just to top up your supplies of English Breakfast tea or something.'

'No, it's fine by me. You do what you want. You've got your own life.'

'Glad to have her back?' Mel risked asking, hearing Gwen banging cutlery around in the kitchen.

'Oh yes. Though . . .'

'Yes?'

Her father hesitated and glanced quickly at the door to make sure he wasn't overheard. 'Sometimes being on your own for a bit is a good thing,' he said. 'It was quite relaxing, really. Not having to set the table properly for a meal, leaving the washing up till morning.'

Mel laughed. 'Mum would say that was the road to ruin!'

'Sssh! Just don't tell her!'

'Now I've mentioned Christmas,' Gwen came back into the room with a chocolate cake, plates and her big silver cake-knife, 'it's been decided this year it's at Vanessa's.'

Christmas. Melanie hadn't even thought about it. It seemed to be a far-ahead group of weeks whose real high point was that Rosa would be back for a while. Last year the family had gathered on the big day at her house. Roger had been there, pretending for a day that he more or less still lived on the premises, for the sake of family peace, but not fooling anyone. Rosa had had a hangover and uttered barely more than a growl all day before hogging the bathroom for an hour, so she could slink out to see Alex in the evening. William and Theresa, Vanessa's children, had eaten their turkey in silence and then immersed themselves in computer games. Howard had fallen asleep with a paper hat over his eyes, while Melanie, Vanessa, Roger and Gwen had kept up a bright and purposeless discussion about falling/rising standards of television programmes. Vanessa's husband Lester had followed her into the kitchen with a view to sympathizing about Roger. He'd got too close, hand squidging her hip, saying, 'Any time you want a little chat, that's what family is for.'

Now, thanks to her mother getting in quickly, it

seemed Melanie was wrong-footed with no alternative Christmas planned and therefore no escape. If she went to Vanessa's, this Christmas would be spent being new, misunderstood things to those she was with. None of these new definitions was superficially attractive: she was, variously, a spinster daughter, a maiden aunt, a lone divorcée, the in-law to be taken in for the day and patronized. If she wanted to be her more positive, single happy self, she and Rosa would have to take off somewhere else. Easier said.

Ten

Mrs Jenkins's house overspilled noisy activity. With Brenda and her family in residence, Melanie could hear constant signs of occupation. From Melanie's side of the dividing wall it was very much like having a television on somewhere in the house that you couldn't find to switch off. Usually Mrs Jenkins was the quietest possible neighbour, but now Mel was being treated to a kind of running, thumping commentary on this long-awaited visit. This was a family that existed at full pelt. Their footsteps pounded up and down the stairs, the front and back doors were crashed shut, the TV was on day and night at a volume that ensured it could be heard from any room in the house, and Barty and Lee-Ann preferred to share their teenage taste in music with everyone within a hundred-yard radius, rather than selfishly keeping it to themselves via headphones. Perfect Patty commented with disapproval to Mel that the neighbourhood was becoming 'rowdy'. Mel couldn't find it in her to agree (they were only visiting for a short while, surely a bit of leeway wasn't much to ask), but it was true that when the family all ventured out, taking in London's sights in the quiet post-tourist-season days, the silence felt unnaturally and eerily profound.

Mrs Jenkins was beginning to look tired. Her jaunty lilac hair was becoming wispy and wild and her shoulders sagged. This visit, longed-for as it was, overwhelmed her by the sheer bulk of her home's extra occupants. Hal and Brenda and their teenage children were built on a bigger scale altogether, as if they'd expanded to occupy the extra space afforded by their vast home nation. Where Mrs Jenkins had small, fragile bones that were almost visible through parchment-thin skin, the visitors' bodies were thickly insulated from the Canadian winters by meaty flesh. Their limbs were chunky and heavy, fervently overnourished by Brenda. She had taken over her mother's kitchen and cooked vigorously, bashing pots and pans around and yelling questions to her daughter, who tormented the poodle in the garden, offering it sticks and stealing them back again till the dog added its voice to the overall volume and yapped itself into a frenzy.

'D'you wanna sandwich, Lee? How about a soda?' Mel could hear it all, for Brenda kept the back door wide open, presumably because the late October chill was considered mild fresh air compared with a Toronto autumn.

Hal was eager to be busy and found things to mend around the house. As he fixed the downpipe back to the wall and cleared pigeon nests from the guttering he exchanged manly comments about tools and ladders across the fence with Max, who toiled below in Mel's garden.

From her study window Melanie could see that Max's fair dreadlocks were darker now, as the sun no longer bleached them. He was turning up in sweaters for a colder season, ones with felted wool, clotted and faded by years of outdoor weather. He would be leaving soon, like a migrating bird, returning (he'd promised) to finish the job in spring. The work for now was almost done – there was little left to do except buy the plants and get them into place. There was, though, a problem with Melanie's garden wall, down at the far end. 'It needs repointing,' Max told her one lunchtime. 'Look, all this section where I've pulled the ivy away, all the mortar's coming out.'

Mel peered at it as if she knew what she was looking for. It was easier just to take Max's word for it, though even she could see that the wall looked as if someone had been stingy with the stuff holding the bricks together. It reminded her of a cake, a Victoria sandwich that had been meagrely filled with the kind of cream that disappears to nothing.

'Will you be able to fix it?' She hoped he would. She'd got used to having him around. Like the best kind of domestic pet, Max was no trouble, even quite a comfort on occasions. He kept his distance in the mornings, answered the phone if Mel was out, and had fixed the dripping kitchen tap without fuss and without being asked. He'd buried the badger, too, when the ground he'd previously dug so thoroughly had been too fine and mobile and refused to stop caving back into the hole. She knew he liked coffee with no sugar but two spoonfuls in tea, and that he had to stop doing anything noisy at 12.55 p.m. to listen to the shipping forecast on Radio 4. The idea of bringing in a set of new workmen and getting used to their preferences did not appeal at all.

'Of course I can do it. Hey, I'm a landscaper, walls come with the territory. It's whether you mind me being around even longer. I mean, plant-wise we're nearly there. We can have the outing to the Palm Centre and do the buying next week. We can't put many of them in the ground, of course, but we can get them into position and just leave them for the winter and then when frost danger is past, that's the time to plant them.'

'If they make it through the coldest bit. It would be typical crap luck if we get one of those "coldest winters on record".' Mel was feeling glum. Tina Keen was having problems with the pursuit of her murderer. There might have to be one last victim so that things would shake up enough to be possible to resolve, and Mel was feeling unusually squeamish about the idea of setting up another killing. It would have to be someone who was already in the book – she was too far in to introduce a new major character. It could be the café victim's best friend, perhaps: the girl she'd run away from the children's home with and who'd managed to give up heroin against all odds and pressures. It seemed a wicked betrayal to kill her off after all her good efforts, but it might have to be done.

'The plants will be fine. Cold damp wind is the worst enemy and you're really sheltered here.' Max was reassuring. 'There's just one thing, though. I have to take some time out, I can't be here every day.'

'Another job?' Melanie imagined him, suddenly, making himself at home in some other woman's kitchen, leaving his unmatched wellies by a different back door before padding across an unknown floor in his tweedy socks to fill a kettle. It would be like . . . what? Not infidelity?

Max grinned, gazed at the floor and looked as sheepish as a caught-out child. 'Not exactly. I'm going on

Who Wants to Be a Millionaire? Bit embarrassing really.' He was practically shuffling his feet around now. 'I don't suppose I'll get past that first eliminator speed-round but if I do . . .' he went on, 'would you consider . . .'

Oh, not the frantic-partner-in-audience role, she thought immediately, before just as quickly dismissing the idea: he'd have a wife somewhere for that one, or a girlfriend, boyfriend, she didn't know. Perhaps she should know, by now. He knew an awful lot about her – things were a bit lopsided here.

'Would you consider being one of my Phone A Friends? We're allowed up to five. I thought you might take on the dodgy literature questions? Book-wise I only really know about sci-fi.' He finally got the words out.

She laughed, part relief and part amazement. 'What, me? That's a dire responsibility!'

'Is it? I mean, don't if you'd rather not. But I won't hold it against you if you get a question you can't handle. I mean, that'll make two of us, won't it, by definition.'

'Well yes, I guess it would. But if you win a million you won't want to come back and finish my garden, will you? Or anyone else's. So if I get asked who the madwoman in the wedding dress was in *Great Expectations*, I could just decide to plump for "Miss Faversham" instead of Miss Havisham.'

'I trust you,' he said. 'You're a book person, who better?'

'Could be a big mistake!'

On the day that Neil Nicholson was to come to her house in the evening and cook, Melanie went early to the gym. On the way she picked up Ben from the bus stop. He was huddled into a fat puffa jacket, staring at the pavement as she pulled up beside him.

'Getting colder,' she commented to him, wondering why it had evolved as a British habit to make pointless observations about the weather.

'Too right. Not that the school cares. We got a lecture yesterday about wearing "the right sort of coat".'

'Well that one's OK, isn't it?'

'Not according to them.' Ben laughed. 'You wouldn't believe the verbal circles our head went round in, trying to avoid saying that we're not allowed to look as if we go to the comprehensive!'

'What are you supposed to wear, then? A big tweed coat? A Barbour?'

'Well, a few of us thought we might go round the charity shops and see if we could find those big camel-type things like Del Boy wears in the programme.'

'You'd need a cigar to match. And a flat cap.'

Ben laughed again. 'Great. That would wind them up.'

Nothing seemed to change over the years, school-wise, Mel thought after she'd dropped Ben off. When she'd been at school there'd been a craze for short PVC macs, the sort she still selected occasionally for tarts patrolling wet night streets in her books. They'd been noisy, slippery garments. She remembered one late after-school afternoon when she'd had a play rehearsal – *Antony and Cleopatra*, a bit part as Charmian, a handmaiden. Neil Nicholson had been leaving the school late, too, and had stopped at the bus stop in his slinky MG, telling her to get in, quick. She assumed the urgency was to do with the pouring rain getting into his adored car. As Rosa would put it: naive or what?

He'd had music on loud, a cassette belting out Whitesnake. The car, the music were exciting stuff, in a highly fancied young teacher. When he'd dropped her off outside her house, that had been the first time he'd kissed her – nothing to object to (well, not back in those days), just a brief electrifying brush of his lips against the corner of hers. His hand had rested on her leg, pale against the black shiny fabric. And she'd felt selected, special. Her seventeen-year-old ego never questioned whether there were others picked out like this. He'd been, for Mel and her hormonally-pent-up peers, the very stuff of solo sexual fantasy – the perfect aid to sleep. She hadn't thought at the time to question the state of *his* ego, the confidence he must have had that his chosen girls wouldn't fail to keep the secret. How carefully had he chosen them, she wondered?

At the gym there were further signs of winter. On the notice board as she went in was a huge poster depicting fat snowflakes and an even fatter Santa Claus, advertising the Christmas party. Christmas was a sneaky thing, Melanie had decided over the past few years – tricking its way in from September onwards, while families were still adjusting to Back to Skool. The earliest signs were workmen taking apart corners of department stores, lugging in bare plastic-leaved Christmas trees and boxes of baubles that were left around in innocent piles, still closed, for a few days, waiting for their moment. Before you knew it entire shop floors were transformed into grottos, awash with glitter and tat and the tinny background of carols. Melanie stared at the poster and wondered whether Roger should be still on her present list. What would the Gift Guides suggest as perfect for the ex-husband? Perhaps someone made an alimony-payment reminder, a silver beeper that went off when a cheque was due.

'Can I sell you a couple of tickets for the party? You and your husband?' chirpy blonde Tanya on the reception desk asked Mel.

'I don't think so, thanks all the same,' Mel told her, imagining a bar full of overexcited twenty-somethings drunk on Bacardi Breezers and the probability of sexual conquest. It was at just that kind of party (amazing what happened backstage at staid insurance underwriters) that Leonora had shown Roger her own Christmas stockings, beneath a boardroom table.

'Oh, shame!' Tanya's bright lipsticked smile faded for a second, then revived quickly. 'Or are you going away? Somewhere nice?'

'No, no I'm not going anywhere. Just to my sister's on the dreaded big day.' The smile hovered uncertainly as Tanya sympathized, 'Oh a nice quiet time for you then,' which somehow managed to sound as if there'd been a death. Mel hurried away to stash her bag in the locker room and found Sarah drying her hair.

'Hi! So tonight's the big night! Looking forward to it?' Sarah yelled over the sound of the hairdryer. Heads swivelled to look, women towelled less vigorously, sensing gossip.

'Ssh! It's no big deal! Only supper. In fact . . .'

'What? Tell me!' Sarah switched off the hairdryer and replaced it in its holder on the counter top. 'Do you want knicker advice? All I can say is don't wear those big beige pants. In fact, throw them away.' She shuddered. 'How Neil can still want to see you again after he's seen those . . .'

'Hey, he won't be seeing my underwear – I've done that phase. I'm on to "Just Being Friends". A new maturity.'

164

'Can't be done, sweetie. They don't know the rules to that game. Now look, you need to be ready for . . .' Sarah lowered her voice and glanced around quickly, pulling Mel into an unoccupied corner of the changing room.

'Ready for?'

'Anything. Just in case. You might change your mind. I mean, look around here, take a peek. What do you notice?'

'Women? Some dressed, some not? Cool gymwear? Expensive shoes?'

'Look at the *not-dressed*. With subtlety, obviously – you don't want to be misinterpreted,' Sarah whispered. 'They've all gone into *winter plumage*. Frightful. Just because they're not sunning themselves on some beach doesn't mean they don't need to keep up with the bikini wax. I mean, some of the sights . . . I hope you've booked a trim, darling. You don't want to be falling out of your lace thong.'

Melanie giggled. 'I've always thought there's not much that can't be achieved with a Bic disposable. Not that it matters, I mean, no-one's going to be . . .'

There was a shocked intake of breath from Sarah. 'Are you mad? You'll have a stubbly undercarriage! How unattractive is that? And suppose you got run over by a bus?'

'You sound just like my mother! Except in her case she only went as far as insisting on clean underwear, not a brutally executed Brazilian wax complete with token Dali-esque wisp. And if I got run over, surely I'd want a bona fide orthopaedic bod to look at me, not one who fancied a spot of voyeuristic gynaecology on the side.'

'I give in. You're a lost cause – almost. Toenails,

then. Just because it's now tights weather . . .'

Mel obediently kicked off a shoe, pulled off a sock and showed Sarah a neatly painted set of cerise nails.

'Phew, well, that's one good thing, I suppose. But remember what I said. When you're on the market you've got to make the best of yourself At All Times. Listen to your Aunty Sarah, she knows.'

'She doesn't know everything,' Mel reminded her, as she refastened her trainer. 'She doesn't seem to understand I'm not on the market.'

Sarah put an arm round her shoulders and leaned close to her. 'Then what are you doing in here?' she asked.

'Keeping myself in good nick. For me. Just me,' Mel told her.

'Yeah, I know,' she said, patting Mel as if indulgently pitying her. 'Of course you are, sweetie.'

Neil was taking quite a chance, Melanie considered, as she parked her car close to the delicatessen. He didn't know how well or how badly equipped her kitchen was. She might, for all he knew, be the sort of woman who lived entirely on Count on Us Meals for One from Marks and Spencer and didn't possess a single sharp knife, a bottle of olive oil or a decent chopping board. On the other hand, perhaps she was the one taking a chance. The height of Neil's culinary repertoire could well involve defrosting a couple of portions of supermarket chicken Kiev and spreading oven chips across a baking tray. It was a strange thing to do, really, to offer to cook in someone else's kitchen when you didn't know them that well. Somewhere along the way there must have been an assumption that was based on the two of them being of the same . . . well, it could only be called class, really. If you were cooking for someone at your own home, you could impose your own tried and trusted favourites on them and trust your guest at least to be polite about it. If you went to a restaurant, you could express preferences via a menu. This way, it was an odd and slightly uncomfortable merging of tastes.

Mel was beginning to feel as if this non-relationship had been pushed several cogs forward while she was looking the other way. What she could do, at least, was make sure she'd got something that would redress the balance a bit. She'd find some really good bread, fat, fresh olives, a dense, rich pâté – perhaps put together a pudding, even though she wasn't that keen on them herself. And then there was all that wine that Roger hadn't yet collected. The thought of making further inroads into that, with someone Roger would consider an ill-intentioned interloper, quite cheered her.

'Hello, Melanie – we don't often see you in here.' Perfect Patty was by the organic yogurt section, clutching her big wicker shopping basket in front of her.

'No. I'm more of a dash-round-Waitrose woman usually. When you're living by yourself you don't need so much stuff. When I think of the hours I wasted shopping in the past . . .'

'Of course, I was forgetting you've got an *empty nest*. Sorry,' Patty half-whispered, as if Mel was suffering from a tragic disease. It was disconcerting, making her ramble on. 'Anyway, I've got someone coming tonight and I wanted a few extra bits and pieces.'

'Oh?' Patty made the short word last for at least the length of three syllables. 'I mean, oh that's nice. We don't want you to get lonely.'

167

Mel smiled broadly, attempting to dispel any misplaced mystery. 'Don't worry, I won't. It's just an old friend, left over from my school reunion a few weeks back,' she explained.

There was another 'Oh,' from Patty, this one on a down-note of disappointment. 'Oh well, never mind, I'm sure one day . . .' then she rallied quickly. 'Talking of exes, which we weren't, well, not really, that old boyfriend of your Rosa is doing brilliantly at Oxford, I hear.'

'Do you? Who from? And isn't it a bit early to tell?' Mel could hear herself failing in the attempt not to sound waspish. Alex had hurt her daughter badly, he'd zapped away too much of her sparkle – he wasn't to be allowed to get away with being a genius.

'I saw his mother. His brother's in Ben's year. Tipped for a first, by all accounts.'

'Oh well, good luck to him,' Mel said, crossing her fingers behind her back.

'Oh, and talking of boys – which at least we *are* this time – Ben's been spending a lot of time at your house. I hope he isn't getting in the way.'

Mel reached behind Patty's perfectly layered chestnut head for a carton of extra-thick double cream. She'd think of something to combine with it later, something fattening, chocolatey, out-of-season strawberries . . . 'He's not at all in the way, really. Don't worry about that. I like to see him.'

'Hmm. Yes, well,' Patty shifted awkwardly from foot to foot, 'it's just that, well, to be honest, I think he should be doing his homework at *home*. I can't really see why he needs to keep coming round to you. Our computer's always available for him. I mean, it's been almost every evening this last week or so.'

Mel looked at her, very nearly coming out with a true and speedy denial. Ben had only been round twice in the past ten days. What she had caught sight of, though, and obviously Patty hadn't, was Ben sloping past her own gate and up Mrs Jenkins's path. Lee-Ann from Canada was a pretty and very friendly girl.

'I'll remind him he's got a home to go to,' Mel promised. 'Best I can do.'

'Thanks, Mel, I knew you'd understand. *Upsets* during the exam years can be so disruptive, can't they?'

Mel made her way quickly round the store, crammed a random selection of goodies into her trolley and lined up at the checkout behind a boy somewhere around Rosa's age. He had the same dark red hair colour as Rosa, and similar straight wide shoulders. She'd never thought of her home as an 'empty nest' before. Patty's throwaway comment had rattled her. It gave her unwelcome thoughts of baby birds that didn't quite make it – the eggs that didn't hatch, the scrawny weakest babies that died unfed or were pushed out of the nest to land on hard pavements, where curious children poked at the sad damp feathers.

Another lad joined the one in front of her: 'Jim! Long time! What did you get?' She listened in shamelessly, waiting to hear if it was a degree result or A levels they were talking about. It was hard to pinpoint their ages.

'Oh, I got ninety hours community service,' she heard. 'Mick wasn't so lucky, he got six months.'

'That'll be the knife.' The pair of young men did some wise nodding.

'GBH to the filth. They gotta send you down for that. Set an example.'

Melanie felt instantly cheered: that small, solemn

and somehow highly moral exchange had quite made her day.

Rosa was backing a virtual oil tanker out of Poole Harbour. What it was doing there in the first place, she really had no idea. It would have been interesting to attach some kind of story to it, imagine it was on its way back to the Gulf to pick up a million gallons of crude oil. As far as she was aware there wasn't a refinery in the Poole area, though she could be wrong – if there was they should have been told, then they'd know what the tanker was there for, that it hadn't just parked itself at random. She'd been to Poole: when she was small her parents used to make the most of the sunniest days, keep her off school and drive down to Studland Bay to glory in doing nothing at all on a proper English beach. They'd have lunch at a hotel, one that was sniffy about children being in the grown-up dining room. Roger and Mel would ignore rules like that, keep her with them, let her show off her grown-up table manners that owed more to her being repulsed by her schoolfriends' sloppy lunch habits than to her parents' guidance. She'd always been a neat eater and could easily manage a Big Mac without a single bit of onion tumbling from the bun.

The thought of food made her feel nauseous, as did the idea that one day she could, if she pursued this particular module through to the end of the course, really find herself steering a massive tanker, on water, not just on a simulator. She was sharing the controls with people who really would ferry vast container ships across all the world's oceans one day. She was being taught by a man who actually had. The simulator gave little idea of the sea's movement. The students were handling the ship, but not the element it rode on, and it felt a bit like cheating. Anyone can drive a ship on a screen, she thought, as she crashed its bow into the harbour wall. It was like a cartoon: she could back the vessel out now (and she did) and the wall would mend itself. It was no more real than Tom reflating after being flattened by Jerry on a motorbike.

'What shall I wear, Max? Bearing in mind that this isn't a date, not a real one. But I don't want to look . . . slovenly.'

Mel didn't know why she was asking Max for advice – from what she'd seen, he was hardly a model of sartorial elegance. It was nearly six-thirty and they were having a beer in the kitchen. Jeremy Paxman was stretched out across Max's lap, purring and proudly full of the big winter-fat mouse he'd caught that afternoon.

'God, don't ask me!' Max put his hands up, pleading defeat. 'You look OK as you are. I take it you don't want to be too . . . how shall I put it? *Encouraging*?'

Mel laughed. 'That's it in one. This is all a big mistake. We should have gone out – a pub supper or something on neutral ground. It's turned into something ridiculously *intimate*. At least, from my point of view. I don't usually have people I hardly know rummaging through my drawers – kitchen ones, I mean. Or any other sort!' She felt herself going ludicrously pink, over-explaining. Possibly she and Max should stick to discussing whether a *Butia capitata* would prefer a west- or south-facing position.

Max shrugged. 'Tell him you've changed your mind. When he rings the doorbell, be ready with a coat and rush him out to your car. Tell him the cooker blew up

171

but you know the perfect alternative just across town. Easy.' He leaned forward and chinked her glass gently with his own. 'Don't forget, you've only yourself to think of right now. So do just that.'

And it would have been that easy. Mel put on her most comfortable jeans and a longish black cashmere/silk-mix jumper. She chose a pair of unobtrusive, pebble-like silver earrings and made sure she hadn't overdone the make-up. Her jacket was ready by the door, her keys were on the table for Max's suggested swift getaway. When the doorbell rang she almost fell over in her haste to put his plan into action.

'Hi!' She heard herself being over-breezy as she flung the door back – and almost ran into Ben on the doorstep.

'Sorry,' he mumbled. 'Forgot – Mum said you had someone coming.'

'It's all right, Ben. Come in.' She stepped aside and he came into the hallway, clutching a couple of school files.

'Lot of work on?' she asked him, pointing at the files. He was looking twitchy, shuffling from foot to foot and not meeting her eyes.

'Er . . . actually . . .' he started, then hesitated, his face twisting with the effort of choosing words.

'What's wrong?'

'It's Mum. She's spying on me, watching where I'm going.'

'Well, she thinks you come here. Has she said something?' The odd conversation in the delicatessen came into her mind. Perhaps Patty had caught on that her son was seeing more of Canadian Lee-Ann than Rosa's computer.

'I told her I was coming here to do some work and she started clucking about the place, going on. I mean you'd think she'd be glad I was getting on with it, wouldn't you?' He shrugged. 'Dunno what her problem is. Thing is, though . . .' He hesitated, giving her a sideways glance. 'She was watching me so I couldn't, like, go straight to Lee-Ann's. And I'm s'posed to be meeting her.' He speeded up now, sure he was safe from being interrupted. 'So would it be OK if I just go out your back door and through the fence gate into hers?'

At that moment the doorbell rang again. 'Of course it is, hang on, though, the latch is a bit tricky. I'll come and . . . just let me . . .' She opened the door. Neil was on the step, clutching several Sainsbury's bags. He followed her and Ben into the kitchen, and Mel opened the back door. By the time she'd seen Ben safely through the side gate, Neil had unloaded a feast's worth of goodies and was searching in the drawer by the sink. 'Bottle opener?' he asked.

Eleven

Mel didn't have a hangover – that was a surprise. Between them, she and Neil had got through two and a half bottles of wine, so if she was feeling OK she was willing to bet Neil had an absolute stonker of a headache. One of the bottles had been champagne, though, which she didn't really count, from a long-standing and potentially dangerous habit of classing all fizzy drinks in the same harmless category as Coca-Cola. Neil had brought it with him. 'To celebrate,' he'd said, which was rather sweet, as they were both way past the age for getting excited at a bottle full of bubbles.

'So . . . tell us everything!' Sarah and Cherry were waiting in Costa Coffee for Mel to give them a full and unexpurgated account of her evening.

'You two, it's like being with a pair of teenagers!' she said, sipping the powder from the froth on her hot chocolate. 'Anyone would think none of us had ever spent an evening with a man before!'

'We don't do hot dates any more – so you're having to do it for all of us. We're therefore entitled to details,' Sarah insisted.

'I don't *want* to do hot dates,' Cherry said with a slight shudder. 'Can't think of anything worse, in fact.'

'So you won't want to know, then . . .' Mel teased.

'Well, of course I do!' she said. 'So go on . . . did you end up in bed with him . . . again?'

Sarah turned to her, puzzled. 'Again?'

Mel groaned. 'Thanks, Chezz.'

'You mean you still haven't told Sarah? Oh, me and my big mouth! Sorry!' Cherry was wide-eyed. Mel suspected she was overdoing the innocence. Betrayal: that's what best friends are for, she thought, wondering when would be a good moment to let Sarah know that Cherry's idea of fun was injecting pungent preservatives into dead wildlife.

'You had sex with Mr Nicholson (geography)? *When?*' Sarah demanded. A pair of baby-encumbered women at the next table had tuned in and were listening shamelessly. One was tucking her hair behind her ears for maximum reception. Freed from full attention, their infants launched themselves from lap to table. One slammed a fat fist into the sugar bowl, the other dabbled its fingers and the end of a pink woolly sleeve in puddles of slopped coffee.

'Um . . . at the reunion.'

'But how? Where? When?'

'I'll say it fast and just once, which is just the way it happened. It was in the old sanny, remember, that scary little cell of a room with no windows? And it was while you lot were down in the hall singing "Jerusalem" and hearing the old headmistresses talking about their glory days. There's nothing more to tell, honestly, except I now know why it's called a "quickie". I'm not exactly proud of myself but it was a useful experiment. Quite fun, too.'

The women on the next table briskly mopped their babies and gathered their buggies and handbags together noisily and speedily. Mel brazenly stared them out as they gave her many not-quite-covert glances. She half-expected them to put their hands over their children's ears, to protect them from further corrupting revelations.

'How to clear a café in thirty seconds,' she said after they'd swiftly manoeuvred the buggies out of the door and given her sly backward looks.

'So when you came to supper the night your skirt went up in flames . . .' Sarah was putting two and two together.

'Yes, I'm sorry. But you were so excited about thinking you'd set up a big surprise, I couldn't just come out with it, could I?'

'Well, not with exactly what you've just told us, no – I can quite see that, but . . . oh, never mind. But from now it's truth time, OK?'

'Brownies' honour,' Mel agreed, humbly. 'Anyway, in case you're still keen to know, Neil cooked a delicious chicken tarragon thing with cream and wine.'

'So fattening . . .' Sarah interrupted, putting her hand to her concave stomach.

'And we had lots to drink and a silly chat about When We Were Young and old teachers from school, that kind of stuff. It was weird, you know, it was almost as if he'd been one of the pupils, not a teacher. I don't think he ever identified himself with the folks on the far side of the staffroom door.'

'Well, he was always like that, wasn't he,' Sarah agreed. 'You almost expected to find him smoking behind the bugs lab like we did. He was the only gorgeous bloke in a girls' school. Men have fantasies about situations like that. But anyway, what happened and are you seeing him again?'

'He's coming to put up my shelves. I didn't want him to but he was very insistent. I can do that, I've got a neat little Black and Decker, but that's one of those things they never can believe. Nothing sexy happened – truly; I poured him into a taxi at half past twelve. End of evening.'

As the drink disappeared and midnight approached, Neil had been closing in on the sofa. Just when he was near enough for her to pick up the scent of rosemary soap and wayward intentions, Ben had rapped on the window, keen to retrace his steps and go back home by way of the door he'd arrived through. His mother was bloody paranoid, he'd said. He wouldn't put it past her to be sitting outside in the car waiting for him to slink home from the pub with his mates and then lie to her. If there'd been a spell to break, Ben had done it pretty effectively.

On his way out Neil had spotted a flat-pack box waiting to be dealt with. It was a truth universally acknowledged by most men, it had occurred to Mel as she'd climbed into bed, switched on her TV and snuggled down with Jeremy Paxman purring cosily across her feet, that a woman who lived alone couldn't possibly put up a shelf. If only they thought it through, the lone women were the ones most likely to be able to.

Christmas was sneaking across the town, shop by shop. Melanie wondered if it was a sign of age to seethe about its appearance before November 5th was over. That was the sort of thing her mother tut-tutted about, even though Gwen would also have had, for at least a month by now, a juicily traditional Christmas cake secure inside greaseproof paper, foil and Tupperware in the cupboard. It would be reverently taken out each Sunday morning to have its bottom pierced with a knitting needle (size 3 mm) and the holes saturated with brandy. When Mel was a child, the same bottle had been brought out several years in a row, but now, with her father's new-found taste for drink, she wondered if her mother was discovering the level going down faster than any cake could absorb it.

Mel had only once made a Christmas cake. She'd been going through a Happy Families phase in which she assumed that if she did all those proper, traditional, wifey things, as if she was following instructions as per some 1950s situation comedy, her marriage would be magically repaired. Roger had never quite understood that most wives tended to expect fidelity in a husband, and that if this wasn't forthcoming they regarded the relationship as a damaged one. His idea of being faithful was to sleep at home each night. That anyone might object to anything he got up to off the domestic premises never failed to be a genuine mystery to him.

Melanie thought of Leonora, newly married and glowing with joyous optimism. She, full of her baby and fruitful thoughts, would certainly have made a Christmas cake – Roger had hinted that Leonora more than made up for Mel's domestic deficiencies. Odd, she'd considered, in one so young: perhaps she'd read a self-help book about how to keep a second-hand husband and decided that good old-fashioned homecraft could be the key. Cake-wise, Leonora would have followed Delia Smith to the letter and be planning an intricate design for the icing by now. She would have drawn it out on graph paper. There would be a timetable for The Big Day and she'd be thumbing through magazines that were far too old for her in search of ideas for table decorations. In her bitchier moments, Mel imagined her keeping a ring-bound folder, as if her first married Christmas was a school project. It would be decorated with pink Hello Kitty stickers.

Melanie's cake had never been eaten. Her mother had arrived on Christmas Day toting her Tupperware box containing her own cake ('I know you won't have made one, Melanie'), followed by Vanessa with yet another cake in a tin with a picture of Balmoral Castle on the lid. 'Never mind, it'll keep,' both Vanessa and Gwen had said of Mel's offering, not giving a second's thought to the possibility of taking theirs home again. But it hadn't kept, not really. She had been careless with the wrapping and it had been discovered weeks later, rotting pungently at the back of the dresser cupboard, a pale blue-grey mould crusting its iced top quite prettily. Roger had sneered and declared this 'typical', by which she realized that the domestic disinterest that he'd originally considered refreshing and charming now thoroughly annoyed him. He was like a scratch card, she thought: scrape away the potentially exciting surface and beneath you'd find nothing more than a man who longs to be mummied. And of course there were no prizes for that.

She'd have to sort out the Christmas thing. There were two possibilities: either forget about it and simply endure the day at Vanessa's, or arrange something thrilling and non-festive far, far away from it all. She'd ask Rosa.

*   *   *

180

Mel hadn't climbed into any kind of truck since she'd been a teenager and had hitch-hiked with her friend Anna to visit Anna's boyfriend at Magdalen College in Oxford. That time she'd worried about being a goose-berry – about what she was to do all day while Anna and Gerry took to his grubby single bed and made up for several weeks of lost groping time. Anna, fearful of hitching alone, had bribed Mel to come with her, giving her unlimited borrowing rights over her fabu-lous Mr Freedom lime-green velvet jeans with purple contrast stitching. Mel thought of these as she settled in the seat next to Max. How confident, how long and thin and sod-you-all she must have been to strut the streets in such a garment. How safe she played it these days (apart from the tragically ruined net skirt), when all trousers (apart from ancient comfort jeans), an unwritten past-forty rule told her, had to be black.

'Ready?' Max asked, switching on the engine.

'Ready,' she agreed, fastening the seat belt. It was her credit card they both referred to. A trip out to buy a garden's worth of palms and exotics, well-grown enough to survive a British winter, was something that she'd needed to brace herself for financially.

The cab of Max's pickup truck was identifiably Max. It was untidy but not filthy, the dashboard had recently been dusted but fresh mud and curled-up crispy leaves were scattered on the floor mats. From the rear-view mirror, where a cab driver would hang a pungent citrus air freshener, there dangled a twiggy bunch of dried rosemary and sage. Hundreds of tickets from the borough's parking machines were stuck around the windscreen, a deliberate ploy to confuse and delay the district's tyrannical traffic wardens. In the gap in front of the gear stick was a collection of cassette tapes

– not music but radio favourites: Alan Bennett's *Talking Heads*, she noticed, along with an old Hancock series (same one she had) and some Alan Partridge and *Dead Ringers* episodes. There was no hint of wife or family – no photos, no forgotten dolls, Pokémon cards or plastic aliens poking out from under the seats.

Max was a bossy road user, steering his truck in and out of traffic lanes as if it was a hot baby hatchback. Melanie's braking foot instinctively shoved its way to the floor, hard, as they raced round a corner and pulled up sharply behind a line of cars.

'You're surely not nervous?' Max laughed.

'Course not, it's just force of habit. It's ages since I was driven by someone else,' Melanie told him. 'You tend to think you're still in charge of the vehicle.'

'*You* do, you mean. I love being driven. I just relax and let whoever's driving take me where and how they will. I figure they don't actually *want* to die, so they'll get us to where we're going just as safely as I would.'

'I must be some kind of control nut, then,' Mel conceded.

'Yes, you probably are.' He was looking straight ahead, concentrating on whether the hesitant Cherokee Jeep in front of them was intending to turn at the left filter, so she couldn't see if his eyes had their trademark mocking look or not. What she could see was his soil-encrusted hand on the wheel. Even when he'd washed them his hands kept a mildly muddied tone, as if the lines on them had been lightly tattooed with soft pale earth. His clothes were the same: earthy but not unclean. He never smelled repulsively sweaty but you wouldn't catch a hint of biological detergent either. There was something sort of . . . *organic* was the word that came to mind, about him. She didn't know which newspapers he read (a fair guess would be *not* the *Daily Mail*), didn't know anything of his past: not his education, marital arrangements, sexual orientation, nothing. He was just there in her garden, being a perfectly integrated part of the outdoors, smoking neat but skinny roll-ups and passing the odd friendly comment with the cat and the stroppy robin that turned up every time a spade hit the earth. He didn't ask questions about her, either – he was the first person she'd come across since she'd been living alone who hadn't questioned her situation. Perhaps he was just like her, completely content to have a solitary existence and assuming it was as normal as cosy coupledom. As they neared the Palm Centre, she caught herself watching his left leg as it operated the clutch pedal. The thigh was long, encased in denim, at the end of which was an ancient sheepskin boot that had once been purple. She watched the muscles tense and relax as he changed gear. It had been raining and there was a misty, oily scent of damp wool from his sweater.

'Hey, wake up, we're there.' Max was grinning at her as he turned the truck round a sharp bend and pulled up outside a vast glasshouse. Mel, caught daydreaming, was flustered and fumbled with her seat belt. Max took her hand in his, moved it away and unfastened the catch. 'You were miles away,' he said. 'What were you thinking about?'

'Oh, er, nothing. The dreaded Christmas, just stuff like that.'

'Not going to spend it with your new man, then?'

'Don't!' Mel could hear her voice sounding fiercely defensive. 'I haven't got a new man. Or an old one.'

'Just kidding!' Max opened the door and slid to the

ground. 'Want a hand out or are you too independent for that as well?'

But Mel was already out, gazing round at a row of towering Cordylines. Across the path was a massive Queen palm in the biggest pot she had ever seen, its huge, graceful stems waving gently in a breeze that must surely be too chill for it.

'It would be easy to feel bad about this,' Melanie said to Max as they walked towards the covered section where the Phoenix palms were kept. 'These poor plants have been kidnapped from their natural habitat and forced to survive in a hostile climate. It's beginning to feel like keeping an exotic animal caged up in an inadequate vivarium with lights instead of sunshine.'

'Oh God, are you one of those people who thinks plants have souls?' Max groaned. 'Because if you are, I wish I'd known sooner. I'd have ticked the box marked "nutter" the first day I met you and never come back.'

Melanie laughed. 'I'm not even sure that people and animals have souls.'

'Ah, but you might think plants are superior beings to them.'

'Well, some of them are better-looking . . .'

'Thanks a lot! I mean, I know I'm a scruffy sod but I think I compare OK to a turnip.'

'Only just, mate, only just. Come on, let's spend lots of money.'

And it was lots of money. If Melanie ever let her mother know that she'd spent nearly £2,500 on plants all in one go, she was sure Gwen would drop dead on the spot. *Dying For It* was going to have to sell in untold quantities if she had any plans to repeat this kind of cash offload. It felt far more exciting than a tour of posh clothes shops. She was buying something that she'd never be bored with, that would make itself at home and grow (fingers crossed) and fill her garden space.

'Think of it as a piece of art, sculpture or something,' Max said as she looked, with some dismay, at the final tally.

'I am, I am. Though a big metal Anthony Gormley wouldn't keel over and die on me,' she said.

'It might rust, though, given time. Everything's got its lifespan.'

Pink 'Reserved' tags had been placed round the sturdy stems of a good selection of plants, ready for delivery. From the glasshouse Mel had also chosen agaves in various forms, fat-leaved, lethally spiky succulents that were reputed to be easy-going about cold weather, and a selection of phormiums ranging from almost shocking pink (just the colour she needed to recover her ancient chair) to a deep murky maroon. Banana plants, which Mel fancied to fill in gaps, would have to wait now till the spring.

'You will come back and see everything in the summer when it's got properly established?' she said to Max as they drove back to the house.

'Like on *Ground Force* where Alan Titchmarsh and the crew sneak up a year later and catch the garden they've made over filling up with weeds and half the stuff's dead?'

'Yeah, that's the one.'

'Lucky I didn't put in a water feature, then.'

'Too right – they're always the first things to silt up and go weedy. I'll try and do better than that.'

'I know you will. And yes, if you like I'll be back for a tour of inspection.'

It was all quiet again next door. Mrs Jenkins's family had taken off for Paris and Berlin and weren't expected back for a couple more weeks, for just a brief two-day stopover on their way home to Canada.

'They wanted me to go to Paris with them,' Mrs Jenkins reported to Melanie over the fence. 'But I said no. I told them they didn't want an old woman trailing around with them. I'd only slow them down. You do, you know, when you're eighty-one.' Mrs Jenkins looked a bit regretful, and Mel guessed Brenda and Hal hadn't put up quite enough of a fight to persuade her to change her mind. She could imagine Mrs Jenkins in Paris, riding along the Seine in a bateau-mouche and admiring the sights. She would enjoy sitting at a pavement table at the Café de Flore and telling passers-by, '*J'ai quatre-vingt et un ans, vous savez.*' She pictured her looking dignified, contented, as if she was waiting for Jean-Paul Sartre to join her for coffee and a croque monsieur.

'Perhaps they thought you'd like a bit of breathing space, time on your own to recover from their visit.'

'At my age – I'm eighty-one, you know – you get more than enough time on your own,' Mrs Jenkins said. 'It's time *not* on your own you look forward to.'

The Christmas question still hadn't been resolved. If Mel was to avoid being holed up for a long stifling afternoon in Vanessa's peaches-and-cream dining room, enduring her brother-in-law Lester's leery asides about a good stuffing, she'd have to hurry up about making alternative plans. She had e-mailed Rosa more than once but had had no reply. Her mobile phone was either permanently off or was being used so frequently that the message service was the only link. Rosa was probably avoiding the issue – and Mel didn't blame her. Who wanted to be asked what they fancied doing for Christmas when they weren't used to planning further ahead than the next afternoon? Big questions during Rosa's day were more likely to be a matter of Which Pub Tonight or choosing between the blue baggies or the minxy suede skirt.

It was now November 5th. Patty and David were having a bonfire party and had dropped a card through Melanie's door inviting her 'and friend' to join them in their garden for hot dogs and treacle toffee. Melanie had decided to take the 'and friend' literally and rang Cherry.

'Um, I'd love to go but I'm already going out. With Helena, that artist you met at the gallery, we're going to her little boy's school firework display. Sorry.'

Cherry sounded quite flustered. 'Are you all right?' Mel asked her.

'Not really, I'm doing a bat and I can't get its wings into position. It keeps falling over.'

'The coat-hanger technique not working, then?'

'Not funny, Melanie. I've got it stapled to a cake rack at the moment and propped up between a big vase and the toaster, but it's not quite what I wanted. I need a proper all-round view.'

'Can't you hang it from something? Like a model aeroplane?'

'Hmm. Not sure. Hold on a second . . .' The phone clattered to a hard surface – Mel guessed it was the kitchen table. She could hear scufflings and shufflings and Cherry saying a triumphant 'Aha!'

'You're a genius, Melanie, what are you? That's going to work – but I've got to do something tricky with stiff

187

wire. Come round tomorrow and I'll show you. I should have asked you in the first place – being by yourself makes you so resourceful, doesn't it? Who needs men!'

Perfect Patty was looking wonderful in a soft leather jacket the colour of a rich tea biscuit and lined with long-haired furry stuff that Melanie had seen in the window of Joseph the week before, and had thought glamorously louche. At the time it had so thrilled her it had made her heart beat faster, but she'd hesitated over the alarming price tag: with the bill for the plants still in the system, her credit card might explode. Now, seeing that Patty had nabbed it, she rather regretted her indecision: she couldn't get one now, obviously, and felt ratty with envy.

Patty looked puzzled to see Mrs Jenkins with Melanie. 'You said to bring a friend,' Mel reminded her quickly, fearful that Patty's initial surprise at greeting the pair of them on her doorstep might turn to tactless incredulity when she realized Mrs Jenkins really had come to join the gathering, and hadn't coincidentally turned up at the same time as Mel on a quest to borrow a cup of sugar.

'Lovely!' Patty rallied. 'Come through to the back garden! There's a super little bonfire on the go and David will get you both a drink. Mulled wine?' She raised her voice to address Mrs Jenkins, as people do in the company of those they consider truly ancient.

'Thank you, dear,' Mrs Jenkins said to Patty. 'You've got a lovely boy. He says please and thank you.'

'Ben? Yes I know!' Patty beamed, raising her eye-brows slightly to Melanie across the top of Mrs Jenkins's pink crocheted hat.

'I'm eighty-one, you know. He's nice and tall, your boy.'

'Oh, he is!' Patty agreed, taking her arm and leading her firmly through her house to where groups of friends and neighbours stood around sipping steaming scarlet drinks in the garden.

Melanie had met most of the guests before – at Christmas drinks parties, summer barbecues. There was Gerald, retired and curmudgeonly, from next door chatting to Paula and Sean from the house opposite, whose window posters frequently proclaimed their anti-Euro views. The rest were mostly fortyish couples with busy working and social lives and children who were forever being ferried to and from extra-curricular lessons: ballet, riding, piano, county-standard rugby, championship-level tennis, in the manner of all the area's pushed and privileged youth. It was as if, Melanie had often thought, children must be kept occupied at all times in case they sank into terminal couch-potato mode. Given Rosa's capacity for endless sofa-hogging with no more exercise than a finger-twitch on the remote control, this was probably right. The girl was surely sadly lacking in the necessary social arts of today. If she'd lived in Jane Austen's time she would have been an equivalent case, hopelessly untutored in bezique, croquet, embroidery, harpsichord playing or watercolour painting.

Patty's garden fences were prettily strung along their length with fairy lights. The decking she'd had built the year before had a pair of patio heaters blazing out enough kilowatts to keep a good-sized house warm. Melanie took off her gloves and shoved them in her pocket. Mrs Jenkins, installed comfortably at the head of the eight-foot teak table, was unravelling her scarf and helping herself to a sausage from a plateful that had been brought out from the oven. She dunked it into a dish of hot mustard and sucked at it with steady concentration, like a small child being careful with an ice lolly.

'I like your new haircut. Makes you look very young and fluffy.' David, Perfect Patty's not so perfect husband, topped up Melanie's glass of wine and stood too close beside her. Mel shifted her feet – he was practically on her toes.

'On your own tonight?' he went on. 'Oh sorry, I forgot! Roger's moved away, I gather. Oh dear, a faux pas.' David placed a commiserating arm on her shoulder, squeezing and kneading at the base of her neck as if certain she must be sorely missing manly physical contact.

'He's got married again. They're expecting a baby,' Mel told him. She knew he knew this, Patty would have been sure to tell him, but she also accepted that was no guarantee that he'd either listened or taken the information in. Sarah always said they didn't, men. Her theory, she'd told Mel, was that all domestic conversation counted as girl stuff unless it was going to make a direct difference to them in some expensive way.

'You must get lonely, all by yourself with Rosa gone as well. Don't you get fed up on your own? In need of company?'

It was hard to know if there was something he was getting at. If Melanie was one of those women who was utterly certain that she was permanently at the peak of astounding attractiveness, she might assume he was on the verge of being suggestive. He was more likely to be simply making conversation: Patty was not known as Perfect for nothing. David was *not* perfect: for one thing, he was a sweaty man. In all weathers his skin leaked unattractively. Tonight, beneath the massively efficient gas heaters, with the warmth stealing up the garden from the bonfire at the far end where a group of children were gathered, he oozed oil like a slab of haddock from a dodgy chip shop.

'I'm enjoying living on my own. Believe it or not, I'd actually been looking forward to it. I can do just what I like for the first time . . . well, practically ever.' She should get cards printed, it would save trotting out all this same stuff each time.

'And you can see who you like, too. A new man on the horizon, is there? I can't believe a woman like you would be lacking company.' He leaned even closer. 'You must let me know if I can . . .'

'You're right,' she interrupted with a sweet smile. 'You *can* go out with who you like. I do,' she said, indicating Mrs Jenkins, now on her second sausage.

'Darling, a word, do you mind?' Patty, the gorgeous jacket abandoned because of the heat, took David by the arm and pushed him towards the far end of the garden. Then she grabbed Mel by the wrist and hauled her back into the house.

'Just a little word, about Ben. Ben and alcohol, I'm sure you'll understand . . .'

Melanie didn't. 'Sorry, Patty, what about it?'

They were in Patty's silvery-blue conservatory. She had delicate wicker chairs (no sign of any unravelling, who would dare?) with silky-shiny pink cushions – little sparkly beads were embroidered here and there on them. Tiny driftwood picture frames hung in a double row on one wall, each containing just one unblemished seashell.

'It's just that on school nights, we'd rather he didn't drink. You see, the other night I couldn't help but smell it – after he'd been to you – beer on his breath. And he was home awfully late too, which was frankly a surprise after that little chat we had in the deli. Now I know you must be missing Rosa, but, well, you do see my point, don't you? Tempting as it must be to have the company of a replacement teenager – well, I'm sorry but we have to think of Ben's schoolwork. You do see?'

Well, there was a choice. She could protest the truth: that Ben hadn't been to make-use of her computer more than half a dozen times and hadn't had anything stronger than a Coke from her fridge, or she could keep schtum for him and allow herself be thought of as a sad and lonesome old teen-napper.

'Of course, Patty, yes, I completely understand,' she said, seeing Patty's anxious face break into a highly relieved smile. She watched from the window as the first of the fireworks were lit. Above the sound of the collected oohs and aahs the excited voice of Mrs Jenkins could be heard, at last declaring herself to be eighty-two.

Twelve

It wasn't hard to guess where Melanie would find her father. Every day since her early childhood he had walked the dog (from the first crotchety Sealyham to the current toothless fox terrier) along the same route: to the top of the avenue, across the main road, through the park with the luridly clashing begonia beds and out to the edge of the common. From there it was a brief pavement stroll round the corner by the Shell garage and back on the home straight. The suburban parade of shops were on this last stretch, where, when she'd been a child, her father had picked up the evening paper on his way home from work. Now long-retired and out and about by mid-morning, he'd tie the dog's lead to the railing outside the newsagents while he collected a paper (and presumably, if he was still pursuing the soft-porn option, anything else whose front-cover ladies took his fancy). He would then walk the terrier the few yards on to the Three Horseshoes, where the landlord kept a water bowl for dogs beneath the dartboard.

The pub was shabby and scuffed round the edges. No-one had yet seen an opportunity here for gutting and theming. Its buttercream paint peeled and flaked and the carpet was faded and threadbare. The smell of disinfectant saturated the air, overlaid with the scents of a century of spilled ale and exhaled tobacco. Sunlight streamed in through the frosted windows onto the freshly polished oak tables. It was early-morning quiet – Mel could hear no sounds of occupation apart from the rhythmic swish of a floor-mop beyond the door marked 'Gents'. Across the sticky carpet, beneath a lifeless fruit machine, her father sat wearing his reading glasses, immersed in the *Telegraph*'s Deaths column. A few other elderly men were dotted around singly, looking as if they'd been deliberately placed at equal distances from each other, each with a newspaper, some also with dogs lying beneath the tables, both dogs and humans tired from their walks. There were no women: this scruffy pub seemed almost to have had its air of neglect cultivated deliberately, to turn it into a male refuge. It was, it occurred to Melanie, the opposite of the spruce, clean home her mother had created. Perhaps there was a theme here, after all – a kind of grubby anti-domestic atmosphere cleverly designed to appeal to over-fussed retired men like her father, who were forever being asked to move their feet out of the way of a vacuum cleaner.

'Dad? How are you doing?' Howard looked up in astonishment as Melanie sat down next to him. The dog shambled to its feet, wagged its tail briefly and flopped down again.

'Melanie! What are you doing here? Is Gwen . . .'

'It's OK, Dad, there's nothing wrong. I can't pretend I was just passing, so I'll be honest – I wanted to see you without Mum.'

'Oh.' He looked down at the obituary column again, reminding Mel of a sulky child avoiding all-seeing parental eyes.

'It's about Christmas.'

'Christmas?' He looked as if he'd never heard of the word. Mel felt bad – he obviously thought she'd pursued him to his sanctuary on special orders to find out if he was up to no good. It was as if he imagined she'd been following him, sent by Gwen to body-search him for porn mags, and then report back so she could evict him to spend his remaining days in his shed.

'Christmas,' she insisted quietly. 'I don't particularly want to go to Vanessa's. I'm too old to play the failed single daughter – I just can't be doing with it. It was bad enough last year, everyone knowing Roger and I were just about over. Vanessa kept giving me those *looks*. So I'm making a grown-up choice: I'm not going. How do you think that will go down with Mum? She seems to think it's a *fait accompli*. She's not very easy to . . .'

'I know, I know.' For Howard it didn't need saying. 'Melanie, as you just said, you're an adult. You live on your own, you run your own life. You can do what you like.' He sighed heavily, and reminded himself with a wry grin, 'I'm a grown-up too, of course.'

'Do you mean you don't much want to go to Vanessa's either?' She grinned. 'Let's both not!'

'Well. No. Hand on heart, I love to see both my daughters. But it's not as if I have to do anything but turn up in a suitable outfit and sit where I'm told to sit. But . . . that Lester's a dull old bugger, isn't he? And there's something odd about those children. Never a word out of them, a pair of Midwich Cuckoos.'

'So you prefer Boxing Day?'

'Oh, I do!' His face lit up. 'There's racing on the telly, leftovers to eat as and when . . . no fuss. Yes, I much prefer that.'

'We could go to Kempton this year if you like, lose a few quid on some no-hopers, in real life instead of by way of the box. What do you think?'

Howard laughed. 'We could! Let's! What a brilliant idea. Now that really gives me something to look forward to.'

She realized immediately that this meant she couldn't now go away. She couldn't book into a madly expensive health spa or a Maldives diving centre. It was probably just as well. Getting away from Christmas was an idea that only seemed to work in theory. The thing tended to follow you, to get to you wherever you tried to hide. Why else were holidays a hundred per cent price-inflated during the Christmas/New Year fortnight? It was so that hotels frequented by Western travellers at every corner of the planet could justify rigging out their premises with plastic fir trees and glittery baubles. It was so that hotel staff could 'entertain' guests with carol singing and turkey barbecues and Santa in a scarlet and white fun-fur bikini.

So, instead, Mel and Rosa probably would spend the day chez Vanessa after all. Vanessa had a Christmas book that she brought out every October in which she checked off all the things to be done. She always sent out Christmas cards with the current year's specially organized family photo on the front. When the children had been little she'd got them to wear cardboard antlers, angel haloes or Santa hats. Now there was just body language that wasn't even remotely ho-ho-ho. On last year's, William had been scowling, Theresa's vacant eyes had been avoiding the camera and

Vanessa's smile had looked frantic. In this year's, Vanessa could well be hiding a sharp knife behind her back to warn against one of the perfect family smiles slipping. She peeled and prepared the sprouts on 22nd November and stashed them in the freezer. Her stuffing was ready by 15th December. She was probably the one person of her generation who insisted on silence for the Queen's speech. But hell, this wasn't for life, it was only for Christmas. It was just one day. How much could it hurt?

Tina Keen and Melanie were pretty sure by now who had committed the grim café murder. The victim's friend, the young reformed junkie, had been allowed (just) to keep her life, but not before enduring a terrifying, torturous night shackled to a barred window in a cellar. The chill, airless room was beneath a hospital where body parts – amputated limbs, defunct livers, infected, useless kidneys and aborted foetuses – waited like a butcher's special offer on steel trays in irreverent uncared-for heaps, to be bagged up and taken away for incineration. The hooded killer simply sat and watched her, silent, sinister and dangerous. For amusement he played with his knife, testing the blade by slicing a lobe from a diseased lung, then cutting a finger from a hand severed in a meat-processing accident.

Melanie's own fingers hovered over her keyboard, just giving one last moment to deciding which way to take it: whether to condemn the secretive young constable (with the sister-fixated past), or the mortuary attendant with his morbid obsession for making holes in people, to a life sentence of wary terror in gaol. It's not real, she reminded herself; it's only pretend.

Neither of these was a flesh and blood man who was really about to pass many fearful years in a miserable cell. She could flip a coin, let the fates decide which one of the pair was to star in the book's cataclysmic finale.

Mel finished the second-to-last chapter satisfied that as she'd scared herself to the point where she was almost afraid to leave her study, her readers would find it quite gruesome enough. She switched off the i-Book and looked down into the garden. It was dark – a smoky-damp late afternoon. Most of the gardens on either side of hers had long pools of light leaking out from downstairs rooms. Hers didn't – she hadn't been downstairs since the daylight started to fade, and no lights were on. Below, as she left her study, there was a rattle and clatter that almost made her heart stop, but it was only Jeremy Paxman racing in through his catflap. He was being chased, Mel thought, as the adrenalin subsided, either that or it was later than she'd imagined and he was in urgent need of food.

Melanie switched on the kitchen light, opened a sachet of Jeremy's favourite food for him, then took the vodka and tonic bottles out of the fridge and ice from the freezer. She smiled to herself as she pictured Roger with his eyebrows high up like a viaduct arch, commenting, 'Spirits before six, Melanie?' as if she was only a single measure away from joining the winos under the bridge. She poured herself a good strong drink (thinking as she did so of Sarah's useful maxim that if you pour the vodka over ice, you can kid yourself it's only a small one) and sat facing the black, blank window. A branch from next door's buddleia was scratching against the glass. The teenage addict she'd just been writing about, the murderer's chosen final victim, had been watched through an uncurtained window like this one. She too had fed her cat, taken a drink from her fridge, and all the time there'd been a man just the other side of the door, just a pane of glass and some flimsy wood away, excited, elated, craving to do unspeakable things to her.

Someone could be out there now, she thought, her insides tightening as small beads of fear started collecting together and gathering an unwelcome strength. There were no hiding places in her garden for any Tom to do his peeping from. Max had left it stripped and flattened, not so much as a blade of a weed remaining. But someone could be just beside the fence, sneaking along the black edges where the oblong of light stopped. They could have crept up close and be only inches away beneath the window.

Her mother's voice took over from Roger's drink warning. 'You should have got curtains,' it said, 'nice thick ones.' Mel had never seen the point of curtains in a kitchen, thinking them fussy and suburban and likely to get soggy and grease-speckled. Kitchens were warm places, needing more heat to be let out than kept in. She wasn't overlooked by other windows or by passers-by. It occurred to her now for the first time that somebody might take an undraped window for an invitation to peer in and think criminal thoughts.

'Maybe I should write light romantic comedies in future,' she told Jeremy Paxman, who was finishing off the last lickings round his bowl. The cat merely raised his head for a second and then started lapping noisily at his water.

The doorbell ringing almost made Melanie, in her hyped-up state, pass out completely. Her heart was pounding so hard as she went to open the front door that she thought it would crack a rib.

'I thought I'd just pop round on my way home, see how you're doing.' Roger was on the doorstep, shuffling his feet slightly, trying to look nonchalant. Melanie recognized that look – sideways grin, eyes not quite meeting hers – and it didn't convince. She remembered it from when he'd first mentioned Leonora, dropping her name too often and too enthusiastically into a conversation about junk e-mails. 'Just someone at work,' he'd said, when Mel asked who she was. If he'd been a child he'd have been literally wriggling with the burden of the lie. As it was, he'd shifted and twisted and got up for some more wine when his glass was still almost full.

'OK, come in,' she said, rather gracelessly. 'And on your way home from where? You're a long way off the track from Battersea to Esher.' Good grief, surely he wasn't seeing someone else this soon into his new marriage?

Roger slid his coat off and flung it over the banister rail, just as he used to when he'd lived there. 'Oh, just went into the town for something. Couldn't find it, don't remember what it was.'

'You're rambling, Roger. Just admit you've come to check that I haven't gutted the house as well as the garden. Drink?' She led the way to the sitting room, switching on a couple of lamps. As she closed the blue linen curtains she took a quick look outside to the garden. No-one there. Of course there wasn't.

'Oh, er . . . yes. That would be lovely. Only if you've got time though, I don't want to keep you from anything.' He was peering around, she noticed, as she went to the kitchen and came back with whisky, ice and a glass for him. She wondered what he was looking for – signs of another man occupying his former territory? A big fierce dog? Paint charts? He settled himself into the motheaten pink chair and pulled nervously at a couple of loose threads. In spite of herself, she couldn't help watching as he crossed one long leg over the other. She'd always loved the way his muscles went taut. He had, for a man, the most elegant legs, so did Max. Did this, she wondered, make her a 'leg-woman', in the same way that men defined themselves by their preferences as 'tit-men'?

'I've just finished work myself,' she told him, pouring him a Scotch. 'I've got nothing else planned – yet. I might go to see a film later.'

'Oh? Who with?'

'Why do people ask that? Isn't "which film" more to the point? If you really want to know, I'd be going by myself!' She laughed at him. 'Roger, you're as bad as Cherry – she thinks anyone who goes out on their own is terminally sad. Which in her case means she hardly ever goes anywhere.'

'Well, what's on? We could go together.'

She laughed again. 'What, you and me? Like a date? Are you mad?'

'No, not like a date. Like old friends.' He shrugged. 'It was just a thought.' He hesitated for a moment, then looked at her carefully. 'We are old friends, aren't we?'

Melanie felt taken aback. 'Old friends' would not have been her first thought when asked to describe their no-longer-married state. But to call themselves 'new enemies', or just 'acquaintances', would be to cancel out all the years when they'd been contented enough, raising Rosa, putting their home together, planting the now-annihilated garden. And there'd been the shared, well-supported bad times too – the death of his father, the loss of their baby.

'Yes, OK, Roger, we can be old friends if you like. I don't particularly want to go out with you, though, not tonight. Sorry. Anyway . . .' She couldn't stop herself using the defensive, carpy voice she thought had gone for ever the day the decree absolute had come through, as she added, 'Don't you want to rush home to Leonora?'

Ugh – she almost shuddered, wishing she hadn't said that. Now he'd think that somewhere in the corner of her soul there was still a little heap of jealous regret. She pictured it as a small, slightly battered sandcastle on a typical cold English beach just as the sun's going down, everyone has gone and the tide is coming in. At first, when they'd decided the marriage was definitely no longer workable, there'd been a whole massive sandy fortification of the stuff, practically a garrison town's worth – how could there not be? They'd been together, give or take a dozen or so of Roger's dalliances, for nearly twenty years. She was happy to be down to that one last tiny bucket-sized heap, with no flag in the top.

'Actually, there was something.' Roger's foot started twitching up and down with nerves. 'I sort of wanted to talk to you.'

Oh please, she thought, don't let it be some messy personal stuff concerned with Leonora and her pregnancy.

'Roger . . .' she began.

He interrupted quickly. 'No, Mel, just let me . . .'

He fumbled in his pocket, pulling out a crumpled piece of paper. 'Do you remember this?' He passed it to her and she smoothed it out, her hands moving softly and gently as she recognized the pattern.

'Oh, the wallpaper! Of course I remember. Those lovely *Swallows and Amazons* boats. I remember . . . I'm sure you do too . . . we talked about how free they were, those storybook children messing about on the water, no grown-ups, no life jackets, no-one fussing around, telling them not to tack downwind. Have you kept this scrap of paper all this time?'

'No. It's just . . . this is recent – it's still in production. Can you believe that?' He gave a short, brittle laugh. 'There's a book of sample papers that Leonora got. I ripped this one out.'

'What . . . because . . .'

'She liked this one. She'd turned the corner of the page down. I didn't want her to have it.'

'I see.' And she did, perfectly.

'Because it was ours, wasn't it? You understand, don't you? This was to do with us. I know it's just a detail, but those kids in the boats, I remember we saw them as Rosa and Daniel, five years on.' He pulled some more threads out of the chair cover. 'We never even collected the paper from the shop.'

'Er . . . I did, actually.'

'You did? Why? What was the point – Daniel had gone.'

'I know, I know. I was just passing the shop, about a month after he'd died, and I went in, on a sort of whim. I was half-crazed at the time, don't forget, I think we both were. Maybe I thought if I just carried on as if everything was all right, it sort of *would* be. Of course, when I got home, well, even halfway home – no buggy to push, no feed to rush back for . . . I just put it all in the loft, then went off to collect Rosa from school. It's still there, all seven rolls of it.' She laughed, shakily. 'I mean, if you really did want it, you could . . . No, on second thoughts, sorry.'

'I think . . .' Roger took a deep, long breath. 'I think I'm scared it might all happen again. Is that half-crazed too?'

'No, of course not. You know in your heart that it's not even remotely likely, but, well, I'd be amazed if you *didn't* think about it. Don't you talk about all this with Leonora?' She somehow hoped he didn't – Daniel had been *their* baby, their loss, their grief. One and a half pounds of almost transparent humanity. She could hardly bear the thought of Leonora, too young, too uncomprehending, eyes glittery, saying, 'Oh poor Roger, how terrible for you,' but she wouldn't have a clue, not deep down. She pictured her giving Roger a consoling hug, smiling a reassurance that *her* body wasn't faulty, wouldn't fail to let a baby hang in there for the full term. Then she'd switch channels on the TV, time for *Sex in the City*.

'Leonora hasn't even read a single baby book, not even one How To article in her many magazines. I don't think it occurs to her that there could possibly be anything to go wrong.'

No imagination, that's her trouble, Melanie thought, biting her lip to stop the words hurtling out.

'Well, she's probably right – it almost certainly *won't* go wrong,' she told him. 'We were just unlucky, that's all.'

'Yeah. I'm sure you're right. Look, I'm really sorry to have dragged all this up again. I'd better be going.' He looked at his watch and stood up. 'You OK?'

'Yes, I'm fine. I won't sit here and brood about it, don't worry. I have my down moments still, but not many and not for long – his birthday, the day that *should* have been his birthday, Christmas just a bit, you know.'

'Yes, but you're here by yourself . . .' He hovered by the doorway, as if guilty that he was abandoning someone that he'd injured. She felt annoyed suddenly, for it wasn't as if he could stay, even if they both wanted him to. He had somewhere else to be, someone else to be with. As if on cue, the doorbell rang.

'I like being by myself. I don't like having to keep reassuring people about it, though. I won't say it again, actually, it's too much like letting you off the hook,' she said as she walked past him to open the front door. Roger followed her, picking up his coat from the banisters. He looked puzzled, as if he'd patted her gently and she'd turned on him.

'Hi! Shelf-man here for you!' Neil, eager and willing as a soft old Labrador, brought chill damp air into the house with him. He also carried a big blue metal tool box and another one that she could see contained some kind of power tool.

'Oh. I see, so you're not quite as "on your own" as you make out,' Roger said, smirking as he gave Mel's cheek a perfunctory peck. 'I'll give you a call in the week – I was wondering what Rosa wants to do about Christmas. Bye!' and he was gone, swallowed up into the night and his new, other life.

Rosa and Desi lay on his bed watching *Friends*. They'd eaten a chicken stir-fry into which Desi had sliced too much ginger. 'It's good for you,' he'd told her. 'Ginger is supposed to stop you feeling sick.'

'Not *this* much of it, surely,' she'd said. 'Couldn't you have just got me a luscious box of ginger chocolates instead? Really dark, really bitter chocolate?'

And he had. She hadn't actually meant it, but Desi was one of those people who took things literally. In a way it was good, there was no devious thinking about him. You got what you paid for, so to speak. She put it down to spending all those years locked up (well, not literally, but it must have felt like it) at the kind of school where the use of imagination wasn't really encouraged. Sport, religion and a strangely old-fashioned sense of history – that was what he'd been raised on. He'd said he was just going out to the offy to buy a couple of cans of Stella, and he'd come back with a box of chocolate ginger creams. Milk chocolate, but lucky to get that after 8 p.m. on the edge of Plymouth town centre. He didn't want anything in return. He just did it because he liked her. She almost cried.

'You'd better check the sell-by,' he warned now as she reached into the box for her fifth sweet.

'Too late now,' she told him, hugging him close.

Melanie could have done it herself, quite easily. Well, she could have assembled the shelves – getting them to go up and stay up on the wall might have been another matter. Max would probably have obliged.

'It's not as simple as it looks,' Neil told her, in that way men do without bothering to ask first whether you've got a degree in Product Engineering. 'You can't just bash in the Rawlplugs wherever you feel like it.' He went hand over hand along the study wall as if feeling for the catch to the secret passage, knocking gently now and then. Melanie suppressed laughter: the scene was like a play in which a walled-up nun or a prisoner on the other side was likely to knock back. She couldn't think what he was listening for – these were not modern breeze-block and batten walls; as far as she could see the only thing to avoid, drill-wise, was slicing into an electric cable, and it was pretty obvious where they were. Neil looked happy enough, though. Like all men she'd ever known, he'd spread out over the entire room for this so-called simple job. On her desk was the open tool box, exposing an impressive range of drill-bits, screwdrivers, hacksaw blades and chisels that would stock an entire branch of B & Q. His electric screwdriver was charging itself up by way of her computer's mains plug and the packaging from the flat-pack box was strewn around the carpet. Tidy worker he was not.

'I'll get this lot cleared up in a minute,' he said as the last shelf's final fixing plate went successfully into the wall. He looked distinctly proud of himself, Melanie thought, as if he was genuinely thrilled to be fulfilling society's expectations of the standard ideal male of the species. He reminded her of Jeremy Paxman when he brought a bird in through the catflap – all erect head and delighted, challenging eyes.

'It's looking really good,' she told him, feeling conscious that she too was assuming an allotted role. She would now have to cook something – that was the next thing in the script. She wondered if it had been subconscious on his part – turn up an hour or so before the average suppertime and do a manly job so that he could be properly rewarded with sustenance. She could take him out somewhere, she thought, but she was quite enjoying observing Man in his more primitive element, and she didn't want to undermine his mood: if only for the sake of research it was interesting to study him as a stereotype. Besides, for once there was plenty of food in the fridge.

'There!' Neil stepped back and surveyed his work

triumphantly. 'That OK for you?' He turned to Mel.

'It's lovely, Neil, thank you. This has saved me a lot of hassle. Now – would you like some supper, my turn to cook?'

While Neil reassembled his toolkit and swept up the sawdust and plaster, Mel went down to the kitchen and opened the fridge, trusting it to come up with something instantly edible and miraculously simple to prepare yet impressive to serve. There was pasta (of course), three packs of tomatoes of varying ages, romaine lettuce that was a bit droopy in the leaf but crisp enough further down. A bit like me, really, Mel thought, as she took it out and started chopping at it. She was no longer looking at the window, expecting a crazed axeman to be outside, leering in with teeth bared and eyes manic. It seemed as if having a man on the premises was like a talisman against bad luck. The idea that she should acquire one, surrender her independence just to ward off imagined evil, wasn't a welcome one. She would, she thought, prefer to get a large, fierce dog.

It was a simple meal – pasta with pesto and cherry tomatoes – thanks to Nigel Slater's *Real Fast Food* cookbook. Now there, she thought, as she gouged out slivers of Parmesan with her potato peeler, was a man who understood the good things about lone living and eating. Nigel unashamedly praised the virtues of a real chip sandwich – thick white bread, twice-cooked chips, the sort you could really go mad for when you were by yourself. He knew a hundred ways with a single piece of chicken and the best things to put in a for-one omelette. It was all the kind of food that the lone greedy-guts most loved, yet when people were set up into couples and families it was the sort of food they pretended to scorn eating.

Neil wolfed down two platefuls of spaghetti, both the chocolate and brandy mousses Mel had been saving to have in bed after a long evening's work, and helped her to finish another bottle of Roger's best claret.

'Delicious. Thanks, Mel, you know the way to a man's vital organs,' he said, patting his tummy in a manner that seemed strangely elderly and reminded Mel of her father.

'No problem,' she said as she shoved plates into the dishwasher, 'it's just a small thank-you for doing the shelves.'

'Give me a kiss then, say thanks properly.' He had her all wrapped up against him and his mouth on hers before she could say, 'Ah, so that's the catch.'

She didn't much mind kissing him, in fact it was quite tasty and exciting, but it did occur to her that if the going rate for a couple of shelves was a snog, it was possibly just as well she hadn't asked him to construct a double-size built-in wardrobe.

Thirteen

'So how's it going with Neil?' Sarah was one of those annoyingly fit women who could run and talk at the same time. Even at full pelt her voice sounded perfectly normal, as if she was doing nothing more energetic than ambling round Space NK in search of a new lipstick. The gym was busy, humming with full-throttle exercise machines, booming with vigorous gee-up music that seemed to make the pace zap faster, and everyone in the building had skin glistening with the sheen of worthy exertion. Melanie, on the next machine to Sarah, was puffing at a slow trot and wondering why she hadn't simply volunteered to take her parents' terrier and Mrs Jenkins's poodle for a ramble in the park instead. She could have had a lovely child-like kick through heaps of fallen leaves, checked the horse chestnut trees for early signs of next spring's sticky buds and tried to guess which of the early morning mushrooms were the prized magic ones. At least there she wouldn't have to pretend she was in peak physical condition, and could commune peacefully with nature and her own thoughts.

'And what makes you think there's any "it" going

with Neil?' she asked Sarah when she had gathered enough spare breath.

'I called him.' Sarah's voice was loud to overcome the music. 'I asked if he'd seen you and he said he'd been round doing a spot of DIY for you. And we all know what *that* means.' Her eyes met Mel's in the mirror and she gave her a grin full of nudge-nudge insinuation.

Mel laughed. 'It means I've got a couple of nice new shelves where I can stash a few more books.'

'Oh come on, Melanie, don't be so po-faced, I can't believe it was just shelves he was putting up, so to speak.'

A passing staff member, one of the instructors, overheard Sarah. He slowed down, eyed up Mel in a questioning way and gave her a smirk and a leer. He was a well-muscled twenty-something, stocky with cropped black hair and bum-hugging shorts. Gossip in the gym claimed he'd been a pro rugby player until a run-in with an overenthusiastic opponent damaged his knee. He winked lasciviously at Mel via the mirror and she simpered back, just to be obliging.

'Did you see that? Bloody nerve!' she commented to Sarah as the man crossed the room to sort out another woman's confusion with the triceps-extension machine.

'I did and he's gorgeous. Your problem, Mel, is that you don't know when to be grateful.'

'Grateful? God, am I supposed to be? Thanks.'

'Yeah, grateful. Who knows? He might really fancy you. You should go over and give him your phone number; I would in your position. Young fresh blood, you never know . . .'

'Get real, Sarah, you make me sound like a vampire!

212

All that would happen is that we'd see how fast he could run!'

'You're mad. There you are, every young man's dream: an experienced Older Woman with no ties, a comfortable, warm, empty house and plenty of free time.'

Melanie switched off her machine and started on a few calf stretches. Sarah was also slowing down and leapt gracefully to the floor. 'Just imagine, you could have your very own *oooh young man* situation. You could run a string of them,' she suggested.

'Actually,' Mel was thoughtful as they walked to the changing room to get ready for a swim, 'it's only just occurred to me, but I think one of my neighbours thinks I'm up to no good with her son. I've been so caught up with finishing the book and watching what Max is up to in the garden . . . Jeez, she *does* think that. I'm so slow – I've only just realized what she meant.'

'Who? What?'

'Perfect Patty. Number 14. Her son Ben comes in now and then to use Rosa's computer. Except he doesn't come as often as his mother thinks he does, mostly he just used me as an excuse for a couple of weeks so he could go next door and get it on with old Mrs Jenkins's granddaughter. She's gone to Europe for a while, back tomorrow I think. Patty was giving me a warning about "encouraging" Ben. And she thinks I get him pissed. I was covering for him, so I didn't think to deny it. She's been a bit sniffy since then.'

'Well, you're a woman on your own – it's like being the village witch.'

'I've even got a cat.'

'There you are then. This woman will be round any minute checking your shed for a broomstick.'

Mel laughed. 'I haven't got a shed.'

'You're not denying the broomstick, then?'

'Or my trusty cauldron. There's a lot to be said for a good witch.'

The plants arrived in the afternoon. Max and Melanie had been waiting like anxious parents expecting an overdue homecoming child, and they were sitting on the bench under the kitchen window with their third mugs of tea when the truck drove carefully down the narrow alleyway at the back of the house. It was a gloomy but calm day, the sulky sort where you expect rain but it never quite falls, and dusk was already gathering, far too early, as if the sun had given up and gone home. It seemed to Melanie completely the wrong season and weather for the exuberant kind of plants associated with sun, warmth and light. As the truck progressed along the line of back-garden fences, the palms' fronds and the bamboos' whippy stems, safely bound together by tape, were waving their graceful leaves in the breeze like royalty acknowledging an admiring crowd.

'Poor things, they look like brave refugees,' Melanie commented. 'I hope I'm giving them a home they're going to like.'

'It'll be a bloody expensive mistake if you're not!' Max laughed. 'You shouldn't worry so much. They're strong, Mel, don't underestimate them. They've got plenty of resistance. Lighten up and enjoy! This is always the best bit, when everything's been completely prepared and it's all waiting for the final stage.' He looked at her, serious for once. 'I hope we're not going to have a falling-out about what goes where.'

'Wouldn't dream of it,' Melanie assured him.

214

'Anyway, won't it be like your original design? I liked the look of that.'

'Yeah, but when the stuff actually gets here . . . there's always room for a bit of juggling, a bit of artistic licence.'

'Well, you're the artist . . . you choose. I'll just sit here and supervise!'

'Hmm – not sure how that's going to work.'

The plants in their containers were manhandled through the gate by Max along with the nursery's deliverymen. Mel carried in the dozen bamboo plants and arranged them in a line along the back fence where Max had planned for them to go. They were quite small plants now but in the spring would start to grow fast – up to a foot a day, according to Max, though she wondered what he'd been smoking when he worked that one out. The variety of their stem colours was astounding, even in the grim November light – the many shades of yellow, green and black would glisten and change hue like rippled water when the summer sun played on them, and their leaves would shiver and rustle in the lightest breeze. Exchanging the miserably tangled old clematis for this, she thought, as she placed them carefully beside the fence, was like stripping off a stifling tight wool suit and putting on a simple thin silk shift dress.

The truck had a small crane attached to it and when all other possible unloading had been done, the three largest plants were manoeuvred into a roped tarpaulin cradle and winched over the fence. Each of these containers was at least three or four feet wide and of similar depth. It was a delicate, tricky procedure and was also the point at which Melanie realized the operation was being closely watched by just about

215

everyone in the neighbourhood who could get a view into her garden.

Patty was leaning out of Ben's bedroom window. 'Goodness, aren't we going exotic!' she called.

'It's certainly different,' came a gruff voice from next door, which Melanie identified as that of Gerald, a retired tax inspector whose preferences, garden-wise, were fat, velvety roses, hanging baskets and a stripy, close-cropped lawn. The voice didn't sound approving.

'Not your sort of thing, Gerald?' she called over his fence.

'It won't give you much to do outside,' he replied.

'That's exactly what I wanted!' she told him. 'But wait till next spring, when everything's properly in and starting to flourish. You might find you like it.'

'No proper flowers . . .' The disgruntled voice faded away and there was a sound of a door being firmly shut.

'I'll call that a vote against, then, shall I?' Melanie said to Max as he, Pablo and Brian from the nursery unhooked the biggest plant, a massive, many-branched *Chamaerops Humilis*, from the crane and pulled it into place at the far corner of the garden.

'Ooh, look at this! It's like abroad!' Mrs Jenkins came through the fence gate to see what was going on. She was warmly wrapped against the autumn day in her favourite grey fleecy coat and her pink crocheted hat.

'What do you think? Do you like them?' Max wiped his earthy hands down the front of his mud-coloured sweater.

'You need to get your wife to wash that, dear,' Mrs Jenkins told him, pointing her yellow mitten at his chest.

216

'I don't have one,' he replied, with an expression of mock-regret.

'Oh, don't you? Melanie?' she called to Mel, who was talking to the deliverymen. 'Melanie, do you hear that? He hasn't got a wife! So there you are!'

Brian and Pablo looked with speculation from Melanie to Max and back again.

'You are so embarrassing,' Mel told her. 'I've only just offloaded one useless husband, I'm in no hurry to get another!'

'Well, thanks for that,' Max said. 'I do all this work for you and I'm written off with every man on the planet as useless. You wait till spring and you want this lot dug in.'

'The useless referred to husbands,' Mel told him. Max leaned back on the wall and grinned at her. 'Lucky I'm not one, then,' he said. 'Especially yours.'

'Oh good grief, you know what I mean.' Mel stomped into the house, thoroughly flustered. She'd heard the doorbell ringing – two long rings, Sarah's signature tune. As she went back in through the kitchen door she could hear Mrs Jenkins telling Max, 'Brenda comes back tomorrow. They wanted me to go to Paris but I'm eighty-two . . .'

Sarah, Cherry and Helena – the painter whose work Melanie had been to see – were on the doorstep.

'You said this would be plant-delivery day, so we thought we'd come and have a look. And we brought this!' Sarah handed over a Waitrose bag that clanked and bulged with bottles of wine. 'And Neil's on his way over too, he seems to think he might be able to help.' She followed Mel into the kitchen and opened the drawer in search of the bottle opener.

'Does he?' Melanie laughed. 'With what? Telling

Max what to do? I'd like to see him try!'

'Mel, you're mad – Neil's a lovely, available bloke with all his own teeth . . .'

'That I haven't checked.'

'. . . who takes any excuse to be with you and what do you do?'

'Nothing.'

'Exactly.' Sarah stabbed the end of the corkscrew into the first bottle and gave it a vicious twist. She was sounding quite fierce, as if Melanie had a lingering illness and was refusing to try a well-proven remedy.

'Sarah, there's nothing I want to do. I like him as a friend but I didn't ask him to want to be with me.'

'Now if it was me . . .' Sarah wasn't in the mood for hearing reasons or excuses. As she reached into the cupboard for glasses, she looked out of the window to where Max was hauling the last of the three *Phoenix Canariensis* into position halfway along the left-hand fence.

'Well, no wonder!' Sarah declared, turning to Mel with a grin. 'Just look what you've been keeping on the premises all this time! You sly cow! Why didn't you say? Did Cherry know?'

'Hell, Sarah, Max is just the gardener! I *pay* him to be here!'

'Mm, so would I,' she murmured, pouring a large glass of red wine and opening the door. 'Hi!' she shouted. 'Could you fancy a glass of something warming?'

'Sarah's such a lying slapper,' Mel was saying as she took glasses and a bottle through to the sitting room to Helena and Cherry. 'She'd never cheat on Nick – she's just window-shopping and . . .' Melanie's voice wavered. Cherry and Helena were sitting close together on the sofa, holding hands. Cherry looked up, eyes sparkling, her face alight with a new adoration. 'Mel, there's something we want to tell you . . .'

Roger watched Leonora undressing. He lay back on the pillow and tried to remember what she'd looked like when she had a waist. She still wore clothes that he thought were too dangerously tight, as if she was deliberately ignoring her expanding centre. There was a livid dark red band round her middle, the top of her trousers must have been squeezing in against the baby. It couldn't be doing it any good. Which bits would it be pressing against, he wondered, the tiny brain, its tender tummy?

He knew better than to raise the subject with Leonora. He'd said something about maternity clothes just once and she'd laughed. A huge, in-your-face insulting kind of laugh, as if he'd committed the most ludicrous faux pas. Worse, she'd made it quite clear that the term was entirely, utterly out of date, passé, hopelessly from the middle of the last century if not the one before. 'Nobody wears that stuff any more!' she'd shrieked, clutching her sides with sheer hilarity. He'd only meant . . . well, what had he meant? That it looked, to him, more than a bit odd, wearing clingy tee shirts, trousers that followed every line, every curve of the new bump. In the house she was often too hot and wore skimpy little vest-tops that rode up and exposed the tight vulnerable skin. Her navel stuck out like a puppy's nose. There seemed so very little padding to protect the baby beneath. He supposed he meant that she was still going round looking as if – as if she was still trying to attract someone. It bothered him. He knew it shouldn't, he knew it was just what women (especially young ones) wore, but it bothered him.

'I suppose if it was down to you we'd be all swanning around in billowing smocks!' she'd scoffed, curling her lithe legs beneath her on the sofa and delving a spoon into yet another tub of her favourite mint-chip and double-choc ice cream. The baby would be mottled green and brown like a tropical snake if she ate much more of that, he was completely sure.

'Not at all,' he protested. 'I just wonder if you're really comfortable like that, all tight and trussed up.'

'But I'm not all tight and trussed up. That's the miracle of Lycra,' she explained slowly, teasing him as if he was the oldest man on Earth. Sometimes he felt as if he was.

Tonight, watching her pad around the room naked, Roger could feel little desire for his luscious young wife. She wanted sex often just now. Hormones were doing something to her libido, she claimed, and when they made love she seemed to be far away in a primitive, sexually fervid world of her own. He could, at those moments, as he watched her closed eyes and almost snarling, almost animal expression, be absolutely anyone, anyone at all with a fully functioning penis. It frightened him. He wasn't, in the coming years, going to be enough for her. She would move on. He would have been a useful and formative phase. Eventually, he could tell, sometime in years to come he would be living alone. He would end his days in a lonely flat with a cat or two, and the hope that his children would find space in their full lives to visit him. He would stay late at work, putting off the moment of getting home to switch on the lights to a soulless scene where there was existence but not life. He wished he could talk to Melanie about it, but she would be the last one to want to know. He could just hear her now: 'You should have thought of that.' Melanie's unforgiving voice went through his head.

He smiled to himself as Leonora climbed into bed and, misinterpreting his expression, leaned her swollen breasts against him and squeezed his thigh. More in duty than desire, he slid his hands round her eager body.

It was after midnight when the last of them left. By then the house looked as if thirty teenagers had been in having a good time. There were empty bottles all over the place, cigarette ends and Max's roaches in every saucer Mel possessed, and the kitchen surfaces were a sticky mess of toast crumbs, grated cheese, smeared Marmite that had missed its target and crumbs from the chocolate cake contributed by Patty.

'I thought I might as well come with him, see what your computer's got that ours hasn't,' Patty had said when she turned up on the doorstep accompanying a hugely embarrassed Ben and his bag of school books.

'Heard the music and the sound of a fun time, more like,' Sarah had whispered to Mel, as she poured Patty a drink and introduced her to the others. 'Thinks we're going to gang-rape her little boy,' Sarah added. Mel, glad of the very loud music (Max's Nelly Furtado tape from his truck), tried not to giggle. The idea of herself, Sarah and Mrs Jenkins pouncing on Ben and ripping his clothes off must be entirely ludicrous, even to his doting mother.

It had been a long-drawn-out joint effort, getting the plants into positions that everyone was happy with. Instead of simply Max and Melanie deciding between them, Sarah, Cherry and Helena, the nurserymen and

Mrs Jenkins had all contributed their opinions. The original plan had been spread out on the kitchen table and was soon covered in grubby marks where everybody in turn had pointed a finger and said, 'Put that big wandy one there,' or, 'The vicious spiky thing, you don't want that near the path.' Neil arrived in the middle of the discussions and, ever the teacher, tried to take over, waving his arms about as if he was directing traffic.

'That bloke you're going out with, he's a complete tosser,' Max muttered to Mel.

'I'm *not* going out with him,' she hissed back.

'Bloody good,' he said, disappearing behind a *Phoenix*.

Mel tactfully diverted Neil, sending him out to Oddbins as it became clear the beer supply would need topping up. Eventually, after Max had quietly reminded them all that decisions weren't necessarily final and there were still echiums and the more tender succulents to come in spring, it had been time for a celebratory drink. Someone remembered that it might be an idea just to have a quick check on a vital football match that was on TV, and Brian, Pablo and Neil began a long discussion about who were likely to win the league championship.

Melanie accompanied Mrs Jenkins, after a small glass of wine ('I like a drink, but it doesn't much like me, dear,') to her front door and when she came back could see that everyone was now well settled in for the evening. Ben was sprawled on the floor in front of the television and didn't look as if he intended to venture near the computer, and Jeremy Paxman settled himself comfortably to sleep on top of his bag of books on the chair in the hall.

Late in the evening, Patty helped herself to her fifth gin from the fridge and confessed to Cherry, Mel and Helena that she'd once had an affair with a girl at her boarding school. 'I know everyone thinks that all girls at those kind of schools are at it all the time, but . . .' She started weeping silently. 'She was the love of my life!' she sobbed. Mel glanced at the kitchen door, re-assured to hear Ben loudly arguing the case for Newcastle's ground as the permanent site for England home matches.

'What happened to her?' Helena asked quietly, stroking Patty's hand.

'Same as happens to most of us!' Patty wailed. 'She met a man who'd marry her and did it because she wasn't brave enough for any other kind of life!' She stood up and draped her arms round Cherry, who backed away, alarmed. 'I think you're wonderful!' Patty sobbed.

'Get her off me!' Cherry hissed to Sarah.

'You lot all right in here?' Max came in at half-time in search of more beers. 'Oh Lordy – what's up with her?'

'A bit tired and emotional, that's all,' Mel told him. 'Nothing to worry about.'

'Where does she live? Shall I take her home?'

Mel looked at Patty, who was still draped over Cherry. Cherry was trying to disentangle Patty's fingers which were clasped round her neck. 'Might be an idea,' Melanie told him. 'She's just along to the left, number 14. I'll tell Ben she didn't want to drag him away from the match.'

'You know, Melanie,' Patty slurred as Max took over from Cherry in propping her up, 'you're a good woman, very generous hostess. You deserve a nice new bloke. Someone your own age. My Ben's just a little boy. He thinks an older woman is twenty-two, not forty-two.'

'Why didn't she say it a bit louder?' Cherry hissed at Mel, as Max led Patty to the front door. 'Some of the world might not have heard.' Melanie didn't much care. Patty could think what she liked – it was just rather shamingly gratifying that she was not so Perfect after all.

Max came back five minutes later, when everyone but Mel had gone back to watching the match. She was stacking glasses in the dishwasher. Max's nose was streaming blood.

'Bastard hit me!' he said, staggering about in search of something to stem the scarlet flow. Mel pushed him into a chair, grabbed a wodge of paper towel from the roll, ran it under the cold tap and applied it to his nose. His blue eyes looked up into hers, puzzled and affronted. 'Patty's old man, that stocky little prick! He took a swing at me, thought I'd been out getting his wife rat-arsed! As if! She's not even close to my type!'

'So who is?' Melanie quickly put it down to too much wine that she'd asked that question.

Max's eyes were still focused on hers, and he'd got that look that he always had when he was teasing her. He didn't answer her question, which had to be a good thing. Because of course she didn't at all want to know. Not really.

The poodle was barking next door. Melanie, reliving the night before, groaned and shoved her pounding head under the pillow. It was just past seven but still midnight-dark. She hated getting out of bed in the early morning winter blackness. It felt unnatural.

People should be like tortoises, she thought, closing her eyes and trying to get back into a dream she'd been having about a hot sunny beach edged with breeze-wafted palms (elegant *Butia capitata*, she was delighted to be able to identify). People should be capable of slowing right down and sleeping away the sunless hours, digging themselves into a frost-free corner and winding down to a gentle torpor for the winter. As the dog yapped on and wakefulness inevitably took over, it occurred to her that she didn't really have to do this any more. She could, if she so chose, simply take herself off to a sunnier place, either to live permanently or to escape the cold bleak English months. She could rent the house out, sell it, even – go and live in Southern France or on a tiny Caribbean island. Like Mrs Jenkins's daughter, she could live so far away that when she came to visit she would be hugely welcomed by her family and could do nothing wrong – a true prodigal.

There was something not quite right. Melanie snapped back from her sunny reverie, hurled the pillow to the floor and sat up quickly. Mrs Jenkins never let the dog bark for more than a few minutes. She was an indulgent and fond pet-owner and would trail down the stairs at all hours of the day or night to let the creature out if that was what it wanted. And it wanted a lot lately, having got to the age where the demands of its digestive system were urgent and frequent.

Mel dressed quickly, flinging on her jeans and the earth-encrusted sweatshirt she'd worn for moving the plants, and her muddy sheepskin boots. She told herself not to be over-dramatic: there were a good dozen reasons why Mrs Jenkins might be letting the dog bark on. She tried hard to think of them, but not one came to mind. Even given Mrs Jenkins's early-rising habits, she wasn't likely to have popped out to the shops.

Melanie went out through the French windows and opened the gate in the fence. The next-door curtains were tightly shut – Mrs Jenkins was a great believer in keeping the heat in and the draughts out – but the small dog had scrabbled its way under the fabric and was bouncing at the windows like a toy on elastic. Mel tapped on the kitchen door and waited, but there was no sign of life. She was becoming more anxious now and went back through her own house and out of the front door, crossed the low wall and peered in through Mrs Jenkins's letter box, dreading and almost anticipating the classic worst-case scene of the old lady lying stark dead, twisted and bruised at the bottom of the stairs.

The hallway was empty. Mrs Jenkins's old beige jacket hung from the coat hooks on the wall along with her umbrella, the poodle's lead, her collection of scarves and the pink crocheted hat she'd been wearing the night before. Her wicker shopping trolley stood at the ready beside the low table on which sat the old cream telephone, a photo of Brenda and Brian in their infant-school days and a grinning grey china cat.

'Mrs Jenkins?' Melanie called through the letter box and rang the doorbell. Probably she'd frighten the life out of the old lady. She'd have to spend a good half-hour calming her down and filling her with tea and toast back in her own kitchen. The little dog bounded into the hallway, yapping and jumping. Mel backed away from its snapping teeth, leant on the door as she straightened up and found that she was pushing it open. The catch was broken. This was the moment when, if she was putting the scene into one of the Tina

Keen books, she'd have the tension tightening and it would be time to get some back-up. Instead she found herself going into the house, treading carefully in the half-light and keeping her fingers spread across her face in case she needed to cover her eyes from a sight too horrific.

Mrs Jenkins was in the sitting room, lying back in her Parker-Knoll recliner where she liked to rest in the afternoons. Her eyes were closed. Melanie wondered about tiptoeing away again, whether, to avoid terrifying her, she should just let the dog out for a few minutes and leave her to sleep. But there was the broken door-catch, and there was too much space on the mantelpiece, and on the old walnut sideboard where all the best silver picture frames had been there was only a single china Pekinese with a chipped ear. Melanie started to feel chilled and shivery. There was, when she looked closely, a bruise on the old lady's cheek, her hair was matted in dark sticky-looking patches. There was breath, but it was shallow and uneven.

Mel, shaking, ran to get a coat from the hall, draped it carefully over Mrs Jenkins and phoned for an ambulance, asking for police as well almost as an afterthought. Then she sat beside the unconscious old lady, holding her cool dry hand and waiting. She hoped the ginger sergeant, the one who'd been so kind and concerned when her car had been stolen, would come. Mrs Jenkins deserved someone gentle like that, not a brash young detective with promotion and daydreams about armed robbers on his mind.

The ambulance crew arrived first. A strong young blonde girl and a man who looked unnervingly like Michael Caine spoke soothingly to the old lady and treated her with dignity, talking to her as if she was conscious. They told her what they were doing as they checked her pulse, her blood pressure and applied an oxygen mask. The police turned up soon after, screaming round the corner in high drama with the blue light and siren going even though the road was clear and empty, just as the paramedics loaded Mrs Jenkins into the ambulance. Melanie wanted to tell them to be quiet, the lady was sleeping.

'You will be careful with her, won't you?' she said to the blonde girl, who smiled a calm reassurance. 'She's eighty-two, you know.'

Fourteen

'So are we going out to do Ex-muss shopping or not?
What did we decide last night? Call me back and
remind me, soon as you can!' Cherry's bright and
chirpy voice was on the answerphone when Melanie
came back from the house next door. It was still only
just past eight thirty: Cherry must have got up ridiculously early, Mel thought, if she was now ready to talk
about hitting the shops. This must be what this new
love for Helena had done to her, made her eager to
bounce into the world each day and savour all sentient
moments with joyful exuberance. It was quite unnerv-
ing: since Nathan's abrupt departure all those years
ago, Cherry had taken life at a cautious pace, been
wary of enthusiasm. Such passions as she had – and
the collecting and storing of dead wildlife came to
mind – she kept safely to herself. Melanie decided
to wait a while before calling her back – the last thing
she felt like talking about was present-buying and
where to go for a long, chatty lunch.

Mel had brought Mrs Jenkins's orange poodle back to
the house with her, convinced that taking care of the
dog was the inadequate best she could do just now for

229

her neighbour. She could only hope that he wouldn't fall foul of Jeremy Paxman's claws. She also felt a bit guilty – whoever had inflicted this robbery and beating on poor Mrs Jenkins had managed it with flagrant ease under cover of the racket that was coming from next door. A house blaring with music, loud TV and people carelessly getting drunk must be on every burglar's wish-list. The front door had obviously given way with little resistance: Mrs Jenkins was of the generation that talked nostalgically of times when no-one needed to lock their homes. To her, having a small Yale lock represented security on a level that should keep out armies of vandals. It had probably never crossed her mind that one swift kick and the entire door frame would simply splinter. Melanie hoped she'd been knocked out swiftly and immediately, before she had worked out what was going on, and wouldn't have had time to feel deep terror.

She sat, cold and shocked, with her legs curled beneath her, in her favourite pink raggedy chair, hugging the smelly poodle. The dog panted and grinned and tolerated being held tight without protest. It made Mel feel sick and shaky to imagine how bad the attack could have been, and she tried hard, but failed, not to imagine poor Mrs Jenkins facing a thug, perhaps more than one, wielding a weapon, pushing her about, threatening her, not caring if she lived or died. She'd have been confused, unable at first to think the worst, perhaps asking if they'd come to read the meter. She would have told them she was eight-two – just as an innocent point of information, not as a plea for mercy. Mel couldn't recall her ever expressing any fear of living alone. She didn't even have a safety chain on the door. If someone knocked, she opened the door expecting to find a visitor who was to be welcomed; she would consider it bad manners to do anything else. A dread of isolation, of loneliness, had loomed more large than physical danger. If she'd read of attacks on frail pensioners and feared for herself, she had certainly never said so. Mel prayed that the damage wasn't going to be deep and permanent, but knew that, even if Mrs Jenkins recovered fully in the physical sense, she would never again feel safe on her own premises, not when she realized that her generous trust in her fellow humans had been so let down. The burglars had stolen a lot more than knick-knacks and picture frames.

Brenda, Hal and their children were due back before lunch. All Melanie could do was to stay home and be ready to tell them what had happened. They would have to take it from there – Brian in Somerset needed to know, too, and between them he and Brenda would have to work out what to do in terms of caring for their mother. That was if there *was* anything to do – nobody even knew yet if Mrs Jenkins was going to survive this.

The doorbell ringing made Melanie jump. She'd been sitting silent and rigid for so long, simply staring out at the strange new plants beyond her French doors, that she had almost drifted to sleep again. The poodle jumped off her lap and hurled itself, yapping and leaping, at the front door. As she opened it, Mel wondered if she should invest in chains, deadbolts and alarms.

'I know it's early but . . . good heavens, Melanie, what on earth are you wearing? You're not going out like that, surely?' Her mother bustled past her into the kitchen and switched on the kettle. Mel followed dumbly, pushing her chilled hands up inside her fleecy sleeves for warmth.

'This is what happens when you refuse to live with anybody,' Gwen went on, crashing cupboard doors around in search of tea bags. 'You'll end up going out in any old thing, all hours of the day and night. You look like a tramp, quite frankly, Melanie – I'm your mother, it's my duty to tell you straight out. Don't you possess a mirror?'

'I haven't got dressed yet,' Mel said, feeling too dejected to explain further.

'You mean you sleep in old jeans, sheepskin boots and a filthy sweatshirt? And your hair . . .' Gwen looked out of the window and sniffed. 'I see you've been getting on with the garden, such as it is. They'll all die you know, plants like that aren't for cold countries like this.'

It was almost comforting to be harried. It reminded Melanie that whatever else was tearing the world to pieces, some things would never change.

'Anyway, I've come to talk about Rosa and what she'd like for Christmas. I don't know what teenage girls like . . .'

'Teenage boys, mostly . . .' Mel murmured.

'What? Look, please don't be flippant, Melanie, I haven't got time for it. She's the last one I need to buy for – I've more or less got Christmas out of the way. I'm too old to fight my way round shopping centres in December so I want it all done and dusted by the weekend.'

Gwen picked up the boiling kettle and poured water into a pair of mugs. 'No proper teapot . . .' she murmured, as she always did. Mel flopped into one of the wicker chairs as her mother fussed around. It seemed easier to let her get on with it rather than to battle for occupation of her own kitchen.

'Don't you have anyone doing your cleaning at the moment?' Gwen said eventually, as she placed a mug of weak milky tea in front of Melanie. 'This place looks like a bomb's hit it.' She surveyed the array of dirty wine glasses by the sink, left from the night before, Patty's abandoned chocolate cake that looked as if someone had dug impatient, clumsy fingers into its middle, and the sink full of plates. She sniffed the air, canny as a gundog. 'And it smells in here. Cigarettes.'

Melanie almost laughed; it was like being a teenager, caught having a sly cigarette out of the bedroom window.

'I had a few people in last night, that's all. We were celebrating the new garden.'

'Drinking. That's what people mean when they say celebrating. Drinking.' Gwen put a lifetime's worth of disapproval into the word. For her, drink was something people 'took to', something that drove them to ruin and disgrace. Howard had been heading that way, she was sure. It was why they were going to spend a month in Spain - to break the habit. He wouldn't like Sangria or the robust Spanish wines, and by the time she got him home again he'd have lost the taste for that tawdry pub. It wasn't the only habit that she intended to be broken, either, for where was he going to get his hands on filthy magazines in a good Catholic country where girls in photographs kept their clothes on and their legs together?

She glared at the bin bag which waited by the back door to be taken down to the dustbin. It bulged with obvious bottle shapes. A beer can had pierced a hole and poked out, pointing a broken ring pull at her.

'Someone'll cut themselves, taking that out,' she said, indicating the sharp metal. 'You could sever a vein.'

'I know, I know.' Melanie reached across and shoved the can further into the depths of the bag.

'And nobody would know. You could be lying here all alone, bleeding to death. Now if you and Roger . . .'

Mel put her hands over her ears. Huge tears pushed their way out of her eyes and rolled down her cheeks. They felt as big as marbles. She was aware of them individually as they fell, and a weirdly disconnected part of her brain marvelled at how each one formed in her eyes, welled up to overflowing and gradually tipped itself out over the edge, like a reluctant but determined suicide going over a high balcony.

'Gracious, Melanie, what on earth's the matter? Was it something I said?' Gwen sat down next to Mel and put her hand on hers, rather gingerly.

Melanie looked down at the skin on her mother's hand. It was thin, dry, speckled. If you touched it, it would crackle. The folds and lines were rather beautiful, she thought in an odd, detached way, like a dried-out river valley pictured from space.

'It'll be hormones.' Gwen nodded wisely at her. 'You're not getting any younger, are you?'

'It's not hormones. I'm fine,' Mel protested.

'It's the time of year then,' Gwen decreed, risking some gentle patting. 'People on their own do feel it worst around Christmas.'

Melanie smiled at her mother. There was no point arguing this particular toss, Gwen would never believe her.

'Mrs Jenkins has been burgled,' she told her, as she reached across for kitchen towel to blow her nose on.

Was it less than ten hours before that she'd used this paper roll to staunch Max's blood? Where was he? He'd said he'd be back, that there were still things to finish, like wrapping fleece around the plants to protect them from frost. She really wished he was with her now, even if he was down at the far end of the garden doing something loud and messy involving cement and a hammer.

'And whoever did it,' she went on, 'has hit her and knocked her out. She's been taken to the hospital.'

'Oh, so that's why you've got her dog – I thought you'd taken up walking in the park. That poor woman, she'll never feel safe in her own home again.'

Mel wiped the tears away. They seemed to have stopped as suddenly as they'd started, as if there'd been just that amount of spare salt water, no more.

'Look, why don't you come home with me?' Gwen suggested at last. 'Daddy would love to see you and we could have a nice fish pie for lunch. I've got one in the freezer. It only needs mike-ing.' She looked at Melanie intently. 'You know, you could come and stay properly if you like, back in your old room. It's not as if . . . Well, till Rosa gets back from university. You don't want to be on your own.'

Melanie got up and started clattering with the dishes in the sink, shoving them carelessly and fast into the dishwasher. She was touched by the invitation, but didn't want her mother to see how very much she couldn't bear the thought of returning to her childhood home, even for one night, to sleep as someone's child again in her old bedroom. She also caught sight of her mother looking nervous, taking sharp glances at the freezer. Mel could almost read her mind, could sense her wondering whether having her daughter to stay would involve moving the frozen fish pies aside to make room for a bag of dead squirrels.

'It's a very kind thought,' she said eventually. 'But I've got to stay here and talk to Brenda – Mrs Jenkins's daughter – tell her what's happened. She'll be back soon. It'll be a shock for her but she'll want to know the details from me, not from some police officer who doesn't really know. And then there's the dog, and the cat . . .'

Gwen stood up quickly and tucked her scarf round her neck. 'All right, Mel, I expect that's the best plan really, but remember, if you ever want . . .'

'Thanks, Mum, I will. And I'll let you know what happens with Mrs Jenkins.'

'Oh yes, do, I like her. We had a very nice lunch together that day you went out. She might enjoy a visit at the hospital.' The thought seemed to cheer Gwen quite considerably. Mel was glad – her mother was now distracted from her daughter's stubborn solitariness and was mentally running through the choices: whether to take grapes or tangerines, *The Lady* or *People's Friend* on her visit to the hospital.

'And Melanie.' Gwen, by the open front door, turned and spoke almost in a whisper to Mel, as if half the street was all ears. 'Go and do something about yourself. Have a bath, wear something pretty, put some lipstick on. It makes all the difference.'

'I will, Mum, I promise. Thanks.'

Brenda and Hal and their pair of teenagers squeezed their ample bodies out of the taxi and argued loudly on the pavement over who should carry which bags into the house. Lee-Ann's mouth was turned down at the corners in a sulk that almost prompted Melanie to warn her that her face would stay like that if the wind changed. That was, it crossed her mind with renewed depression, exactly the kind of thing her mother had said to her when she was little. Gwen had never said it to Vanessa, not that she could recall, because Vanessa's face had been permanently set in a smile. 'Born to please, that one,' her mother had said, 'born to please.' The phrase, almost sung, would be followed up with something along the lines of 'Now why can't you be more like that, Melanie?'

She hadn't caught Vanessa, behind her back, putting her tongue out at Melanie, digging her nails into her leg, making her squeal as they sat beside each other at the table. Gwen hadn't caught her with a pair of nail scissors, either, cutting small sly holes in Melanie's dolls' dresses, holes small enough to be missed on first looking, so that by the time Mel discovered them Vanessa would be nowhere near either dresses or scissors and suspicion would fall on Melanie herself.

'You were just jealous of her,' Roger had said when she'd described a classic example of sibling rivalry.

'I probably was,' Mel agreed. 'The first child is an only child for a while. It's hard to give up that complete attention you get. Especially when you're only fifteen months old.'

When her time came to have children, Melanie had dreaded a repeat of her own childhood battles and been careful not to produce two of them too close together. The four-year gap had seemed ideal. But then Daniel hadn't survived, and a lot of things were not ideal after that.

Melanie drove Brenda and Lee-Ann to the hospital. Hal offered to go too, but in a manner that suggested he would, if pushed, come up with a lot of excuses not to be there. Mel could read in his reluctant expression that, though he was eager not to cause pain, he knew for sure that hospital beds were female terrain, that he would be in the way there, that this was Brenda's mother, not his, and that he had his own masculine way of being useful. 'I'll stay here, fix the door and put up a chain. Barty can walk the dog,' he volunteered.

In the car, Brenda clutched a box of tissues and her daughter's hand. 'Hal hates hospitals,' she said. 'They make him feel queasy.'

'I don't think anyone's that keen on them,' Melanie reassured her.

'I hate them too. Why'd I have to come?' Lee-Ann whined.

'She'll wanna see you,' Brenda said bluntly.

'Won't she wanna see Barty too?'

'He can come tomorrow. Too many people might make her tired,' Brenda told her, taking a shaky deep breath and becoming tearful. 'If she's still . . . still with us. Poor Mom! We should never have gone and left her.'

It wasn't the moment, Mel thought as she pulled into the hospital car park, to point out that as they'd left her on her own for the last fifteen years or so, they could hardly have foreseen that another week would make such a difference. She remembered, as she went with them along the hospital's corridor, the mental picture she'd had of Mrs Jenkins sipping coffee at a sunny table outside the Café de Flore. Would she really have liked Paris? Or would she have worried about the dog, worried that her arthritis would play up, hated the food, mistrusted the language?

'She's in *here*?' Brenda stopped at the door of the long ward and looked at the double line of beds. She seemed to be horror-struck, gazing around as if she was taking in a scene from a years-old film. The hospital, although impressively rebuilt and ultra-modern at the front, kept a couple of Victorian wings with traditional long wards far away at the back. It was as if they were being kept specially, just till the present generation of old people died out, so that they wouldn't be flummoxed by small mixed wards and high-tech surroundings. Ancient ladies in pastel dressing gowns shuffled around, some laboriously wheeling drips or catheter equipment alongside them. Visitors huddled beside beds administering home-cooked food, spooning it into pale, frail, paper-thin relatives. There was a sad smell of mild decay, of leaked urine overlaid with the aroma of recent lunch.

'Why doesn't she have her own room?' Lee-Ann asked, bewildered by the antiquated scene.

Melanie smiled. In contrast to Lee-Ann, she found the place reassuring. She would have to explain to the girl that sharing a huge, old-fashioned, shabby ward with twenty-three strangers meant that you were probably going to be all right. In this country the occupation of a precious single room on the National Health Service tended to mean only one thing: it was the ante-room to death.

It was a bit late in the day for serious Christmas shopping by the time Melanie went off to meet Cherry. Twilight was already starting to gather as she emerged from the tube at Knightsbridge. She wouldn't get much of it done, but it didn't matter – it was just important somehow to launch herself into central London's careless, brightly lit bustle and join in the annual crazed buying fest. Having spent so long protesting to all and

239

sundry that she relished being on her own, she could hardly wait to lose herself in a crowd and chat with a good friend.

Cherry was waiting outside the Sloane Street entrance to Harvey Nichols. The new radiance that had lit her face the night before, when she'd told Mel and Sarah about Helena, was still there. Even her chestnut hair seemed to shine more richly. Something new in her had been brought to life. It was about time, Melanie thought; Cherry had kept her personal capacity for love locked up and dormant for far too many years. Somehow it didn't surprise her that Cherry had fallen for a woman. After Nathan, she'd seeded and culti-vated a distrust of male-female relationships that was rooted so deep it would take another lifetime to shift it.

'So, how's your poor neighbour? Any news since this morning?' Cherry asked, as they made their way into the cosmetics department. The counters were at least six deep in eager purchasers. Had this been such a good idea, Melanie wondered, feeling the beginnings of claustrophobia, wouldn't it have been more sensible to buy everything she needed over the Internet?

'She's confused, sore and wanting to go home,' Mel yelled to Cherry, over the battle between a woman demanding a Susheimo foundation in Dizzy Peach and an assistant assuring her there was no such shade.

'Will she be allowed to go home?' Cherry shouted back, as she ran her finger over an eye-shadow tester. It was a deep pinky-gold, Mel noticed: things *had* changed for Cherry – usually she never veered from a safe smoky grey.

'I don't know, to be honest. She's turned into one of those parcel people, you know, when the "system" takes over and she has to be assessed? Brenda won't be around to take care of her for more than a few more days, though I think she's trying to change their flight so she can help sort things out. You hear about old ladies walled up in hospital wards for weeks and weeks, waiting to be placed somewhere by the powers that be. I hope she comes back home.'

Mel would miss the old lady a lot if she didn't, it occurred to her. Mrs Jenkins had been around all the time she and Roger had lived in that house, all through Rosa's growing up, through the loss of Daniel. She'd babysat, cat-sat, kept an eye on the house when they'd been away for holidays. She had long been Southernbrook Road's senior resident. If she went, someone else would move up to that position – probably Gerald from the other side of Mel. It was depressing, somehow, to think that in her turn she too could be the lone Elder Inhabitant. Panicking at the idea, she told herself, as she tried out a deep purple lipstick on the back of her hand, that she could move on and away, but then remembered all the lovely new garden. How would she face Max and tell him she was off to start again, casual and heedless, say in a riverside flat with only a titchy plantless balcony? Perhaps he wouldn't care, she thought, as she trailed after Cherry to the outside door. After all, she was only a client, nothing special.

'What are you going to tell your folks?' Rota-Girl Kate was sitting on Rosa's floor. Rosa was stretched out on the bed, stroking her expanded stomach with great fondness. She knew that from where Kate sat the bump would look exaggerated, like when you were lying on the grass at the bottom of a hill and the land seemed to be rising above you forever.

241

'And why haven't you told them yet?' Kate went on. 'Why are you having it? Don't you believe in abortion?'

'Leave off her, Kate. What kind of a question is that?' Desi snapped at her.

'No, it's OK, Desi, they're all fair questions.' Rosa thought for a moment. 'I think I want to have this baby more than I want to do anything else right now,' she said, stretching her arms above her head and yawning.

'You mean you're having it because you can't be arsed not to?' Kate's face was screwed up with over-done incomprehension.

'That's not what I said,' Rosa told her. 'I'll be good at this. I can do it. Mum will be cool about it.' She hesitated a few seconds, then added, 'I think.'

'And what about your dad?' Kate persisted. 'Will he go spare?'

Rosa laughed softly. 'Dad? I don't think he's got any grounds for complaint, somehow, not with his track record.' She laughed again. 'In the space of just a few weeks he'll become a father and then a grandfather. I wonder what his little-girl wife will make of that.'

Tina Keen was all finished with her case. She wound up the paperwork in the office and Melanie, back at her keyboard that evening, allowed her to go out for a celebratory dinner with the chief constable. He was married, of course – Tina's men usually were – it was how it was for women past thirty. In his honour Tina was wearing the kind of underwear Sarah would heartily approve of – solving a case was a massively sexy achievement. Mel had often thought she should look things of this sort up on the Internet or in the library, find out for sure if there was some hormonal trigger associated with success at work that applied to women in the same way that it did, with a testosterone rush, for men. Whichever way it was, for the purposes of the book's ending, Tina was feeling warm and powerful, accommodating and seductive.

Over the sliced duck and sticky mango sauce the chief constable told Tina that he and his wife had 'different interests'. He ran his hand up Tina's silky leg and encountered suspenders, a proper lacy stocking-top and that soft warm strip of exposed flesh at the top of her thigh. She continued to eat her duck steadily while the chief constable kneaded his stubby nicotine-stained fingers into her leg. She really should, she thought as he prodded deep into her flesh, go on a diet.

Melanie stopped typing and looked down into the garden. She'd left plenty of lights on downstairs this time, even though she wasn't writing anything that would make her jumpy. She would talk to Max about getting lights fixed up outside, artily placed ones so that the shapes of the plants would show up like ghostly statues.

Concentrating on Tina once more, Mel let her finish the duck and help herself to extra potatoes – creamy dauphinois ones, for if Tina was to sign up with Shape Sorters she should be allowed a last generous binge. Then she let her take a long, cool look at the chief constable, weigh up the why and why not of the situation. He was sweating visibly now as his hand stroked and rubbed. If Tina knew Perfect Patty's husband Dave, she would be strongly reminded of him.

'Excuse me, just for a moment,' Tina murmured to the chief constable. Ever polite to ladies, he half-stood, clutching his napkin to the giveaway bulge in his trousers as she took herself and her handbag to the loo. She looked at herself in the mirror. Too much make-up, too accommodating, too generous in the choice of underwear, too little discernment in her choice of date. Tina's reflection reminded her of the murder victims she'd just had to deal with. She was now about to have sex with a man she didn't much fancy, just as they all had – the difference being that she wasn't going to get paid. Or murdered. She'd be better off on her own, she thought, as she retouched her lipstick. Melanie provided her with a handy fire exit and allowed her out of the restaurant by a side door. A black cab was conveniently passing the end of the road. It stopped for Tina as she raised her hand, and Melanie sent her home to her flat, by herself.

Melanie raided the fridge and found some bacon, eggs and cold roast potatoes. There was also a bottle of cheap fizz that was perfectly chilled and would do well enough for now to celebrate the completion of *Dying For It.* The real celebration would come later, when her agent Dennis had read it and raved about it and the publishers gave it the thumbs up. She fried up the bacon and potatoes together till both were too crisp for most civilized people's tastes, and then cracked an egg over the top. Just because Tina Keen was about to start a diet, that didn't mean that her creator had to join in as well. The feast was piled onto a plate and Melanie took it through to the sitting room, along with the bottle and a glass. She settled herself comfortably on the sofa, shoved aside newspapers and magazines from the low table in front of her and put the bottle there at the ready. She dug the TV's remote control from behind a cushion and flipped through the channels. *Who Wants to Be a Millionaire?* was just about to finish. Melanie turned up the volume and then sat with the remote control still in her out-stretched hand and watched in amazement as, without needing her after all, without her being his Friend to Phone, Max shook hands with Chris Tarrant and left the programme's studio with a cheque for £64,000.

Fifteen

There was a peculiar noise. A strange beeping woke
Melanie. Surfacing from deep sleep into the early
morning greyness, she at first half-dreamed there was
a sad, trapped bird somewhere in the room, one that
had spent the night quietly seeking an escape route
but with daybreak had been forced to resort to cheep-
ing for help. Then she sat up fast, her thoughts turning
to disaster, to fire and smoke and being trapped alone
at the top of a blazing stairwell. But there was no smell
of smoke and she quickly realized that it was the
phone that was alerting her to its presence. She picked
it up as a computer-generated voice ordered her quite
crossly to 'Hang Up Now'. She tried hard to remember
the last call she'd made. Surely she hadn't been out of
contact since returning Cherry's call the morning
before? Why had the silly gadget not piped up to tell
her off before now? She smiled to herself as she went
down the stairs to make a cup of tea – there must have
been a highest-level phone company meeting at some
time about that. Directors, soberly dressed in proper
suits, must have congregated round a boardroom
table, solemnly discussing how long a phone could

reasonably be expected to be off the hook before a householder should be jolted into reconnecting. The women would opt for a longer time than the men, she decided, as she stacked last night's abandoned plates and cutlery in the dishwasher. They would be able to imagine plenty of situations where someone might want to leave the phone off the hook. She thought the men would be more reluctant – some might go for a ten-minute maximum, not because of a need to be contacted, but through a general shakiness about having something electronic in the house that was less than fully functioning.

Mel yawned and stretched, catching sight of her tousled bed-hair in the mirror on the dresser. Even though her new edgy hairstyle was meant to look as if she'd been dragged through a bush, this amount of matting and tangling would only look sexy on someone under twenty. Perhaps her mother had a point. How seductive was it to pad around the house in the early morning in a pair of ancient (but free) Virgin Atlantic in-flight oversized grey pyjamas? But then, unless she invited Neil to share her nights, who was there to be seductive for?

When she turned round again, Max was looking in at her through the back-door window and she could feel all her nerves leap at once. 'God, Max, you made me jump!' she said as she unlocked and opened the door.

'I could see that,' he said with a grin, coming into the kitchen and kicking off his muddy wellies. 'I thought you were going to hit the ceiling! Sorry. You look nice,' he commented, grinning at her in what she took to be mock admiration.

'Sure I do,' she replied, thinking she could do without sardonic humour at such an early hour. He reached across and switched the kettle on again, then helped himself to a mug from the cupboard and a tea bag from the jar. 'You do, actually, but you're so sodding defensive I won't bother saying it again. It's bloody cold out there. One of those days when I'm sure I'm in the wrong job. I nearly stayed at home to do the VAT and I don't often consider that to be an attractive option.'

'I didn't think I'd see you again,' she said as she pushed a couple of slices of bread into the toaster, 'not after your big win.' She tried hard, but could feel herself failing, to keep out of her voice a note of slight acidity. It was a thing that didn't matter, really it didn't, even though he'd asked her, even though she'd allowed herself to feel a bit flattered, almost honoured. If he'd decided he had more reliable, more trustworthy, probably in truth more downright knowledgeable Friends to Phone than she was, well, that was his choice. It had obviously paid off. Being told now that she 'looked nice' felt a bit like being a dog thrown a very tiny bone.

'It was a big enough win, and a hugely welcome one, but hardly enough to retire on! If I'd only known for sure, and I should have done, that chloroplasts were not present in animal cells . . .' he laughed. 'Still, it's enough to take time out for a bit of travelling. I quite fancy a gap year. I don't see why kids straight out of school should have all the fun.'

'Are you leaving right now or will you find a minute or two to wrap up my plants?' Ridiculously, Mel felt close to tears. She occupied herself quickly, taking the butter and marmalade from the fridge, clattering about with cutlery.

'Of course I'm not leaving right now. I'm here,

aren't I? Reporting for work? I just wondered . . .'

'Yes?'

'Why were you gossiping on the phone yesterday morning? I really needed you and I couldn't get through. In the end I had to ask my sister which writer Elizabeth Jane Howard used to be married to.'

'Kingsley Amis,' Mel answered promptly.

'I knew you'd know. She wasn't sure if it was him or William Golding. It cost me a fifty-fifty lifeline. If you'd been available instead of yacking all day I might be looking at a cheque for a million.'

Melanie laughed. He didn't really sound as if he minded too much. So he *had* tried to contact her. She felt a bit pathetic that such a small thing sent her spirits soaring. Perhaps her mother was halfway right, hormones might be involved. 'The phone got left off the hook. It was an accident, I was a bit distracted by events, I'll tell you about it. Though I was rather surprised to see you on the programme, I only caught the part where you were going off with your cheque. You never said the day before that you'd be on.'

'I didn't know! It was recorded that morning, all very, very last-minute. They keep a couple of spare contestants ready in the studio in case someone keels over with nerves. But during a break the night before, four of them went and pigged out on dodgy chicken burgers from a van outside the studio and got instantly ill. I was only called in because I lived near. And then, well we had to put four Welsh towns in alphabetical order. Abergavenny, Aberystwyth, Abersoch and one I can't remember and I did it fastest.'

'That was clever of you. I'd just rush it and get it wrong.'

'It's from looking in plant directories – I'm always searching the index for stuff.'

'I thought you'd changed your mind – that you'd decided you didn't need me.' She hadn't at all intended to say it. The words had just let themselves out without any help.

'And you minded?' Max looked mildly incredulous.

She shrugged. 'Yeah, well, just a bit. Not a lot, you know.'

'Yeah, I know. Go and get dressed, Mel, you can help me wrap these plants.'

Mel was in the shower when Neil phoned. He left a message on the machine saying he'd be round that evening to take her out for supper, and that he wasn't going to leave her a number and give her a chance to think up an excuse not to see him. Bloody control freak, she thought, cutting off her options. Perhaps she could just go out, or hide in bed with the lights off. On second thoughts, going out would be good for her and possibly good fun too.

'I don't know why he bothers,' she told Sarah on the phone, 'I haven't exactly been over-encouraging.'

'Well, you did have sex with him the first time you set eyes on him after more than twenty years,' Sarah reminded her, rather unnecessarily in Mel's opinion. 'Perhaps he thinks that as you're so impulsive, your impulses in the old sex department might just kick in again at any moment.'

'I don't think they will. Definitely not here on home territory anyway – I'm keeping my bed as a personal man-free sanctuary. Anyway, why I phoned is, do you have a number where I can reach him? You must have had one for that time you invited him to the dinner at your place.'

'Sorry sweetie, would love to be of use but it was on a tatty scrap of paper and I've lost it.'

Melanie couldn't help picturing Sarah with her long skinny fingers crossed. She could almost see the bronze-varnished nails flashing as they moved swiftly to placate the gods against the lie. She felt inclined to drive round to Sarah's immaculate, brilliantly organized house, open her desk drawer and look under 'N' in her address book. Sarah didn't go in for 'tatty scraps of paper'. Neil would certainly be listed there, address and phone number neatly noted down by Sarah's Mont Blanc fountain pen and luscious purple ink. Mel couldn't be cross with her, though. Sarah liked everything properly arranged. She was simply doing her best to tidy Melanie away into convenient coupledom. It was too late now to insist to Sarah that she didn't want to tell Neil that she wouldn't go that night – she only wanted to know what time they were going and where to. Clothes-wise, it would make a difference. She didn't want to wear jeans and a snug old sweater to the Ivy or her little black suede dress to Pizza Express.

Mrs Jenkins's son Brian was even bigger and sturdier than his sister Brenda. He squeezed through the gate in the fence into Melanie's back garden as she and Max draped thin layers of protective fleece carefully around the *Washingtonia* and secured it with string. Brian was wearing a huge plaid woodcutter's jacket that Mel guessed had been sent by his sister from Canada, probably at a time when he'd been a good bit thinner. He moved slowly across the garden, treading warily and staring with suspicion at the palms. The poodle, expecting to follow him as he used to with Mrs Jenkins, yapped furiously from the other side of the closed gate.

'I saw you from the upstairs window,' he told Mel. 'I didn't think you'd hear me if I rang your front door-bell.'

'That's OK,' Mel said, wiping her earthy hands on her scarf. 'How is your mother?'

Brian shoved his hands deep in his pockets. He gazed at the ground and scuffed at the pebbles with the toe of his shoe, kicking them up into a pile and expos-ing the layer of black fabric beneath. Mel glanced quickly at Max, who was looking at Brian with an expression of furious outrage, like an artist who finds someone in their studio casually picking chunks of oil paint off a precious canvas.

'She's not very well,' Brian said eventually. 'She's had a big shock to the system and she's going to need full time care.' He looked terrified by the prospect, as well he might, Mel thought: he'd be her only relative in this country when Brenda escaped back to Canada.

'So we thought – we might do a bit to the house.' He gestured with his shoulder towards his mother's home. 'Tart it up and sell it. It'll pay for her keep in a home down near me.'

'A home?' Mel said, astonished. 'Like a full-time residential place? Is she really as bad as that?'

'Well, she can't look after herself, that's obvious – her eyesight's rubbish and the knock on her head, well, they think it might have triggered a minor stroke. We can have her for a little while, just till she's properly herself again, like, but . . . well, there's the wife.' He was starting to sound angry now, defensive, as if Mel

253

had put up a series of arguments against what he'd decided. 'I've got to think of the wife. She's not well herself.'

'Oh really? I'm sorry about that,' Mel said.

'It's her nerves.' Oh, is it? Mel thought, feeling anger rising which she tried hard to quell – after all, who was she to say who should or shouldn't share their home with Mrs Jenkins? Unless she herself was prepared to take her on, it didn't exactly do to criticize others.

'And I'm working, it would all fall on her. Mum'll be all right. We've found somewhere she'll like.'

'Have you?' Max chipped in. 'My, that was quick.'

'Yes, well. We've kept an eye on things. Doesn't do to be unprepared, does it?'

'Oh no,' Max agreed, turning back to securing the last of the *Washingtonia*'s bonds. 'It doesn't do at all.'

'We'll take the dog on though, that's something.'

'Mmm. Yes, it almost is,' Max muttered.

'If she stayed here in her own home – I could keep an eye on her,' Mel suggested.

'But you already have,' Brian pointed out. 'You've been a good neighbour, she said so. Brenda said so. But this *still* happened. And next time she might fall down the stairs or something. And what if you're away? On holiday or something?'

'She could have one of those alarms, the ones that go round your neck, you know, just in case.'

Brian laughed. 'She wouldn't use it. She'd think she was being a nuisance.'

He was right, Mel knew he was. Mrs Jenkins wouldn't come back to her home. She'd leave the hospital in Brian's car and go and live in a Somerset town where she knew nobody. She and Mel would send Christmas cards to each other. Mel would write now and then and let her know what was going on, tell her when Roger's new baby was born, when Rosa graduated. Gradually, as time passed, little of it would make sense to her former neighbour, but she'd be thrilled to receive the letters. Mel knew how excited she always was about the post. An assistant at the home would read them to her – she might even find her frequently-mislaid reading glasses for her so she could, at last, do it herself. She would tell people she was eighty-two, and with luck might remember when she got to eighty-three. Then one day Mel would have a short note from Brian saying that Mrs Jenkins had died. He'd say 'passed away'. The funeral would already have taken place, and none of her former friends and neighbours would have been there to send her on her way over the horizon to the next life.

Brian went back through the fence gate to start packing away his mother's possessions. Mel hoped he and Brenda wouldn't simply throw most of them away carelessly, but, on present form, she wouldn't be surprised to see a skip outside before the week-end.

Mel was on her way out to get her manuscript photo-copied in the town when Ben called round. 'Oh, you going out?' he said, catching her at the door already wearing a coat, scarf and gloves.

'Sure am, Ben, do you want to use the computer?'

He shuffled his feet about on the path. 'Well, if you don't mind . . .' he said. 'I won't touch anything.'

'It never occurred to me that you would,' she told

him. 'Come in, help yourself to tea or coffee and biscuits. I'll be about an hour.'

What on earth did he imagine that she'd think he'd want to 'touch', she wondered, as she drove into the town and parked at Waitrose. Perhaps it was that teen-boy thing of having so much sex on the brain (and nowhere else) that he imagined she'd think he'd be rifling through her knicker drawer as soon as she was safely round the corner. Well, Patty had been clear enough about that – she didn't need to be convinced that Ben would have no interest in her and her underwear at all.

Christmas was in full swing in the town. Dickins and Jones's windows were full of fairy lights and outfits of the glitter-and-velvet combination that turned up every year for what magazines called the party season. It was strange, Mel thought as she walked past, how the same clothes, the moment Twelfth Night was past, looked overdone and faintly ridiculous. It was like leaving the decorations up for too long. Possibly it was even unlucky to go out in a velvet and diamanté frock after 6th January, especially if the dress was scarlet and strappy and teamed with a sequinned pashmina, as was the one she'd stopped to look at.

'Looking for something to wear tonight?' Sarah appeared next to Mel.

'Oh hi, Sarah. Tonight? No! I was just wondering who on earth buys these things. And where do they wear them?'

'They are corporate wives who go to Botox parties and they wear them to the firm's annual Christmas dinner dance. The pashmina isn't to keep warm, it's to obscure flabby arms.'

Mel laughed and continued, 'But after a few drinks,

when it gets a bit hot, the pashmina falls to the floor and . . .'

'And Mrs Corporate Wife takes to the dance floor to shake it all about to "Dancing Queen".'

'Does she know all the words?'

'She does and she sings them. I know. My name is Sarah and I am that Corporate Wife.' Sarah pulled a face of mock tragedy.

'Get lost, you don't have the arms for it.'

'That's true.' She took a last look at the dress as they moved on. 'And I'd have it in black, not red. One is not Santa Claus. Let's treat ourselves, Mel, seeing as it's only a few short hectic weeks till Christmas, let's go in All Bar One and have a spritzer.'

The place was busy, loud with post-lunch lingerers and shoppers surrounded by bags, who, having achieved a serious amount of purchases, were recharging themselves for another few hours battling in the stores.

'Two spritzers please!' Melanie yelled over the racket to the barman.

'I'll bring them, find a seat!' he shouted back.

'OK, we'll be just over . . .' Melanie said as she turned to look for a table. 'Well, just look who's here,' she said to Sarah, spotting Neil at a table with a woman a good few years younger than themselves. 'Let's go over here by the window, I don't much want to see him right now so . . .'

She shouldn't have mentioned him – in this crowd Sarah might not have noticed. But it was too late. 'Oh yes, so he is! And there are spare seats at his table.' Sarah either wasn't listening or didn't hear and marched across the bar, picking her way between bags and people.

'We'll be over there at that corner table,' Mel told the barman, racing after Sarah, hoping to catch up with her before she said anything mad, ambiguous or downright incriminating.

'Hello Neil, mind if we join you?' Sarah was saying as she arrived.

'Oh!' Neil looked up, instantly flustered. 'Er, hello Sarah, Mel, are you well?' he asked.

Mel slid into the seat opposite Neil's companion, who was looking bemused. She was an attractive woman, mid-thirties Mel would guess, with chin-length blonde hair so flat and straight it looked as if someone had carefully ironed it. She wore a black suit that Sarah was blatantly pricing up and clearly guessing between Whistles and Joseph.

'And are you friends of Neil from work?' the woman asked.

'Oh no!' Sarah began. 'We know him from . . .'

'Actually, Charlotte,' he cut in, rather rudely, Mel thought, 'these are two of the students I used to teach a long, long time ago. We ran into each other at a reunion not long ago.'

'You used to *teach* them? So how old are you?' Charlotte's question was addressed not to Neil but to Sarah, who blinked hard and looked stumped for an answer.

'It was his first job.' Sarah wasn't about to part with a number, not unless someone pulled out all her perfectly manicured nails first. 'He was newly qualified, just a babe in arms. Putty in our hands,' Sarah told her with a suggestive smirk.

'Two spritzers?' the barman arrived. Mel felt uncomfortable and started gulping her drink. She'd quite like to leave, escape to some fresh air.

258

'Putty!' Charlotte pouted her slicked lips at Neil. 'I wouldn't have thought that was the right word for you, darling.'

Sarah narrowed her eyes. 'Neil, you haven't properly introduced us to your friend. I'm Sarah,' she said, not giving him a chance to make up for his bad manners, 'and this is Melanie . . . and you are . . .'

'Oh, I'm Charlotte. Didn't he mention me at your "reunion"? I'm his wife.'

Oh right, thought Mel, of course you are. Silly me – no wonder he didn't leave a phone number.

'Time to go, sweetie,' Charlotte purred to Neil. 'Pick up the kids . . .'

'Ah. So I take it that dinner tonight is now off?' Melanie said calmly to Neil.

It was hard to make a dignified exit, encumbered by a coat and by having to squeeze through the crowd, but as she took a deep breath on the pavement she didn't regret what she'd said.

'Ooh, that was brave!' Sarah squealed as she caught up with Mel outside Matches.

'No it wasn't. It was spiteful and childish,' Mel told her. 'But I don't in the slightest bit care.'

Well, the day couldn't get much worse, Mel thought as she drove home. At least *Dying For It* was now safely in the post to Dennis. There was nothing more she could do with Tina Keen for the moment, except hope she and her latest case would get a completely fabulous reception from the people who mattered.

There were lights on in her house as she drove up. It meant Max was still there, which was good, though she couldn't imagine what he was still finding to do. Perhaps he'd had a tricky time planting the bamboos and spent many an hour arranging and re-arranging them. Or maybe his newly fixed wall had fallen down. Whatever it was, she would be very happy to see him.

The sound of raised, angry voices could be heard as she approached the front door. One was a woman, high-pitched and shrieky. A slow, male tone seemed to be doing its best to be calming. Don't tell me, Melanie thought as she pushed the key into the door, that Max too has a wife and she's shown up to see what was keeping him on a job that should have only taken a fortnight at the most . . .

But it was Patty at the bottom of the stairs, yelling at her son, who was standing on the landing above her. Max was beside Patty and was clearly preventing her from racing up and clouting someone. Ben was shield-ing Lee-Ann from next door – not very effectively, given that she was twice his width and looking beauti-fully pink and round-limbed in only her purple bra and thong.

'And when I've told that little tart's mother what was going on . . . !' Patty was yelling, then, as Melanie appeared behind her, she turned her attention to her. 'And *you*! I blame you! Letting young boys come in here and use your place like a knocking shop! Do you know how old he is?'

Melanie did. What she didn't know was what had been going on while she'd been in Richmond, though she was catching on fast.

'Why don't we go into the kitchen . . .' Mel took Patty's arm and tried to shift her away from the hall-way.

'And what? Have a nice cup of tea?' Patty was almost spitting with rage. Behind her back, Max shrugged at

Mel and mouthed, 'Sorry!' though Mel didn't know yet what for.

'Yes. A nice cup of tea. I want one even if you don't; so come on.' Then to Max she whispered, 'Get those two sorted out,' pointing up the stairs. He nodded.

She pushed Patty into the kitchen and almost hurled her into a chair. 'Now, what's happened?'

'What's happened? It's obvious what's happened! I came round here looking for Ben. He *said* he had some work to do, he *said* he'd got some French to finish . . .' She stopped and muttered, 'Yeah, I bet he was laughing at me as he said that. Very funny. Very droll!'

'So you found him . . .'

'Your gardener friend let me in. And brazen as you like he says, "Oh yes, Ben's here, he's upstairs with that girl from next door!"'

Melanie tried hard not to laugh. Poor Patty, discovering her adored baby boy in the fleshy clutches of Lee-Ann. She heard scuffling in the hallway, the front door opened and some muffled goodbyes were said. Max and Ben came into the kitchen. Ben looked sheepish, pink in the face, and had clearly dressed in a tearing hurry.

'We'd better go home,' Patty said dejectedly. 'I need hardly say he won't be coming here to do his homework again. Like I said, I blame you . . .' She pointed at Mel.

''S not Mel's fault,' Ben protested, bravely, Mel thought. 'It's nothing to do with her. She didn't even *know*.'

'Allowing the premises to be used for . . .'

'That's when it's drugs,' Max said, opening the fridge and taking out a beer. 'Anyone else fancy a drink?' he asked. Patty ignored him. Mel nodded and he handed her a second can. 'You can hardly be prosecuted, or even slightly told off, if a pair of perfectly legally aged people have a spot of nookie in your house.' Max was also trying not to laugh. Ben snorted and started a deep, uncontrollable fit of chortling.

'Out of here, Ben. Now,' Patty said, standing up and poking her son hard in the shoulder. They left, Patty still furious, Ben still giggling.

'Well, that was fun. What happened?' Mel swigged the beer straight from the can and glanced into the fridge to see what there might be for supper, now that she wasn't to be wined and dined and wooed and pampered by adulterous Neil. It looked as if it was going to be a combination of cheese, pasta and mushrooms that were a bit past their best. Never mind.

'Dunno. Lee-Ann came in through the fence gate and met Ben. A bit later Patty arrived and as they weren't anywhere downstairs, I told her they must be upstairs. Perfectly logical. So up she goes, taking the stairs two at a time, and catches them at it.'

'Poor kids, I hope it doesn't have a permanent effect on their sex lives,' Mel commented.

'And then she came down again as fast as she went up. I was just making a cup of tea.' He looked at Mel, his face breaking into a grin. 'I did offer her one.'

'One?'

'Tea, you daft tart, tea.'

'Why did Patty come looking for him, do you think?' Mel wondered aloud. 'She could have just called his mobile.'

Max looked hard at her for a few moments. 'Because she wanted to catch him at it,' he said.

'With Lee-Ann? Poor kids.'

'No, not with Lee-Ann. You might have forgotten

what she was on about the other night when she was pissed, but it was still on her mind. To her you're one of the weird brigade – an attractive woman, happily existing by yourself. She thought she was going to catch her darling son at it with you.'

Sixteen

It was the last day of the university term. Roger had volunteered to go and fetch Rosa and some of her belongings home from Plymouth. Leonora was sulky about this and complained, 'That's one day less from your annual leave. What about me? I'll need you to take time off for *me* when the baby arrives.' 'Well, I'll do that, when the time comes,' he told her. 'Today I'm taking time off for my other child, OK?'

He wasn't going to change his mind, however much Leonora gave him the silent, pouting treatment. He missed Rosa – it was a long time since he'd played a real, active role in her life. Obviously part of that was because she was more or less a grown-up now – things were bound to be more distant. It occurred to him that he'd only really known her in the casual, relaxed day-to-day way, when he'd been part of the Roger-Melanie couple. When you live on the premises with someone, you can have periods when you share the space but take little notice of each other. Since he'd left, time together with Rosa meant time in enforced conversation, oddly synthetic. If they'd separated when she was a young child, he'd have been used to being with her by herself. Even if he'd only been a very part-time, alternate-weekends type of father, they'd have had lots of practice at being on their own together. They'd have evolved their own father-daughter code, there'd be just-the-two-of-them running jokes. Now, since he'd left, he seemed to have to work at how to be her father.

She hadn't come home once during this first term. He and Melanie had agreed that was a good sign – she must be having a terrific time. The ones to worry about were those who kept turning up back home, clutching bags of laundry and pretending they just fancied a proper meal. They weren't out of touch entirely; sometimes Rosa would send him a cheery e-mail at work. He was flattered that he was even on her list of friends for forwarding silly jokes. He'd send replies, though he didn't really have her generation's easy way with that form of communication. His messages always sounded slightly stilted, as if they should end with 'yours sincerely'. If he wrote something that was supposed to be funny he felt he had to add half a dozen exclamation marks, in case it might be taken the wrong way.

The journey home from Plymouth would be a good chance for a bit of new bonding. He hoped Rosa would be ready to leave – they could have lunch on the way back, do some proper, intense catching up, just the two of them. Then he'd hand her over to Melanie and go home to wonder why he still didn't know what she wanted for Christmas. He'd hope it was because they'd talked too much about other things, that it just hadn't had time to crop up.

Leonora had grown a lot bigger in the past couple of weeks. Her face had filled out so that her stark cheekbones had gone soft, and she spent every evening lying on the larger of the two sofas with her swollen feet propped up on the arm. She'd taken off her wedding ring and put it back in its little velvet bag in the drawer where she kept her best underwear, for her hands had swelled up and it was now too tight. On her finger where the ring should have been there was a faint pale line, contrasting with the remains of her honeymoon tan. 'It's just a bit of water retention,' she told him when he started mentioning blood pressure and pre-eclampsia. 'All this extra weight will come off again once this thing is out of me.'

It wasn't her weight Roger was worried about. If she'd read even one from the heap of guide-to-pregnancy books that lay unopened on the table beside the bed, she might have had a clue about what was happening to her body. She was due for another check-up on Christmas Eve so perhaps someone, at last, would get her to understand that there were hazards in being pregnant, even for a woman as young and fit and oblivious to complications as Leonora.

He set off for Plymouth before it was fully light, leaving Leonora still snuggled deep into the duvet. There were only six more weeks to go till the baby was born, and he could hardly begin to imagine how he was going to cope with the lack of proper sleep that was coming his way. It was just one of the many aspects of baby-life that he'd long ago deleted from his memory. And he'd been comparatively young the last time – now he tended to wake slowly, feeling slightly confused. He hoped he had the energy for this. Leonora had hinted that she expected a large degree of parental input from him – even though she wasn't the one who then had to get up before seven and put in a profitable day's work. A nanny would be a good idea – Leonora had dropped a few heavy hints about that, too. More expense. More complications. Sometimes he almost envied Melanie, living all alone with few responsibilities and no-one to please but herself.

She shouldn't have left it so late. After an initial flurry of hyper-efficiency in which Melanie had convinced herself that she was well ahead with Christmas shopping and there was no need to panic, she now had less than a couple of weeks left and most of the important people still to buy for. In the days following the despatch of *Dying For It* she had bought, written and sent all her Christmas cards, ordered ham, a small turkey (just for the treat of having it cold on Boxing Day, with fried potatoes and spicy red cabbage), and made a couple of dozen mince pies. She had also been to three parties, a carol-singing fundraising event, Sarah's children's school carol service and had bought lots of edible goodies, massive bunches of lavender and overpriced, overscented soap at the annual French market in the pub car park. Now, before Rosa got back late that afternoon, she found herself buffeted about in the crowds in Harrods, wondering what on earth in that huge emporium would suit her finicky sister. Having a hangover didn't help – her mouth felt dry and her head was threatening to explode out of its paracetamol-induced fuzziness back into full-scale hammer and throb mode.

The party the night before had been conveniently nearby, just across the road within tottering distance of home. It was one of those gatherings of neighbours and friends where everyone lives close enough to be able to chat to each other on an almost daily basis, with no real need to have let's-catch-up conversations. Instead, Melanie found she was exchanging with the guests, almost word for word, information that had come up at the same party the year before and the year before that, with only slight alterations to allow for A-level results, holiday venues and the new, sad absence of Mrs Jenkins. It was the third party she'd been to in a fortnight, and she felt as if she could simply have printed out a general list of answers to Most Frequently Asked questions and passed it round. This time she'd also spent much of the evening reminding those who got drunk enough to ask where he was, that Roger really had permanently gone, he was not working late, working away or otherwise temporarily occupied. She'd have thought they'd have got the idea from her Christmas cards, signed simply: 'Melanie and Rosa'. Almost all the ones she'd received so far had been addressed, either in hope or ignorance, to 'Mr and Mrs'.

There had been two distinct reactions from those to whom it was news that she was divorced: the women tended to say, 'Oh, we must find you someone new *at once*,' just as Sarah had. They looked glittery and excited as they said it, as if it was a challenge they'd enjoy, almost as if they were window-shopping for their own requirements. Perhaps they were, Melanie thought, looking at the greying, waist-expanded specimens that they were living with. Or they might have considered her a prowling and predatory threat to their own marriages and be keen to see her safely shackled again. She felt like pinning notices to all the trees in the road, like people do with lost cats, stating that 'Melanie Patterson is happy living alone and is not looking for a man. Thank you.'

Most of the men, and just a few women who might have been wondering about being in the same situation as her, simply asked, 'Isn't it a bit lonely on your own?' Adding, as a sort of more politically correct afterthought, 'Now that Rosa's gone as well?'

In truth, as Melanie was going home alone feeling more than slightly drunk, she had thought for the first time that it was all a little bleak. She had had one of those 'Is this it?' moments, when the future spread ahead like a long, dark tunnel with too many hazards in it that she'd have to deal with by herself. She put it down to drinking champagne, which some people said was guaranteed to lead to gloom, and to the bleakness of the house next door, which had been packed up, stripped out, emptied and scrubbed thoroughly, ready for sale in less than a week. Mel had never thought she'd miss the yapping of that orange poodle, and she certainly missed Mrs Jenkins yelling her age by way of a greeting over the fence. She wondered how the old lady was getting on, if she was spending Christmas with Brian and his nervy wife or if she'd already been handed over to the care home. Mel imagined her informing a roomful of aged folks that she was eighty-two. That might be comparatively young: she could well be rewarded with an unimpressed chorus of 'So what?' Or perhaps they all did it, calling out their ages at varying times of the day like badly synchronized clocks chiming at all the wrong moments.

Jeremy Paxman was asleep across her duvet and had kept the bed warm for her, but for once she felt it would have been comfortable to have someone there, just to pick over the evening with, someone to say, 'Did you see Marcia's incredible cleavage? *That* wasn't there last Christmas.' Silly things like that. And in the morning, it would have been nice not to be the one who padded down to the kitchen and searched every cupboard and drawer for the last of the Paracetamol. She missed having Max on the premises for these small moments. He was always handy with the kettle in the mornings, and knew just when restorative tea was required. And in the late afternoons, if she wandered into the kitchen looking tired, he was equally handy with a corkscrew, knowing, and not commenting with either judgement or sarcasm, that her body clock was decreeing it was time for a drink. Mel knew that these were the reasons why she was battling round Knightsbridge, getting on with things. She was running away from the niggly and unwelcome thoughts.

Rosa would be home later that afternoon. Melanie had bought presents for her already – something gorgeous and warming from the Brora cashmere catalogue, and a small television for her room at the college. She'd sounded a bit glum in her e-mails recently. There'd been hints along the lines of whether the course was really what she wanted or not, as if she was asking for her mother's collusion in a decision to change. She'd started mentioning art and drama, how she missed having a broader range of studies. Melanie wasn't particularly surprised about that: the course was Marine Science, and Rosa's interest in the sea, so far in her life, had extended to admiring it from a comfortable lounger on a holiday beach, glimpsed over the top of a magazine. A bit of early childhood paddling and fishing in rock pools didn't really seem a lot on which to base one of life's major decisions. It would work out, one way or another, Mel thought, as she shoved her way through the perfume hall and almost choked on the clashing scents, it would work out.

A present for Vanessa was still a problem. Losing her sense of direction slightly, she found herself at the

Tiffany outlet in the store. It was full of delicious and expensive sparkly goodies and she thought of Roger's phone call about a present for the matron of honour at his wedding. What was it he'd thought of? Wasn't it a silver yo-yo that he'd bought for Leonora's friend? It suddenly seemed like the best possible choice for Vanessa. Melanie's heartbeat lightened and skipped as she went to the counter and picked out what she wanted. Vanessa wouldn't have a clue what to make of it. She'd think Melanie had lost her brain cells entirely, yet the item was beautiful, frivolous, totally unlike anything Vanessa would ever choose for herself – exactly what a present should be. The assistant went to the back of the store to pack the present, placing it in its soft turquoise bag, then into the distinctive Tiffany box. Finally she handed the package over to Mel. Good, she thought, that is something perfect.

Melanie called in to see Cherry on the way home, to collect a painting Cherry had been doing for her to give to her mother for Christmas. It was of the bouncy fox terrier, a portrait of him from photographs rather than from life (or even death, the way Cherry worked) but Mel knew Cherry would capture the exact doggy likeness. Gwen would like it – she kept a special photo album with photos of all the dogs she'd owned, but this would be the first one to have its own properly painted portrait.

Cherry's house smelled of home baking. It was also immensely and unusually untidy. There was a skateboard in the hallway, wrapping paper was strewn across the normally immaculate sitting room, clothes were abandoned on the sofa and a pair of trainers was threatening to topple someone who didn't watch where they were going on the stairs. The whole place felt warmer than it usually did. Mel would have said that if Cherry was wine, she'd be a well-chilled white, but something had changed, and the Cherry who let her in and invited her for mince pies and a drink in the kitchen was more of a full-bodied exuberant red.

'Looks like you've been busy,' Mel commented inadequately. The kitchen table was covered, not with Cherry's usual impeccably detailed paintings and superbly neat watercolours, but with huge sheets of cartridge paper, stamped over with bold Santas, mistletoe leaves and holly.

'Potato prints.' Cherry pointed to the palettes of bright poster paints and abandoned cut-up slabs of potato that waited by the sink to be cleaned up. 'Remember doing those when you were little? I wish we'd known then they're not just good fun for kids.'

'So you made all these?' Mel said, admiring the pages.

'No, not just me, I was helping Carlos, Helena's little boy. He wanted to make loads of it to sell at his school Christmas fair. We did pretty well, I think, and now he's doing some for us. My contribution to the fair was a hundred mince pies. Well, it would have been, Helena and I ate about twenty as soon as they were cooked. We've got a few left, have one.' Cherry opened a cupboard and pulled out a big Tupperware box, moved the artwork carefully aside and put the pies on the table.

'Drink?' she asked, pulling a bottle of red wine from the rack.

'Do you mind if I have tea?' Mel grimaced. 'I've got a bit of a fuzzy head still from last night. I went to a party across the road. One of those where the person who's walked past you every day for twenty years asks if you live locally.'

'Ugh! Horrible. I went out, too – Helena is a great fan of *The Archers* and she took me along to an Archers Anarchists quiz night. Great fun. Our team won. Helena's part of the West Kensington gay and lesbian faction. We filled an entire pub basement near Oxford Circus.'

'Well, it sounds a lot more fun than where I was.'

'Yes, it probably was.' Cherry looked more contented than Mel could ever remember. She didn't fidget, didn't frown, didn't keep looking around as if there was something she'd forgotten, like she used to.

'Chezza, when . . . how . . . how did you and Helena get together? I mean, it's all a bit of a surprise. Hope you don't mind me asking.'

'Of course I don't mind! You'd have asked sooner if she'd been a man, admit it.'

Mel shrugged. 'Well, possibly. Yes, probably. Anyway, tell me.'

'It was just before that exhibition really, I've been seeing people from an art group for ages and then suddenly Helena was one of them. We went out sometimes, all of us together, men as well, it isn't just women. Then a few times she couldn't go because of babysitters for Carlos, and I found I'd rather stay in with her than go out with others.'

'So it was a lot like falling for a man?'

Cherry considered for a minute. 'Well, no, not really. With men I always used to fancy them first, you know that daft feeling you mistake for love, and then it was a toss-up whether it ever was or wasn't the real thing. But this way round, well, I didn't even know I was going to fancy her. I didn't even know she was a lesbian. This kind of thing hadn't crossed my mind . . . well, not for years, not since I really liked a girl at college – she was completely straight, though – it was just a crush thing then, I thought.'

'I can see that you're really happy,' Mel said.

'Oh, I am, I am. I'm me, the real me for the first time in years and years. Oh, and I must show you this!' Cherry leapt out of her chair and went to the fridge. She opened the freezer and pulled out a small plastic box. Mel shrank back, expecting the worst. 'Helena got me this for Christmas! Isn't it wonderful?' She removed the lid. Inside the box lay a small curled-up creature.

'Isn't it perfect? A beautiful weasel! And whole – not a mark on it! Her brother found it lying by a dustbin. He thinks it must have been poisoned.'

Melanie looked closely at the little animal. It was, or had been, quite lovely. Now it was a love token – not a life wasted, then, she thought.

'You'll have no surprises on Christmas Day!' she laughed, feeling that if she didn't make a joke she might just burst into tears. The champagne effect was lasting far too long.

'Well, she could hardly wrap it and put it under the tree, could she?' Cherry pointed out.

'True. Listen, I'll see you before the dreaded day. Thanks for doing the painting, my old mum will be thrilled. And send love to Helena when you see her again, won't you.' She hugged Cherry. 'I'm so glad to see you happy.'

'Oh, me too!' Cherry's eyes shone. 'And Mel, I know you like being on your own but . . . well, I've got an awful feeling I might have wasted years by actually *insisting* on it.'

275

'Don't worry, I'm fine on my own,' Mel said as she walked down the path. It sounded like a mantra that had gone meaningless with overuse.

'And wave your broomstick at that horrible Patty woman for me!' Cherry called as Mel got into her car.

It was getting dark outside. Gwen closed the curtains and switched on the Christmas tree lights to make the place look a bit more cheerful. She'd stapled the cards onto ribbon and hung them from the picture rail in the hall and the house was looking quite festive. Even so, she'd be glad when Christmas was over – it seemed like a suspension of real life that went on longer and longer each year. She preferred it afterwards, the sales, the bustle, the knowledge that spring was coming again. As soon as Christmas itself was finished, past Twelfth Night, you could feel the days getting longer. Then she and Howard would be going away for their big break. Perhaps Melanie would come out and visit for a few days – that would be nice. And she could do with time off, Gwen couldn't remember when Melanie had last gone away for a proper holiday. That was one of those things nobody liked doing by themselves, though she wouldn't put it past Mel to take off for a fortnight in Barbados all alone and then insist it was the best time she'd ever had. Gwen would find that hard to believe. Perhaps next year she'd meet someone new. She shouldn't be quite as picky as when she was young – you could live with almost anybody if you were prepared for a bit of give and take. When it had come down to it, she'd rather live with Howard and all his faults than struggle on without him. What would be the point of that?

*　　*　　*

Max was on the doorstep when Melanie got home. In the dark, for there were no lights on in the house, she almost didn't see him. He was hidden by a massive, densely branched Christmas tree.

'I wasn't sure if you'd have one yet, so I brought you this. It's a Norwegian Blue,' he said as she fumbled in her bag for her keys, trying to hide her face, sure he'd be appalled at how delighted she felt to see him. Her expression might give it away, she'd look beaming and silly.

'The garden centre always sends them out to their trade customers. I've had three. This might be a bit big.' He sounded diffident, slightly awkward.

'It's fabulous, Max, thanks! It's very . . . well . . . big isn't adequate to describe it, in fact it's massive!'

'I could help you set it up if you like? Would that help?' Max dragged the huge tree into the hallway. It could go in the front sitting-room window, Mel thought, where Roger's bloody piano had once had pride of place.

'Why don't you stay and help me decorate it?' she suggested, then wondered if that was a suggestion too far. He might think there was something a bit intimate about inviting him to share a Christmas ritual like that. Tree-decorating was something families tended to close in together to do. She didn't know what happened with singletons. All the ones she'd known had either had tiny token trees as if apologizing for joining in with a season aimed at families, or, like Cherry previous to this year, they'd ignored Christmas altogether at home and simply tagged onto someone else's, decamped to a parent, a sister. For this year, at least, Mel still had Rosa. Rosa was not a tree-decorator, taking off for an essential visit to Gracie or Charmian the moment the boxes of baubles rattled into the room, but she did like it once it was done. Rosa would be home in an hour or so – the thought gave her another delighted tingle.

Max and Melanie manoeuvred the tree into the stand that Mel found in the cupboard under the stairs, and then Max opened a bottle of wine in the kitchen while Melanie found the decorations in the loft.

'The lights are the first hurdle,' she said as she accepted a glass of red wine.

'I'll lay them out on the floor, we can switch them on and see what's working.' He was, as ever, a highly efficient worker. The lights were fine – a miracle, Mel thought, casting her mind back to the silly bickering between her and Roger every previous year about who forgot to stock up with enough spare screw-in light bulbs. Together, the two of them worked steadily, hanging scarlet balls, balding Santas, lopsided cardboard angels that Rosa had made in primary school and the contents of a big box of chocolate stars that Mel had bought that day in Harrods. When it was finished and the tree lights were on, they stood together in silence admiring their handiwork, surrounded by empty boxes, tissue paper and fallen, sweet-scented pine needles. Mel found herself wondering what Max was doing over Christmas, whether he, like Neil, had a sneaky 'significant other' and family tucked away somewhere. She didn't think he had, he'd said he wasn't anyone's husband. He somehow had the same look as her, the same air of wariness about being attached.

'There's just one other thing I brought,' Max said, going out to the hall. 'Another Christmas essential.' On his way back in he switched off the room lights so only the tree lights were on.

'What is it?' Mel asked. 'What have you brought?'

'Just this,' he said simply, holding mistletoe above the pair of them. 'Some traditions are worth keeping up.'

Max was still kissing Melanie when the doorbell rang.

'Shame,' he whispered, his mouth close to her ear. 'Perhaps next year . . .'

'Wait . . . what are you doing over Christmas?' She was reluctant to let go of him, even to welcome her much-missed daughter.

'Escaping. Going up a big hill with a bunch of atheist anti-festival climbers. And you're going to your sister Vanessa's.'

'Hmm. Boxing Day?'

'Anything you like.'

'You're on. I'll see you then.'

Max and Roger collided as Mel opened the door and Roger almost fell in. 'You won't believe this . . .' he started, then stopped, gesturing back towards the gate.

Rosa was on the path just behind him, carrying a bin bag which Melanie guessed contained laundry. Rosa looked different in the half-light, softer in the face, peculiarly substantial. She's not been starving herself then, Melanie thought, very slowly adjusting to Rosa's unfamiliar new shape, and even more slowly working her brain round to the realization that it was nothing to do with what she'd eaten.

Rosa pushed past Roger, dropped the bag into the hall and towed another person in after her. 'Hi, Mum.' She reached forward and hugged Melanie. The newly expanded middle of Rosa was squashed against Mel. She wanted to touch it, check that this was what she thought it was.

'I think what Dad wants to tell you is that I've left uni, I'm six months pregnant and I've brought someone home to be with me.' Rosa stepped aside and put her arm round the boy she'd brought in with her. 'Mum, this is Desi. Can he stay?'

'Um . . . Good grief, look, come in first, bring your stuff . . .'

'Well, that'll take all sodding night – they've brought everything they possessed. *Both* of them,' Roger grumbled. 'Look, can we get this bloody car unloaded? I need to get home sometime today.'

'Good thing it was Dad's car. We'd never have got it in yours.' Rosa, still clutching Desi's hand, started wandering towards the kitchen.

'We'll give you a hand with the baggage,' Max said to Roger, almost pushing him out of the door and at the same time detaching Desi from Rosa and dragging him along with him. Mel smiled her gratitude at Max and was left alone with her daughter. Rosa was indeed pregnant. She wondered if she was supposed to feel furious, let down, disappointed. All she could feel was . . . strangely excited.

'Alex's?' Mel ventured, looking at the bump.

'Yes. I hope you don't mind too much.'

'I don't know what to think yet – you'll need to give me a day or two to work out what's real!' She switched on the kettle and opened a new box of tea bags. Typical, she thought, to resort to good old-fashioned British tea-drinking at a time of crisis.

'Sorry to give you such a shock. I just thought . . . well, I haven't been thinking at all for some of the time. I thought if I tell people then it will be true. Then I began to be happy with the idea. At first I thought I'd have an abortion, but then I got all upset about it.' She shrugged and gave a quavery grin. 'I just couldn't do it. It would have been a real, tiny baby . . . like . . .'

'Like Daniel was,' Mel finished for her.

'I think that must be it.'

'So what will you do?'

'Well – I have done some thinking. I could get a job till it's born, then in September I could do a teaching degree here in London. And Desi wants to stay with me and I want him to as well – would that be OK? You'll like him, honest, and he's really tidy! It's just . . .'

'Just what? Is there a problem?'

'I hope not – I mean, you were really looking forward to time on your own and then we all turn up. You will say if you'd rather we found somewhere else?'

Mel hugged her. 'Somewhere else? There's plenty of room here. It's fine. I feel very happy that you want to be here. To be honest, I was beginning to work out that being on your own too much is a bit overrated.'

'Everything's in, your ex has gone off in a fury, so I should probably go too,' Max said. Desi followed him into the kitchen, looking nervous.

'It's OK,' Rosa told him. 'Mum's cool.' She glanced out of the window and gasped. 'Shit, Mum, what've you done to the garden?'

'What's wrong, don't you like it? This, by the way, is Max, and it's all his brilliant hard work.'

'Hi, Max.' Rosa shook his hand and grinned at him. 'Garden's great. But . . .' she stroked her expanded tummy. 'It could really do with a lawn, space for a swing and a sandpit, something child-friendly, you know?'

'Oh heavens,' Max groaned. 'Right that's it, I'm off. Happy Christmas, folks!'

*   *   *

281

He'd been here before, not to this hospital, not to this Special Care Unit, but to one a lot like it. He'd sat staring into a plastic crib, hours on end, marvelling at the fragile limbs. A Christmas Day baby – poor little thing, he'd be complaining about that to his parents for evermore. Roger could hear him now, 'Only one day for presents! It's not fair!'

The big difference was that he'd survive, this one, this time. He was early, an emergency Caesarean to save both him and his mother, but he was comparatively big and sturdy and would be out of this plastic box in a few days and they'd be going home, this new family of him, Leonora and . . . well, he hadn't got a name yet. Perhaps he should get together with Rosa as well and they could make sure they didn't pick the same ones. It would be funny, this baby having a little niece or nephew only three months younger than him, but it would be good, they could see a lot of each other, be brought up more or less together. Leonora didn't want any more, she'd said. Once was quite enough. That was OK by him.

'So that's that for another year,' Howard said as he, Melanie and Max made their way on foot to the race track from the makeshift car park by the A316. Everyone for miles around seemed to be on their way to Kempton. 'Another Christmas, another year gone, another turkey guzzled. Wasn't too bad, all things considered, was it, Mel?'

'Well, there were quite a lot of things *to* consider,' Mel said.

Howard chuckled. 'Hmm – I wish I'd taken a photo of Vanessa's face when she realized Rosa was pregnant and not just plump.'

'That was funny,' Mel agreed, recalling Vanessa prodding Rosa's middle and saying, 'Been overdoing the stodge at university?' then flicking her hand back as if Rosa had given her an electric shock.

'Mum was great,' she added, still astounded at her mother's reaction to the news of the baby. She'd been unhesitatingly delighted: 'You're at a perfect age for having a baby!' she'd said, hugging Rosa (and the very confused Desi too, assuming it was his). 'All these older mothers, people leave it far too late these days!'

'Vanessa liked your present, though,' Howard said. 'She was thrilled, she said it was just what she'd always wanted.'

Mel sighed; it wasn't very noble of her, she'd admit, but accidentally giving her sister the exact thing she'd wanted was not terribly satisfying. 'I don't know how the packages got switched. I didn't at all mean to get her a Tiffany cruet set.'

Max laughed. 'And someone else must have unexpectedly unwrapped a silver yo-yo. I wonder how that got explained away.'

They'd reached the course, paid their entrance fee and picked up their race cards. Mel looked quickly through the list of runners: several serendipitous names caught her eye – Keen Detective, Big Max, Sweet Baby Blue, The Phoenix. They all had to be worth a good each-way bet.

'I'm feeling lucky today, Max, how about you?' she asked.

He pulled her close against him and said, 'I'm feeling very, very lucky.'

THE END

NO PLACE FOR A MAN

Judy Astley

Jess has just waved goodbye to her darling son, off backpacking to Oz. She's left with two teenage daughters and husband Matt – all of whom find themselves regularly featured in her popular and lighthearted newspaper column in which she conveys to her readers an enviably cheery muddle of family life.

Things become less rosy when Matt, after twenty years with the same firm, is made redundant. Only Jess sees the potential calamity in this. Matt is delighted with his new freedom and takes to hanging out at the local bar with others of the male barely-employable tendency, drinking and drifting and dreaming up hopeless schemes to make them all rich. Daughter no. 1, meanwhile, has taken up with a mysterious boy living in an abandoned car on the allotment, and her younger sister is over-burdened with a surfeit of secrets. For Jess, trying to hold everything together and missing her first-flown child, it becomes ever-harder to maintain the carefree facade for her readers. Of course she could just tell them the truth . . .

'DELICIOUS DOMESTIC DISHARMONY'
Woman and Home

0 552 14764 8

BLACK SWAN

SEVEN FOR A SECRET

Judy Astley

'IF YOU LIKE THE EASY STYLE OF JOANNA
TROLLOPE, THEN JUDY ASTLEY . . . IS FOR
YOU'
Today

It was Heather's silver wedding anniversary. But
this important milestone did not mark her marriage
to Tom, her often-absent airline pilot husband and
father of their two teenage children. It was for her
first marriage – a wildly romantic, secret affair,
when she and Iain – twelve years older than her
and the heir to a Scottish baronetcy – had eloped
immediately after her final school speech day. She
was just sixteen at the time. The marriage had not
lasted twenty-five weeks, let alone years, and it
was, as her mother firmly announced, As If It
Never Happened. But secrets have a habit of
coming out, and when a film crew arrived in the
attractive Thameside village where Heather and
Tom lived, Heather was horrified to find her ex-
husband amongst them.

As Heather and Iain met again, many secrets
jostled to be revealed, including Tom's own highly
secret life. Heather, her daughter Kate – the same
age as Heather was when she embarked upon her
disastrous elopement – and her mother Delia all
had to reveal things which they never thought
would need to be revealed, and their peaceful
Oxfordshire village community buzzed with
speculation and scandal.

0 552 99629 7

BLACK SWAN

EXCESS BAGGAGE

Judy Astley

A Proper Family Holiday was the last thing Lucy
was expecting to have. But as a penniless and
partnerless house-painter with an expired lease on
her flat and a twelve-year-old daughter, she could
hardly turn down her parents' offer to take them on
a once-in-a-lifetime trip to the Caribbean. She'd
just have to put up with her sister Theresa (making
no secret of preferring Tuscany as a holiday
destination) and brother Simon (worrying that
there might be some sinister agenda behind their
parents' wish to take them all away) with their
various spouses, teenagers, young children and
au pair.

In a luxury hotel, with bright sunshine, swimming,
diving, glorious food and friendly locals, any
family tensions should have melted away in the
fabulous heat. The children should have been
angelic, the teenagers cheerful, the adults relaxed
and happy. But . . . some problems just refuse to be
left at home.

0 552 99842 7

BLACK SWAN

JUST FOR THE SUMMER

Judy Astley

'OH, WHAT A FIND! A LOVELY, FUNNY BOOK'
Sarah Harrison

Every July, the lucky owners of Cornish holiday homes set off for their annual break. Loading their estate cars with dogs, cats, casefuls of wine, difficult adolescents and rebellious toddlers, they close up their desirable semis in smartish London suburbs – having turned off the Aga and turned on the burglar alarm – and look forward to a carefree, restful, somehow more *fulfilling* summer.

Clare is, this year, more than usually ready for her holiday. Her teenage daughter, Miranda, has been behaving strangely; her husband, Jack, is harbouring unsettling thoughts of a change in lifestyle; her small children are being particularly tiresome; and she herself is contemplating a bit of extra-marital adventure, possibly with Eliot, the successful – although undeniably heavy-drinking and overweight – author in the adjoining holiday property. Meanwhile Andrew, the only son of elderly parents, is determined that this will be the summer when he will seduce Jessica, Eliot's nubile daughter. But Jessica spends her time in girl-talk with Miranda, while Milo, her handsome brother with whom Andrew longs to be friends, seems more interested in going sailing with the young blond son of the club commodore.

Unexpected disasters occur, revelations are made and, as the summer ends, real life will never be quite the same again.

'A SHARP SOCIAL COMEDY . . . SAILS ALONG
VERY NICELY AND FULFILS ITS EARLY PROMISE'
John Mortimer, *Mail on Sunday*

'WICKEDLY FUNNY . . . A THOROUGHLY
ENTERTAINING ROMP'
Val Hennessy, *Daily Mail*

0 552 99564 9

BLACK SWAN

A SELECTED LIST OF FINE WRITING
AVAILABLE FROM BLACK SWAN

14721 4	TOM, DICK AND DEBBIE HARRY	Jessica Adams	£6.99
99822 2	A CLASS APART	Diana Appleyard	£6.99
99564 9	JUST FOR THE SUMMER	Judy Astley	£6.99
99565 7	PLEASANT VICES	Judy Astley	£6.99
99629 7	SEVEN FOR A SECRET	Judy Astley	£6.99
99630 0	MUDDY WATERS	Judy Astley	£6.99
99766 8	EVERY GOOD GIRL	Judy Astley	£6.99
99768 4	THE RIGHT THING	Judy Astley	£6.99
99842 7	EXCESS BAGGAGE	Judy Astley	£6.99
14764 8	NO PLACE FOR A MAN	Judy Astley	£6.99
99854 0	LESSONS FOR A SUNDAY FATHER	Claire Calman	£6.99
99840 0	TIGER FITZGERALD	Elizabeth Falconer	£6.99
99898 2	ALL BONES AND LIES	Anne Fine	£6.99
99795 1	LIAR BIRDS	Lucy Fitzgerald	£5.99
99760 9	THE DRESS CIRCLE	Laurie Graham	£6.99
99883 4	FIVE QUARTERS OF THE ORANGE	Joanne Harris	£6.99
99887 7	THE SECRET DREAMWORLD OF A SHOPAHOLIC		
		Sophie Kinsella	£5.99
99938 5	PERFECT DAY	Imogen Parker	£6.99
99909 1	LA CUCINA	Lily Prior	£6.99
99952 0	LIFE ISN'T ALL HA HA HEE HEE	Meera Syal	£6.99
99819 2	WHISTLING FOR THE ELEPHANTS	Sandi Toksvig	£6.99
99872 9	MARRYING THE MISTRESS	Joanna Trollope	£6.99
99864 8	A DESERT IN BOHEMIA	Jill Paton Walsh	£6.99
99723 4	PART OF THE FURNITURE	Mary Wesley	£6.99
99835 4	SLEEPING ARRANGEMENTS	Madeleine Wickham	£6.99
99651 3	AFTER THE UNICORN	Joyce Windsor	£6.99